MORE TALES OF PAST AND PRESENT

HENRY TEDESCHI

IUNIVERSE, INC.
NEW YORK   BLOOMINGTON

More Tales of Past and Present

iUniverse books may be ordered through booksellers or by contacting:

iUniverse
1663 Liberty Drive
Bloomington, IN 47403
www.iuniverse.com
1-800-Authors (1-800-288-4677)

Because of the dynamic nature of the Internet, any Web addresses or links contained in this book may have changed since publication and may no longer be valid. The views expressed in this work are solely those of the author and do not necessarily reflect the views of the publisher, and the publisher hereby disclaims any responsibility for them.

ISBN: 978-1-4401-2696-3 (sc)
ISBN: 978-1-4401-2697-0 (ebook)

Library of Congress Control Number: 2009923913

Printed in the United States of America

iUniverse rev. date: 3/27/2009

CONTENTS

THE ESSENCE

Deborah woke up with a start, a moment of utter confusion — a warm male body next to her in the bed and a tousled dark head on the pillow — the new day peeking through the curtains faintly illuminating the scene. A stranger, she remembered in panic. He had said his name was Paul. There had been passion — sex almost violent in its intensity. All started by a charming smile — glib flirtation. The drinks and her troubled state of mind must have colluded.

Now loathing and fear. Loathing for herself. Fear of him. How could she have let anything like this happen?

He stirred, then moved toward her with a groan — leaned over and kissed her. Her unresponsive lips were held together tightly. But the masculine voice was warm.

"Good morning darling."

She hated him — hated herself. She bounded out of bed and sat naked on the couch. Then sobs took over, unsummoned, unwanted, multiplying her shame and distress.

The voice was warm. "Don't blame yourself. Wait until you see everything in the proper perspective."

She didn't look at him and even resented his insight.

Not a word came to her. At least she stopped crying and silently went into the shower in the adjoining bathroom, trying to wash away the whole experience — her whole shame.

Out of the shower, she dried herself hastily and got dressed. Last night's clothes. She couldn't help feeling that they were grossly soiled.

He was fully dressed. "I'll take you home."

There was nothing exceptional about him. He was indistinguishable from any other man she had ever met.

"I'm going to take a taxi. I don't want to see you again. Ever."

"I want to make sure you're safe."

Passively, she accepted his hand as he guided her into his car. She was spent and chose the path of least resistance.

At the door of her house he kissed her forehead chastely.

"Good luck."

"I don't want to hear or see you ever again."

"I'll respect your wishes. Here is your cellular phone. You were leaving it behind. I programmed my phone number under Paul. If you ever have a serious problem you can count on me."

Stupid male conceit, she felt. "I don't want to hear or see you ever again."

"As you wish," he repeated.

******

Deborah Weston and Frederic Means had been lovers. At least that's what she had thought. They were from different worlds—both employed at Agolyle, Inc. For a time she had enjoyed the formal engagement. The ring with a very large diamond. The notoriety it brought — uncomfortable as she might have been with the tennis set, the high-class partying, the highfalutin discussion of the latest play or novel. But it had all been an illusion, a sham as it had become painfully clear.

"Deborah, you'd better do what I tell you."

"Why is that?"

"You're my woman. If you want a future you'll simply forget it all. After all you're becoming part of my family."

"I don't want to be part of a fraud. It's not much of a family if it tolerates fraud."

"It tolerates survival, the life they are accustomed to."

"No dice!"

He hadn't believed her at first but finally days later he'd erupted in a nightclub of all places. "You ungrateful bitch. I should have seen you were just a plain unfeeling slut the moment we met!"

Without a word, she passed him the ring that had made her so proud. Perhaps she had counted too much on her illusions. Totally devastated she was left feeling vulnerable. Without hesitation she had passed her knowledge onto the District Attorney. Still she was left in pain. Any future she might have had at Agolyle was entirely gone. Surely, she would be fired.

Even Bob Trevail, avuncular Bob, the doyen of the group, her sponsor in the company, middle-aged and with a reputation for common sense, tried to dissuade her. "Don't be foolish and give away your future. Look what we did for you. You were promoted quickly to a remarkable position and salary. Don't throw it away for some meaningless technicality."

"I wish what you were saying were true. But you and I know that they are not meaningless technicalities."

Trevail was very angry. "You're behaving like a total idiot."

She never saw him again.

After the breakup with Fred, she hadn't meant to go to a party. It had been at Denise's insistence that they'd gone. They had been friends from college and leaned on each other whenever needed.

"It doesn't pay to obsess about the inevitable. You need distractions."

That's how she had met Paul. Now she regretted that moment.

She had quickly entered the second phase of her distress. Fired — a search for a new job had become necessary. Scouring the "Wanted" section of the newspaper, she suffered along with all the other unemployed. Uncertainty is hard to take. It's another form of humiliation. In a telephone conversation with a cousin twice removed whom she hardly knew, Olga, had suggested looking into a job at the University.

"Oh God!" she had piped, "I only have a Master's degree. And in English at that."

""I didn't mean an academic job. I heard of a manager job in the Chemistry Department at the University."

"My knowledge of chemistry doesn't even reach Lavoisier."

"There you go with a lie. If you were such an ignoramus you wouldn't be dropping names like that. Besides, it's an administrative job. How to make things run smoothly. You could give it a try."

Debbie feared reporting her difficulties to her mother who she visited every few weeks. The idea of conveying the news by telephone didn't seem appropriate; her mother would fret even more. The trip through the mountains was harrowing and she knew that her mother would be extremely worried about her unemployment to the point of acute anxiety. She could well imagine her mother's troubled face when she told her about her problems. It was like being a teenager all over again. She resolved not to tell her until she had found a new job.

Pride made her respond to the challenge of the chemistry position. She wondered why she felt so nervous when her letter applying for the job was answered with an appointment for an interview. It didn't help to assure herself that she didn't give a shit whether she got the job or not —after all it was so far removed from her expertise! The anteroom to the site of the interview was plain with one upholstered modern couch on which she was sitting. The walls were painted white with one photograph of a patrician looking fellow of yesteryears — from the days when women had to stay home. Not an encouraging omen.

After a short wait she was summoned by a woman dressed in a business suit. Deborah entered the conference room to face a group of men around a table. With a thump in her heart she recognized Paul "What's his name" among them. What the hell was he doing here? she wondered. In a formal well-cut suit and tie he looked quite different from the man she had met. She felt herself blush. Shit! She didn't have to be so transparent. He was quite handsome in a very unconventional way — masculine but not otherwise remarkable. With that recognition she knew that her chances of getting hired were entirely gone. She was introduced to the group. Paul's name turned out to be Paul Harroway. He didn't show any sign of recognizing her. The names of the others left her mind as soon as the introductions were over.

She was asked to sit down with them at the table. After the first painful throb she felt only anger. Coward she was not and would give her misfortunes a good fight. That seemed to translate into an effort to make the best impression possible. The questions hurled at her had to do with her previous experience, her ability to get along with people with different backgrounds with a strong hint that many of the members of the department she would have to serve were definitely weirdos (or in their words, "eccentric"). At the end of the questions, one by one they shook her hand and thanked her for coming. Paul hadn't said a word throughout.

"Oh, thank you for considering me." What was going through her mind was "fuck you all."

Days later, an impersonal phone call, she presumed from the person who had directed her to her interview informed her that she had gotten the job. Her happy surprise was only surpassed by her dismay at finding out how wrong her expectations had been. She was losing her touch. The job paid well, the benefits were substantial and the hours just nine-to-five. The salary didn't compare to what she had received from Agolyle, but she told herself, for a change it was honest work. Elation took over whatever had been going through her mind.

Giving in to an insane impulse, she phoned Paul Harroway at his office with considerable trepidation. She had remembered that he worked at Safeguard, Inc. When she heard him say "Harroway" she hastened to say, "This is Deborah Milton. Thank you for not blackballing me."

He said nothing for a moment, she figured her call had been unexpected. "Oh, my dear, why would I do something so awful? I recused myself, after all I had met you before. I think that I can tell you that Agolyle was not very kind in their letter, but your former coworkers and supervisor went to bat for you without even having been asked."

Well, that was flattering and took some of the bitterness out of her recollections.

******

Debbie's first day at work was painless. Actually, unexpectedly she found it pleasant. The woman she was replacing, Michelle Elwin, was very pregnant — ready to drop, Deborah judged. Her small size and slenderness made her bulge seem even more prominent. Michelle laughed at what must have been Debbie's startled expression

"You don't have to worry. I won't be coming back. Will be too busy making babies. Phil and I saved six years for this."

Deborah smiled and felt a friendly wave course through her.

Despite the bulk she was carrying, Michelle was unexpectedly lithe. She showed Debbie the routine: ordering supplies and equipment for the department, carefully checking the specifications and entering records in the computer. After illustrating each step, she took Debbie for coffee in the University cafeteria and introduced her to a number of friends who greeted Michelle with affection. Debbie hoped they would eventually treat her with the same degree of friendly enthusiasm.

After their coffee break, a tour of the various offices and laboratories followed and Michelle introduced her to the faculty and technicians. Some of the professors looked very young — like anybody else in other walks of life and without the professorial veneer. There were only two women. Michelle had whispered that it was a very male dominated field, but giving way. The two women were young, with short dark hair and intense expressions. Debbie wondered whether they ever smiled. Others were clearly "eccentric" as she had been told. Meeting so many people at once confused her. Remembering all the names seemed a hopeless task. Even with a list of the staff it was difficult for her to match names with faces.

After lunch, Michelle explained what was not obvious. "The job is not as cut and dry as you might think. There are ways of stretching out money. That's the creative part I like most." She pulled out papers from a tray. "This order is pending. I got a 20% discount by fusing several separate purchases and then threatening to yank out the fifty thousand dollar equipment order if they didn't give me a good price. I have been stretching our money that way since I started here. Sometimes you have to evaluate the quality as well. Best to do it after consulting with the faculty, but with a grain of salt, in some ways they are experts, in others they have prejudices like everybody else." After a pause. "I had to take the purchase orders out of the usual Purchasing Office routine. They don't understand the need for speed. Delaying an order even if you get a better price can be fatal to a project. An idle technician or a delayed scientific experiment is also money wasted. For some reason they don't understand that."

Michelle looked at Debbie with a very amused smile. "The job is not without power. Some of the faculty ignores rules for dangerous or radioactive chemicals. The Safety Office is hopelessly ineffective in enforcing regulations. For some mysterious reason the orders from a recalcitrant chemist that reach my office get lost until the offending scientist complies. A strange phenomenon." Debbie loved to hear Michelle's amused laugh. She felt she had known Michelle all her life.

Somehow the occasion arose for Deborah to satisfy her curiosity. "I was interviewed by a bunch of professors and a Mr. Harroway. What's his role? Do you know?"

"Oh, sometimes he represents the board of trustees. He's some big deal in Safeguard, Inc., a security company ... you know protection of businesses, personnel and academic buildings."

Debbie felt a smile forming on her lips, "In other words, a protection racket!"

Michelle responded with a laugh. "Don't let anybody hear you say that. They are big donors to the University! Half of the fellowship funds come from them. And besides Harroway is a good guy."

Debbie had been relieved not to feel self-conscious with her question about her "Paul", but curiosity egged her on. "How is that?"

"He's well regarded by all the people working for Safeguard. Phil, my husband, used to work for Safeguard. Did very well. A good salary, good benefits. But loathed his job — checking whether references were genuine and interpreting letters of recommendation. Harroway got to know Phil very well. He's that kind of guy. He guessed Phil's attitude toward his work and found out that he had artistic talent and training. He helped him set up his art store. You know, cosigning loans and stuff like that. The store sells good solid paintings from promising painters, plus he offers framing, art lessons and then paints when he gets a chance. He's been a different person since then. I'll be eternally grateful to Harroway for that."

Debbie was pleased that she had been able to put together the identity and some of the character of the mysterious Paul that had caused her so much anxiety.

Days went by and Debbie was surprised to see Michelle still coming to work.

"You know Michelle, I can function now. You must have a lot to do in preparation for the great event."

Michelle chuckled, "We have been preparing for several years! Nothing left to do but the great deed itself! But I'll have to stop coming soon or to get here I'd have to roll like a ball."

Returning to the office from an errand, Debbie found Michelle in the company of a pretty teenaged girl with an unappealing pout. Neither acknowledged Debbie's entrance. Michelle was giving the girl a good natured dressing down.

"Look. He might tell you what to do all the time. That simply means that he loves you. You don't know what not being loved means. Nobody ever loved me until Phil came along. It's a lonely, painful road. You can accommodate some of his wishes. You know that for anything important you will be soon free to go your own way."

"Oh! Fuck. You say the same thing everybody says."

"It might mean that there is some truth to it. And don't forget you came to me. I didn't pursue you with my opinions."

"Can I still come just to talk?"

"Any time. But you know, I'm due in two weeks. After the baby comes, I'll have other concerns."

"Good-by."

The girl left after giving Michelle a hug, somewhat hampered by Michelle's protrusion.

Debbie felt like commenting, "I guess it's not that bad after all!"

"That's Monica Harroway."

"Mr. Harroway's daughter?"

Michelle chuckled. "He's not married, he's a widower, no children. She's his little sister. He's been raising her. Not an easy task now that she is a teenager, particularly for a bachelor."

What an unusual situation, Debbie reflected.

Michelle missed coming for two days. Debbie wondered whether it had become too arduous for her to travel or whether the baby had finally arrived. The information finally came from some of Michelle's many girlfriends in the department who couldn't contain their excitement and loudly cruised the hallways with the happy news. The baby was a little girl, 6 pounds three ounces. Michelle had named her Miranda after Phil's grandmother.

Debbie could hardly contain her own enthusiasm after hearing the news. She was dying to see mother and child. After she judged that Michelle must have gotten organized and after a phone call, she embarked on a visit with balloons, a mobile, rattles and a sort of sac she was assured would fit any baby and was always needed. She had really started to miss her friend's presence at work. She never would have expected to have become so fond of her in such a short time. On the phone, she offered Michelle any help she might need.

Michelle laughed her funny laugh. "Too early for babysitters. You might not be so enthusiastic when she starts crawling!"

Upon entering the living room she first saw Michelle proudly holding the baby. There were several women from work and in one corner the father, Phil, with a big grin pasted on his face. Debbie judged that he was even more gaga than the mother, if that were possible. She dropped the packages next to Michelle and her friend acknowledged them with a smile and a nod.

"You know everybody here, don't you?" intoned Michelle.

Looking around, with a start Debbie realized the Phil was sitting next to Harroway, a totally unexpected surprise. She had forgotten that the Elwins and Harroway were friends. She felt a tremendous unease. Harroway must have felt the same way because he suddenly got up.

"We'd better be going."

Michelle intervened. "You said you wanted to hold Miranda and you're not getting to leave until then. I would be insulted."

"I certainly don't want to insult you or Miranda, but the next thing you'll ask me to do is to change her diaper."

"Are you kidding? Aside from Phil, I wouldn't trust any man with that task. You guys are too clumsy."

Harroway went to her chair and held out his arms, carefully accepting the precious cargo.

Debby found the expression on his face mystifying. It bordered on admiration and delight. His unease at her presence seemed to have disappeared entirely. Monica, his teenaged sister, who Debby hadn't realized was also there, detached herself from the group sitting next to Michelle. "May I Michelle? May I?"

"Be sure you support her head with your arm."

Debby was surprised at the look of delight on the girl's face while holding the baby.

"She's so cute!" expressed Monica's tender feelings.

Harroway's face also conveyed delight as he looked at his young sister with love and devotion. How could Monica herself fail to notice such an emotion in her brother? Then Debbie remembered her own adolescence, its doubts and torments and understood.

After Monica held the baby for a while, Debbie found herself extending her arms and accepting Miranda after Harroway had sent an inquiring look at Michelle. The two of them, Debbie and Harroway looked at each other with a trace of a smile on their faces. Based on her previous experiences, Debbie was relieved that despite all the activity Miranda hadn't bawled. She must be a very placid or very sleepy baby, she thought.

A few days later, Debbie visited Michelle and Monica on her own and admired the routine adopted by the mother who was breast feeding the baby with a look of contentment.

"Thank you for all the goodies you brought me last time," Michelle said.

After a while, somehow, Debbie steered the conversation to Harroway.

"Very sad! He married his childhood sweetheart. She had leukemia. They knew it when they got married. She died several years ago. Rather heroic of them, I think. Why do you ask?"

"Just curious. He seems to be an interesting person."

"Be careful! Many women have set their cap for him and it always comes to nothing. It's not that he's rich or handsome. He just seems to be very successful and is very comfortable with that without any burning ambitions."

Debbie's opinion of Harroway's handsomeness differed from that of her friend but she didn't feel like contradicting her. Strangely, she felt much better about their tryst. In her mind it was no longer the sordid affair she had imagined — he hadn't been just a lecher in search of pleasure. And she must have been just insane.

******

Debbie read with trepidation the summons a messenger had brought her. She had been asked to testify at the trial of the executives of Agolyle, Inc. She had thought her role in reporting their deeds to the DA had fulfilled her obligation. According to the media their records had been seized in a raid. She could have done without the promised notoriety and disruption of her work, not to mention the nervousness that enveloped her. But there were two more weeks before her new ordeal so her thoughts and worries on the matter could be pushed aside momentarily.

A frightening and sudden reminder came from an unexpected source. As she was taking the elevator up to her apartment, the man joining her had looked ordinary. But he suddenly pulled the emergency switch stopping the elevator between floors. She looked at him in surprise and that's when he seized her and from behind held a knife to her throat. The blade was very sharp and with difficulty she forced herself not to squirm and to remain totally passive.

In a thick raucous voice he threatened, "If you don't leave town immediately and not testify, this will be for real."

He threw her to the ground and reversed the switch. At the next floor he leisurely walked out as the door of the elevator closed behind him. Terrified, she got up painfully when the door of the elevator opened on her floor. Her hands trembled so badly that she had trouble directing her key into the lock. She rushed to the phone to dial 911. Her voice had difficulty forming words but finally she could describe what had happened.

******

Debbie didn't think the police had found the perfect solution to her safety. They assigned a detective to follow her around. Alicia Prim was a small, delicate looking Asian-American. The police captain who had made the assignment chuckled on seeing Debbie's surprised face.

"Don't you worry. Detective Prim is a karate black belt and a sharpshooter. She can follow you around during the day. I'm assigning somebody else to watch your apartment at night from a distance. You'll be covered for 24 hours each day."

"Isn't this a bit excessive? It's like having a permanent appendage."

"Not really excessive. And Detective Prim can be very unobtrusive. Besides, the DA insists on this kind of arrangement. I don't know why protection troubles you. Wasn't the knife sharp enough?"

Debbie couldn't suppress a shudder. She felt cold all over and didn't protest further.

Any doubts Debbie might have had about Alicia Prim were erased one morning when she went to work. The usual homeless person with a threatening appearance who accosted passersby, quickly disappeared after Prim interposed herself in front of Debbie. There was something about her that wasn't obvious but must resonate with some street people and hopefully villains who might come out of the woodwork. It was hard to believe that such a slight woman could be intimidating.

The time came when she was expected at her parent's house. Debbie knew that her visit, as inevitable as it was, would open a can of worms. She'd have to explain Alicia's presence and go into the whole sordid story.

On the phone, her mother had been firm. "It's time that we spent some time together. I'm beginning to think that something awful has happened and you're keeping it from me."

Mother didn't know how right she was. Debbie denied any problems, preferring to discuss them personally. She hadn't even informed her mother of the breakup of her engagement. No doubt that event would raise more wails than anything else, including her daughter's dangers.

Debbie didn't cherish the long ride along the mountainous road. She didn't understand why her parents felt obligated to hide themselves in the summer months in what wasn't much more than a large log cabin. She wouldn't go through tortuous mountain pathway unless she felt up to the challenge — not at night or when she was tired.

Alicia laughed at Debbie's warning about her mother.

"You think I don't know mothers? My Korean mother asks me when I'm getting married at least once a week. She even went as far as to buy me a traditional Korean wedding outfit that makes the bride look like a balloon!"

After packing and loading the car with enough clothing for the weekend, Debbie warned her companion to pack a sweater or perhaps a warm anorak. It could get cold. Once in the car they hastened with Debbie at the wheel, hoping to reach their goal before dark. The mountains were spectacular with trees in full foliage. Occasionally the highway went over bridges spanning angry torrents, or kills as they were called on that part of the country.

After about two hours, they had reached the local road. To Debbie's surprise another automobile was following closely. The road usually was not well travelled, and in the past Debbie remembered rarely sighting another car, usually going in the opposite direction. When the curves became sharper and the road had abrupt drops on both sides, the other vehicle approached theirs too closely, as if it intended to ram them. Debbie wasn't sure that was what the other driver had in mind. But, Alicia had her police experience in good stead and pulled out her handgun. Debbie struggled to keep the car on the road. The other car slammed into theirs twice. A loud report came from Alicia's side. She was leaning against the seat rest with her gun pointing toward the other car. On the third clash their car left the road. The car hit the rocks below at full speed with a crashing sound, then Debbie passed out. When she came to, Debbie was totally confused but there was no way of mistaking her quandary. She was trapped and couldn't move. The air bags must have been able to mitigate some of the effects of the collision.

"My God," she thought, "what happened to Alicia?"

Debbie could move her arms and explored the space next to her. She felt Alicia's inert body and was sure that she was dead. There was no time for sentimentality although tears crowded her eyes. Debbie herself would be soon dead if she couldn't pull herself together.

Could she alert the authorities with her cell phone? Her phone was in the pocket of her jeans. Could she get to it? In pain, she strained until she had it out. Its face was illuminated when she pressed the start button. Suddenly hope! Pushing the buttons to summon the emergency number, 911, didn't seem to work. Incapacitated by sobs and despair she was motionless for several minutes. She didn't think she could punch in her parents' number of several digits. Her arms hurt and it was too difficult. She had to keep calm and think. Some solution might come to mind.

After a while, she remembered that Paul had programmed his number on her phone. Under the circumstances, she couldn't take his offer of help too seriously, but she didn't have any other alternative. Her need had become desperate and she had to press only one button. Could he be useful? Would he be able to act? It seemed highly unlikely. She squinted to see Paul's entry and pressed the button. Holding the phone next to her ear, she heard ringing.

"Please God, let him answer."

When she heard his voice she wasn't able to assemble her wits right away.

"Hello! Hello!" he yelled impatiently.

She could only murmur rather than speak. She wished she could yell at the top of her lungs to communicate the urgency, her danger. "This is Debbie Weston. I have been in an accident. I'm off the road and incapacitated. I can't get 911."

Paul responded immediately. "Where are you?"

She explained the best she could and then added, "The car is in a ravine next to Walnut Road."

"Are you hurt badly?"

"I think so."

"Don't move as long as the car is stable. I'm calling for help. I might get to a rescue team and I'll see if I can come. I'll try to get hold of a helicopter."

Although she concluded that help from him didn't seem likely, there were no other possibility. She could do nothing but wait.

The pain had become excruciating. With the lack of sunlight it was getting cold. In the dark, she became unconscious again. She revived just as a flickering light illuminated part of the car. The car door was opened carefully and the top light was still functioning. Paul looked at her intently.

"Oh my God! Please don't move. The rescue team will be here in minutes. I'm sorry it took so long. It's pretty dark and we had to find the tracks where the car left the road. I see your escort is dead. I'm so sorry!"

Illogically, anxiety came back in full force. "Please don't leave me!"

"That will be the day! I found it too hard to get here. I'm no mountaineer."

"Please hold me!" She needed reassurance. Without comment he put an arm around her. He couldn't do more without disturbing her position.

After a while they could hear unfamiliar men's voices. "That's sure a bitch of a descent! Carrying all this shit!" "I've seen worse." And then they were there with a litter and ropes. They transferred her onto the litter with infinite care after removing part of her seat. A perfusion bag was immediately attached to her arm and she was conveyed up the mountain. In a panic she realized that she had no sensation in her legs, and then she passed out.

When she regained consciousness, she recognized she was in a hospital room. She was told later that she had been moved by helicopter. When Paul noticed she had become conscious he tried to make conversation, probably so that her mind wouldn't dwell on her predicament. Her pain had abated somewhat. Probably because of drugs.

"I've been with you all along. They let me because I told them I was your husband!"

She giggled, perhaps the consequence of the sedatives. "Isn't that putting the cart before the horse ... or is it the horse before the cart?"

"Nothing to do with carts or horses. Just you and me."

Some time went by. "Don't let them call my parents yet."

"Not much danger there. They are not in their home on Long Island. And that's the only phone number we could find."

He didn't speak for a few minutes, perhaps searching for a suitable topic. Then he continued. She imagined he thought that with the drugs they had pumped into her, she wouldn't remember what he was saying. Her half-closed eye lids enhanced that impression.

"To talk about our first encounter, I'm sorry I didn't realize how vulnerable you were. I should have held back. I never meant it to be a one night stand. I knew a lot about you. Agolyle has been under surveillance for a while under several warrants. There was more than one video camera at different spots. The phones were tapped and at least one room was bugged. I had to go through all the recordings for the police. They gave me a thorough picture of you. I admired your integrity and courage. And of course, in person you looked even prettier than on the tapes. I think I was already a bit in love with you."

"You're fantasizing. They must have given you some of the same sedative they gave me. Just shut up and hold me."

But he had to talk some more. She guessed there had been lapses in her consciousness. "One of your vertebrae has been displaced and is pressing on the spinal cord. They wanted me to sign a release and other forms as your husband so that they can operate. Obviously I thought you'd better do it. Are you up to it?"

She chuckled, "Why not. Do you think I've been in a serious accident or something?" Then after a pause, "Do you think I should?"

"Debbie, you'll have to decide. I know you're groggy and it isn't easy to concentrate on anything this important. I'm really not your husband as you might remember. They think they might be able to relieve the pressure and re-establish function. I don't see where you have a choice. I can tell you that, as a friend who is totally unqualified to give medical advice."

"If you were my husband would you consent?"

"I would just state my opinion. I really think you should decide."

And so she was wheeled into the operating room.

After she had spent some time in the recovery room, Paul gave her more details on what had happened. The murderer was now dead himself. Alicia's shot had found its target and his car had followed theirs into the ravine. The searchers found it not too far from where she had been found.

"Well? Do I know the man?"

Paul hesitated. He thought she would be hurt by finding out that detail. She waited nervously.

He finally spoke, "It was Bob Trevail."

She was relieved that it wasn't her erstwhile fiancé but the information was nevertheless shattering. She had thought of Bob as a good, although misguided friend. They were both silent for some time.

Days later, she was moved to a rehabilitation hospital close to her home. The physicians who cared for her had prescribed a series of supervised daily exercises she didn't cherish. Paul had said his good-by. "I don't think you need me anymore." For some reason she felt abandoned and resented his disappearance.

There hadn't been any problems with her job. Michelle had agreed to substitute temporarily and the new mother was told that she could bring the baby with her.

The visit by her parents hadn't been as bad as she had imagined. Her mother, of course, had been in tears. There was little they could say or do except reiterate their love and support. Debbie suspected that despite everything her mother was still sorry that she had broken her engagement.

One of the first things she felt she had to do was to contact Alicia's parents to express how sorry she was at her death. The two insisted on visiting her. They came with flowers — two formal, very slight Asians with very limited English. Ironically, it was Mrs. Prim who embraced her and tried to console her.

"That's what she wanted to do with all her heart. She performed honorably."

"Heroically!" interjected Debbie.

Their visit remained in her mind for a long time.

During the trial of the executives of Agolyle Inc., Debbie was allowed to testify in a wheelchair. Although she resented the limelight, her ordeal lasted only a short while. The prosecutor needed little detail and the defense didn't want to arouse counterproductive sympathy for her.

In the hospital she found that she missed Paul terribly — she had learned to count on his unfailing, unquestioning support. Her request to be left alone, uttered well before the attempt on her life, hounded her. How stupid can you get!

Monica Harroway was a surprise visitor. She knocked and peeked through the partially open door. Surprised, Debbie invited her in. Monica spoke shyly of many trivial matters, mostly about how cute and accomplished Miranda had become. But then she turned to the purpose of her visit.

"Debbie, I know you must think I'm empty-headed and a pain in the ass but I promise you that I will be very nice and well behaved if you latch on to my brother."

"What do you mean, 'latch?'" Debbie was amused.

Monica blushed, "You know ... have a relationship."

"What are you talking about?"

"I think he's very much in love with you and you would be a fool to ignore it."

That, of course, was the opinion of a very inexperienced teenager, but nevertheless it set Debbie thinking. She was very polite to Monica but didn't comment on her conclusion. Adolescents think they know everything, she thought. Yet she couldn't forget what Paul had said before her operation. The drugs hadn't erased her memory after all.

She phoned Paul. "Could you please come and see me?"

Debbie waited nervously. When he came, she didn't know where to start or even what to say. The idiot just gave her a weak hello and didn't even kiss her.

"Have you forgotten all about me?" she asked.

"Do you need me?"

"Damn right!" She thought for a moment. What exactly did she feel? "Oh, God. I don't know. I can't function without you. Do you think that could be love?"

"Isn't that a definition of love?"

"I'm so confused! I would want a lifetime stand. Would you be amenable to that?"

She had to stop talking because he was kissing her and she reciprocated unexpectedly and passionately.

THE CROSSING

Elvira never would have thought of knocking on the door of the *osteria* if she hadn't been frightened out of her wits late that night. First hiding in the school, then under a culvert, her shoes and socks had become soaked and trying not to give away her hiding place had caused her to wet herself as well. She had been able to run out of the back of her house while their maid Tommasa had blocked the way to the men in black uniforms. Elvira had been entrusted to Tommasa while her parents were away. Elvira hoped the punch in Tommasa's face hadn't hurt too much. Surely they thought that a young girl wasn't capable of such trickery as to use the back door. While hiding, clutching the silver cross her grandma had given her hadn't helped. Fear and humiliation overtook her. Yet, she knew that the men searching for her would be well pleased to get hold of the daughter of General Altardo. Although only sixteen, she understood the price of defeat.

There was a moment when the streets had appeared empty, and she had scrambled out of her hole and run.

"Please open!" she implored.

It was ironic. The man who opened the door was one she had been warned against. Not respectable, somebody outside acceptable society. She had seen him before and had to ignore his leering. The few times she had seen him he'd had a toothpick in the corner of his mouth or a lighted cigarette hanging from his lips. She had heard that he had returned from the Russian front with severe wounds and a bum arm but that didn't make him any more respectable. Somebody had told her that he might have joined the resistance, whatever that meant.

This encounter wasn't much better.

"Oh! The pretty *bambina*!" and he pulled her in. For an instant he held a leer on his face. But he must have known her situation because he asked, "Where were you hiding?"

"The school first."

"Anybody there now?"

"No, they all left."

"*Vediamo ... vediamo.*"

He directed her up a short ladder to a space right under the roof. She felt like shrugging away the firm grip on her shoulder guiding her, but he didn't have anything untoward in mind as she might have suspected. She was too scared to protest. The darkness enveloped her along with the smell of mold and dust. If she hadn't been so terrified, she would have tried to get away. The banging on the door made her shudder.

There was the sound of several booted men entering.

"Oh! Madonna! What's the matter? You can see I already served my country."

"Where is the girl?"

"Oh, *cazzo*, I haven't had a good fuck in weeks."

"You're Maldonato aren't you?"

"Yeah, and what's your name?"

She heard a slap and then the sound of a blow.

"Oh! *Porca miseria.* You're just jealous because the girls don't fuck you. You should take your boots off when you get into bed."

This was followed by the sound of several punches.

"You know the Russians do this much better. That's why you fuckers are losing."

More blows. Elvira was terrified. There were desperate yells and more moans.

Then after heavy breathing, "She ain't no friend of mine. I'll tell you."

"If you're shitting us you'll be more than sorry!"

"She's at the school. The janitor's closet. Don't blame me if you waited too long."

The sound of boots again. Then the little attic door opened again.

"Amateurs! They didn't leave one of their idiots behind."

He expected her to come down on her own since the ladder had been placed at the opening. But this time he didn't help her. The descent was labored, she was afraid of falling. When she finally faced him, she saw that he was still bent over in pain. She wanted to say something. Thank him or tell him how sorry she was, but no sound came out of her mouth.

He handed her a pistol. "Here! Get going. No time to lose. Remember there are fates worse than death. But if you decide to die take a few of them with you."

"Aren't you coming?"

"Too hard with a bum arm and a broken leg. They sure did a fine job." More heavy breathing. "You don't have to worry about them chasing you.

They won't be able to get very far." Terrified she took the weapon which felt even heavier than she expected.

"What are you going to do?"

"You'll be able to see. It will happen when they all come in. And I'll be laughing my guts out sitting right on that chair. Don't they say that whoever laughs last laughs best?" And then after a short pause , "Five for one, not a bad deal."

He continued, "Try for Fiesole. Salvatore Romano. Just ask around. It will take you a few hours, but you're young." Those were the last words she heard from his gruff voice

She quickly departed. She hid the pistol under her clothes. Already at some distance, she received the final message from him. An explosion rent the air. Elvira knew that Maldonato had gotten his way.

THE RING

The relationship between Susan and her husband, Elliot, had hit rock bottom. He had said unforgivable things and she had replied in kind. When their relationship had come to a pass, they started sleeping in separate rooms. One night he had simply stomped to the guest room. At better times they actually had had guests!

Apart from a glimpse of him in the morning she didn't see much of him, except for a real contact, once a week or so when they would briefly discuss who had to pick up one of the children or who would go to the PTA meeting or the appointment with a teacher. Thank God, he was still very much involved with the children. Their exchanges were conducted with a minimum of words and indifferent expressions. The family had their meals together and the two of them tried to present an amiable front for the children. These conversations were carefully acted and studied. They were demonstrations of their dissembling ability.

Because of their deteriorated relationship, she was not at all surprised by what her friend, Alice had to tell her. He hadn't even deigned to remember their wedding anniversary that had just passed. Elliot didn't know Alice well and didn't realize she was in the shop. She had caught a glimpse of him purchasing an expensive emerald ring at Budenstein, known for its unusual designs and steep prices. Clearly, he must have acquired a new girl friend. Presumably, thought Susan, that was to be expected. At that point she could hardly hold it against him as much as she hated him.

The nature of the gift said a lot. She'd bet that the bitch looked much like herself. A dark blonde with a somewhat dark complexion which would be brought out by the green of an emerald. She had heard it said that the woman in a second marriage, although much younger, often resembles the first wife.

Well, she told Alice, "That's par for the course, isn't it?

Alice had known of her troubles and had acidly commented before that she should leave such a monster. Susan had simply replied that she wasn't prepared for that yet. That was true. However, she knew the ways of the world and had hidden a voice activated tape recorder in their summer cottage. She might need evidence of a tryst for a favorable divorce settlement and what better place to carry out an affair than in their summer cottage? Not too far away, it offered unlimited privacy. She had considered an affair there herself to get even with the bastard. But she simply didn't know any man she cared for. Besides, she wasn't that kind of woman. One man at a time was her way, even if she wasn't in speaking terms with the present one.

She checked on the tape once a week, sometimes once every two weeks. She could hardly take herself very seriously. You might have called it a hobby! She only played the tapes when Elliot wasn't expected until later and the kids weren't home yet. There was never anything of significance except some undefined noises of short duration, but then eventually voices were recorded. She quickly perked up when she heard a woman voice on the recorder but then she was disappointed, it was the voice of Elliot's sister as clear as if she had been in the living room. Why would they meet at the cottage, she wondered. But then it occurred to her that it was halfway between their houses in separate towns.

She wouldn't have bothered listening if she hadn't realized that the conversation was about her.

"So why diddle-daddle. These things happen and they are irreversible. And you're no prize yourself."

"I like to understand what has happened. I keep thinking of the sweet woman I first met. And am I such a monster?"

"You're wasting your time. What's done is done."

"What makes you an authority in marital warfare? You have been happily married for years. No divorce in sight"

"That's precisely it. Having a happy marriage gives you a good perspective of what can go wrong, even if such things don't happen in one's case."

"I've been looking back. I made many mistakes. I didn't realize when she needed support. She was smothered by the lack of freedom when the kids were younger. But that was precisely the time where I had to make my mark. I don't think it was ambition in my part. The system is such that you either make it to partner or you're out. I wanted to make sure that I could support them. Now that I have the money, I seem to have lost what was most important. Except of course the kids I can still see. Talk to them. Enjoy them. But it's not the same thing."

"You never really were a realist!"

"I know one of the things that bothers me most is that when we arrive at a crisis, she seems to count me among her enemies."

"That probably goes back to when she was a kid and she didn't get the support she needed. And you probably don't voice much sympathy. You're such a slump!"

"You're not much help, are you?" After a pause he continued, "You know, when I received the award from the Bar Association, I wasn't even able to give her the news. She said 'Don't bother me with stuff that has to do with your work You know what I feel about it,' before I had a chance say anything."

"We are not teenagers anymore. Then you could have come to me for meaningful advice. Now it makes no sense."

The troubled situation between the two of them came to a head one night when he came into their bedroom and without a word enveloped her in a bear hug next to the bed. His intention was clear. She wrenched herself free.

"Do that with your chippy or mistress or whatever you call her. I wouldn't want to catch a disease."

She thought for a moment he was going to slap her. But apparently he was able to contain himself.

"And exactly what does that mean?"

"Don't act the innocent. I know and you know you have a girlfriend."

"What gave you that idea?"

"As usual you think you're the only person in the world! Alice saw you purchasing an expensive ring at Budenstein."

"You shouldn't listen to gossip."

He looked at her intensely, then leaned over, opened a drawer in the night table and pulled out a small jewel box. "Here it is," and he handed it to her. The ring was truly gorgeous and would look beautiful on her finger

"Look on the inside of the ring."

The engraving said, "To Susan with love."

"I wanted to give it to you for our anniversary two weeks ago, but you were so unfriendly that it would have been a travesty."

Susan gulped. She couldn't be more confused. The poor man, as mean as he was, had tried to patch their differences.

She carefully placed the ring in the box and handed it back to him. That gesture just gave her enough time to think how to salvage the situation, at least in her eyes.

"Let's plan on a whole day. You bring me flowers first. Then you entertain me in the most fancy restaurant in town. Then you can give me the ring with a flourish. And I can thank you the way you deserve."

Perhaps she looked desolate, suddenly overcome by regrets, suddenly shy. He didn't know, but he took her in his arms and felt her reciprocating, first reluctantly. Then passion followed. She thought for a moment that she should warn him to be careful not to tear her nightgown, it was her favorite but it seemed to be the wrong thing to say and it made little difference because it was off her an instant later.

In the morning they looked at each other sheepishly. Elliott spoke first.

"Let's see if we can straighten out our mess. That should be our top priority."

She couldn't have agreed more.

IRONY

Life is irony, Jason thought. Behind bars, he sat on his hard lumpy mattress. Knowing that he would be released soon, he could contemplate a possible future. Marty, his roommate of sixteen months, stretched out on his bed, stared with a smirk on his saturnine face.

"Betcha first thing you do is get laid." He smacked his lips and gave him a tawdry wink. His unshaven face and prison pallor contributed to his malevolent expression. That Jason had been imprisoned without having committed a crime was beyond Marty's comprehension. "Contempt of court" was not in his vocabulary. Why Jason was being released was to him another mystery.

Jason felt his own appearance must not be much different than that of his companion. Much younger and clean shaven, he hoped his jail-time expression of unfocused despair had disappeared with the good news.

Soon he'd be out of his depressing surroundings — the smelly cell, gray and without any amenities. The small barred window offered little relief. Not much better than cells in another era — except for the unshielded toilet. The daily one hour outside the confines of the cell had done little to lessen the drabness or the monotony.

Jason smiled at the thought of freedom. He had no idea what portents it would bring. But surely, he would regain some of his past triumphs. As a journalist, Jason had exposed accounting frauds that had tainted two of the most important pension plans in the state. What he did best was investigating and exposing. To him it was an intense game and he had no sympathy for the villains. His motivation had been reinforced by the knowledge that innocents were hurt. There are so many paths to success or at least survival. No matter how smart or important you are, cheating makes you an inept fool, he thought, a schmuck in today's language.

Not too long before his incarceration, he had been the toast of the town. Even the mayor had made speeches about his courage and incorruptibility. Jason could still envision Mayor Evans's bloated red face and large pate surrounded by a crown of short gray hair as he voiced hypocrisies from the podium. Evans's smile had been well rehearsed. A dark suit and red tie hadn't done much to improve his appearance. During the speech, Jason's wife, Mariana, sitting in a prominent position with her eyes proudly on Jason, had looked more attractive than ever. In the well-lighted hall, supplied with several TV cameras, the crowd had laughed at Evans's well-timed jokes. Then, His Honor had proceeded to tell them that in this day and age heroism came under many guises. The audience had applauded wildly. Whether the applause had been for Jason or the mayor, Jason had no way of telling. Where had Evans been for the past few months? He certainly didn't speak about Jason's heroism or principles anymore. Jason's heroic stands had somehow become "stubbornness."

At that time, Jason had been married to one of the most attractive women he had ever met, Mariana. High society, no less —accustomed to the best. Her beauty was spectacular. She always managed to be dressed in good taste — always perfect with the right finery and adornments — the fashionable cut of the dresses, the colors that enhanced her beautiful complexion and raven hair.

She had probably married Jason on a whim. He had been successful — considered attractive. Toying with danger, as he did, has always been assumed to be appealing, even if most would be unwilling to be put to the test. For his part Jason had been unable to ignore her desirability. Neither of their two separate motivations could lead to stability. Yet, having partaken from the fountain of success even temporarily it still seemed to have been worthwhile. The two of them had been admired, even envied. Attended by many luminaries, Mariana's parties had made the two of them feel like royalty. They truly enjoyed each other's company. He remembered their well-satisfied feeling as well as the envious looks of some of the onlookers. Even the occasional reluctant appearance at the parties of Mariana's little sister, Penelope, seemed to enhance her older sister's status. Penny admired her sister greatly. She wasn't plain or uninteresting, but it was clear that she didn't care how she looked and what was fashionable. In many ways, she was the inverse of her sister. Yet Penny had a charm of her own — a vitality that couldn't be suppressed — a self-knowledge which spoke of an unpretentious self-confidence. Her spectacles communicated the stereotype that she was interested in intellectual pursuits as she actually was.

When it had become clear that Jason was to be jailed for an undetermined length of time the break between Jason and Mariana took place without drama or recriminations.

"You know, I really couldn't take that!" Mariana had declared.

She had never lied to him. He had just smiled although his heart had been awash in regret; he knew that she was saying all the truth and nothing but the truth as he had understood all along. Was it his heart or his vanity that had suffered a blow? He had agreed to a Reno divorce. A sort of "a no fault" affair. There had been no great problems —almost all the money had been hers and there hadn't been another man, at least then. She had even offered him financial support for when he was eventually released. Although he had known his enforced absence would decimate his finances, his male ego couldn't possibly allow him to accept.

After a few days in jail he suddenly understood the meaning of the sensory deprivation that was used as a form of torture or responsible for unpleasantness of the milder isolation of mothers with young children.

Surprisingly, it was Penny who had made his incarceration bearable. With a shy smile and rather formal behavior, she had visited him with some regularity. Through the screening process of the jail, she brought him magazines and mysteries which in many ways had saved him from the void that could have threatened his sanity.

Penny's conversation was generally impersonal — news of the outside world. Mariana was never mentioned. He had often wondered what was motivating Penny. He doubted that she could have been acting for her sister. In his mind, she always been Mariana's little sister, to be revered with distant affection. Perhaps she was the victim of a juvenile crush. In fact, when they had first been married, Penny had not been far from adolescence. But then his conclusion might have been just a reflection of his own vanity, if he had any left.

He thought she didn't know how grateful he was for her visits. Whenever her presence was announced he'd feel a surge of affection and gratitude. He hoped she hadn't noticed that her presence also elicited a wave of desire. Involuntary isolation seemed to enhance that drive. Aside from his susceptibility, there was no question that she had become a very attractive young woman. She dressed modestly but what she wore didn't hide her mature body. Her friendly smile was something he had learned to cherish. Not that he had completely ignored her charm before. He remembered well her cute face in moments of unexpected intimacy in their past. Once Jason had been waiting for Mariana to go somewhere or other and Penny was on a brief vacation from college. Jason and Penny had been sitting across from each other in the elegant living room. He had found himself advising her on an oral presentation for some college course. First give some idea of what you're going to talk about. Then present each separate thought by itself as you would in writing, with each thought in a paragraph. Then bring the presentation to a dramatic end, a sort of climax in which the various thoughts are brought together. Her presentation must have gone well because the week after, she thanked him warmly.

Then there had been the time when the two of them waited anxiously in the emergency room after Mariana had been thrown by her horse. Holding hands had made the wait bearable. There were people going in and out showing anxiety or boredom while they waited for news about their patient. Then, finally, a favorable prognosis and report. Mariana had only cracked two ribs — a painful but not dangerous condition. They had actually hugged when they'd heard the news. Concern had brought them together.

While Mariana recovered at home, Jason had taken over from her maid and attended to her comfort hand and foot.

Sitting in jail, Jason thought of the event which had led to his imprisonment. The incident had occurred so quickly that he had been unable to separate what had been recorded by eye and brain and what had been surmised in those few seconds of drama. The platform at the station of the elevated track had been crowded although there was enough space without contact between strangers. After a long wait, the train had finally rumbled as it approached. Wouldn't you know it — it had turned out to be an express train that wouldn't stop. Jason had gotten the distinct impression that a man next to him had lifted a young girl, perhaps eleven or twelve, with the intention of hurling her into the path of the train. Jason had grabbed her with both hands. While still pushing the girl with one hand, the man had hit him with the fist of the other. In avoiding the thrust, Jason had felt himself falling onto the track with the girl in his arms. Instinctively, he had turned in mid-fall so that the girl wouldn't be slammed onto the ground. The impact had jarred his back. The thought came to him in a flash, how a real hero in the New York City subway had jumped onto the tracks to save someone who had fallen, allowing the train to pass over them harmlessly. Terrified, Jason went through the same motions and had held the girl tightly against the ground. He wasn't sure what followed, although there was the grating sound of metal against metal and then the train blocked the light of the day. He had lifted the girl to the platform and somebody had helped him up saying, "Are you alright? Are you alright," until it became obvious that Jason was intact. The terrified girl had not been harmed. Her face was white and she'd started crying uncontrollably. Many well-wishers or curiosity seekers had crowded around them and the train had remained idle. Jason had left as the wails of an ambulance approached them and before anybody could identify him. The girl surrounded by people had been safe from another attack. He had left certain that he didn't want to appear a hero where only serendipity and some primitive reflexes had sufficed. Not surprisingly the incident escaped the attention of the media, so he hadn't been able to find out who she was. He had only told Mariana about his action. His wife as usual was impressed, yet concerned about his impulsiveness.

"One of these days you'll really get into trouble," she murmured.

A few days later, Jason had gone to the newspaper office to leave a small article about recent scams. The editor-in-chief, Marlowe, had been discouraging.

"It doesn't have the pizzazz of your previous series. This is not what we need!"

"I can't offer perfection every time. It's still better than your usual shit."

"I always find your modesty astounding!" the editor had quipped with sarcasm and malice.

Marlowe's eyes were slits, covered by the thick spectacles worn on a lean face. Sarcasm was one of his weapons. Jason admired his ability as an editor but never would have admitted it.

As he was walking away from the building, a black Cadillac with tinted windows had kept pace with him. It had all the markings of another era, when gangsters were more visible and threatening. With trepidation he realized he was not far from wrong. A burly man had stepped out and opened the backdoor.

"The boss wants to talk to you."

Jason had hesitated a moment. Was this going to be the legendary "being taken for a ride?" What choice did he have? Who of his many enemies had he irritated enough for this? With his heart pounding he'd gotten into the car where a dignified elderly man was sitting in the back seat. He gave him his hand which Jason felt compelled to shake. Was this the equivalent of the Mafia ritual where the victim is first kissed? he mused. As the door closed, the car sped away.

The old man, formally dressed in a dark suit and tie, had white hair neatly combed back.

"I'm Barcolino," he had said. Even after many years he had managed to retain an accent. Jason had no clue about what was happening. The name of course was familiar to him. Rumor had it that despite his advanced age, Angelo Barcolino was still the dominant crime figure in the small part of the city to which he had retreated. His dominance elsewhere had long since gone.

The little girl, Gianna ..."

Totally confused, Jason couldn't make a connection between past and present. Barcolino had continued. "She's my granddaughter," and after pause, "I owe you," Barcolino had seemed to hesitate, "As if they could intimidate me! There used to be honor in my generation. Now that's gone. I'm going to strike back."

Jason remained silent and without any real understanding had nodded. The old man must have been referring to the train episode.

"But I learned something in my old age," Barcolino laughed —a full belly laugh. "Here is my deal." He had pulled out a package tightly wrapped in a plastic sheet and handed it to Jason. "This is all you need."

After a few seconds he had continued, "How old do you think I am?"

"I wouldn't know."

"Eighty-eight, my boy. I'm still doing alright. But at my age you have a total different way of seeing. There couldn't be much time left. But enough ... enough."

Jason had been puzzled by the exchanges but hadn't dared interrupt the man or break his mood with questions. His answers probably would not have enlighten him and he still wondered about his own safety.

Barcolino had rapped on the window separating the passenger compartment from the front. For a short while, the car sped on. Then it stopped in front of Mariana and Jason's house and the burly driver had opened the car door and a baffled Jason exited.

Before he could make any sense out of the episode, he had to learn more about Barcolino. Jason had learned a long time before that there is always at least one person capable of providing information on any selected topic. His colleague Joseph Rovair was the person most knowledgeable about organized crime. Not really friends, they mostly ignored each other since they had entirely different interests. The fact that Jason was almost never in the newspaper offices made any contact difficult. However, he eventually found Rovair at his desk. With a red face, graying hair and an aquiline nose, Rovair had a diabolical look with flashing eyes and thin disapproving lips. He was reputed to have a fiery temper, although Jason had personally never felt its lashes.

"Barcolino? Strictly a has-been. Still has some hold in the South Side, but that will be ousted soon. The Avanti folks are moving in. He's too old-fashioned! Imagine, he just got involved with drugs in the past year. But I'm afraid it's too late! He's a has-been, as I said. I predict they'll take over his whole organization, the whole caboodle!"

With his curiosity aroused, Jason decided to examine the contents of the package. The sheets of paper were covered by old-fashioned cursive handwriting. The list included names and amounts, a list of sites and routes involved with "candy". It took him a long time to decide that the information was genuine. But why would Barcolino betray his own organization? Jason had been reluctant to make a move. He had been aware that he was sitting on a bomb, and bombs can't be used carelessly.

Rovair's prediction had been prescient. Barcolino was shot just a few days later. The likelihood that he could direct his shrinking empire from a hospital bed was remote. But Jason felt that the old man was smarter than most. Barcolino must have meant for him to use the information in his possession, as soon as his organization had been taken over.

After a week or two, Jason had started writing articles exposing each facet of the information one at a time. First the bent police. Later the locales where drugs were stored followed by the names of all the men involved in their distributions. Cautious, he had sent the written reports to the DA before publication. Julius Emmett, the DA, was an ambitious man and had taken immediate action. The series of arrests, some by the city police, some by the FBI, some by agents of the Bureau of Alcohol, Tobacco, Firearms and Explosives, and some by the state's Organized Crime Drug Task Force had followed the publication of each article.

There had been little doubt that the information was correct. Material evidence had been quickly collected by the authorities. However, when several cases came to court, Jason was asked to testify and reveal his sources. Obviously he had to refuse. The information accumulated had been sufficient to convict and his testimony was totally unnecessary and even irrelevant. "But so it goes," to quote the incomparable Kurt Vonnegut. And that is how poor Jason had found himself in prison.

After Barcolino had died of his wounds, Jason who had been in jail for all those months was ready to testify. However, he had to be released. And not surprisingly, nobody was interested in his testimony. Most of the defendants had already been convicted without his contribution.

On the day he was released, the presence of Penny at the exit was a welcome surprise. Standing there patiently waiting for him, with a bright smile, she looked particularly prim and endearing. Without any makeup, she was dressed simply, in a skirt and blouse. He couldn't suppress his sudden unexpected impulse to hug her and he found her in his arms. She was blushing from head to toe.

"You have to come with me," Penny stated firmly.

Jason hadn't made any arrangements and probably would have had to stay at a hotel but the possibility of spending time with Penny was enticing. He realized that coming from jail he was not exactly attractive and possibly repulsive. He had carefully shaved in preparation for his release but couldn't ignore that he must have carried with him the obnoxious smells of his cell.

"Only if I can use your shower," he quipped.

"I got the clothing you stored in the newspaper locker. Not much, but it should be enough for a few days." In her apartment he immediately showered. Under the stream of water he had a chance to reassemble his thoughts. Was it really wise to stay with Penny? Was it fair to her? His thoughts were confused. He probably was in love with her. But was that really what it was? Isolation from human interactions and women certainly may have altered his good sense.

After emerging, dressed in jeans and t-shirt, he immediately broached the subject of his brooding.

"Penny, I'm not sure I should stay here. I'm a very confused man."

"I think you have Victorian values. What's wrong with staying here?"

"Look, I'm all mixed up. I can't even figure out whether I'm in love with you. I love you that's for sure, but that might not be enough. Should you really spend time with such an idiot?"

"I have been in love with you off and on since I first met you as a teenager. I have no doubts."

She solved the problem of his concerns by suddenly removing her spectacles and hugging and kissing him passionately. His response matched passion for passion. Penny without detaching from him gently led him to the bedroom. Some arguments have no possible retort.

THE HIDDEN CARD

Recondite are the ways of life and love
Old saying

In a game of cards you don't know your opponent's hand while in life your own cards might be a mystery.

Consider what happened to Kevin, not so long ago. Kevin had never had the muzzle of a handgun pointed in his direction. He couldn't have been more surprised. In front of him, his friend Mark held the weapon. Kevin gulped. In an instant fear savaged his gut. What was happening seemed entirely illogical. The two of them were in a deserted warehouse, an improbable meeting place that had been selected by Mark. Death comes to your door when you least expect it, Kevin thought. The ceiling was high and light filtered through the broken or stained windows making everything appear gray. Darkness and death seem to go together.

Thoughts crowded Kevin's mind. Past events flashed by. What had brought them to this pass? Kevin had collected a lottery prize for Mark as if it were his own—after taxes a cool two million, give or take a few thousand. The proceeds were passed to Mark who hadn't wanted to collect the prize himself. He had many outstanding debts. Why alert his creditors? Avoiding taxes also might have been one of his aims. Or perhaps Mark intended to hide his assets in a divorce settlement. Whatever the reason, the maneuver certainly skirted the law. But nobody was going to get hurt and the fifty thousand dollars promised were enticing to Kevin. The financial struggle to complete his education had been daunting.

Facing the handgun, Kevin's mouth felt pasty. He forced the utterances of what he hope were calm words. "What's up Mark?" He thought he had to gain some time. As if that would change the outcome!

Mark smirked. "You don't think I could let you go on your own way knowing something that could fuck me up and gain me some inside time, do you?"

"Mark, don't be stupid. If anything happened to me, they would suspect you immediately thinking that you'd stolen my money. You can't transfer cash without leaving traces."

"That shows how stupid you are. First they have to realize that you're dead. The warehouse belongs to Angelo Salmone. He's not going to be released from jail for another two years! You think I'll be sitting around waiting for them? I'll be gone. Out of the country and away. As free as a bird."

They were not alone. A woman, Maureen, was present in the warehouse but remained some distance away. At one time Kevin had been in love with her. Along with the fear, he felt the pain of her betrayal. Maureen seemed to be in cahoots with Mark. She offered no hope. Even before this moment of truth, she had avoided his glances. At other times, her eyes were hard and empty of sentiment. She had taken care of the electronic transfer to one of Mark's accounts and accompanied Mark most of the time. Kevin thought about her with regret.

Kevin had met her years before and still had pleasant memories of what he had thought was love, possibly because it had been his first romance. From the very beginning all he could have said about Maureen was that she was all spontaneity without any artifice. You couldn't call her voluptuous, but she certainly had a touch of the sensuous in her bearing— the light and graceful way she moved. She wasn't even pretty — her features were too irregular. What one noticed immediately were her wide laughing mouth and twinkling brown eyes. All in contrast to her bearing now that she was with Mark.

Kevin had been on night watchman duty. Accustomed to the lumbering form of Herrera at the intersection of their patrol paths, Kevin had been taken by surprise by Maureen who was also in the watchman uniform.

All he could say was, "What happened to Herrera?"

"I guess he quit. You'll have to put up with me."

Between patrolling, he'd used to spend some time in the common room with Herrera discussing over coffee what men talked about when together--football scores, baseball and little else. The room assigned to the watchmen was not comfortable but it had to do. It had a television set, a coffee machine, several chairs and a beat-up table.

With Maureen everything had changed. He had found her teasing, charming, vibrant. He had had very little to do with women previously. His chosen path and taking care of his grandma before she'd died hadn't left much time for friendships or romance. The information they had exchanged was very rudimentary at first. Maureen had originally been with the police. But she had been dismissed under painful circumstances so that Kevin didn't try to pry.

One time, when their watchman routines were almost over, Maureen had looked at him intensely. She'd then proceeded to kiss him on the lips. Kevin had never been aware that kissing could involve the whole body. She asked him to go with her to her home. He'd met Maureen's sister, Liz, and Eleanor, a girl of about nine, he judged. Maureen and Liz were raising the little girl, the daughter of another sister.

Maureen and Kevin had then walked Eleanor to the school. Eleanor had looked him over surreptitiously. Kevin had also stolen some glances in her direction. She seemed to be a very serious and pretty little girl.

When they returned they had the apartment to themselves as Liz had gone out. Kevin had never thought they could contain so much savagery and tenderness. Then and many times afterwards, between the physical delights, they often murmured about their dreams and thoughts while in each other's arms.

Kevin had been deeply in love and hadn't expect their relationship to terminate abruptly, but Maureen had a surprise for him.

"We have to stop seeing each other. I didn't tell you the whole story. As you know, I was with the police. A detective of all things. I killed a man in self-defense while on duty. He was socially prominent, so you can imagine what happened. I'm out on bail. I'll have to do three years for manslaughter. I should have told you before. I don't want you to wait for me or visit me in prison. Let's just call it quits. It will be less painful."

None of these memories were helping him. Mark again raised his gun. Kevin's insides knotted. He might as well die trying and prepared himself for a leap to grab the gun. Before he could spring there were two shots. To Kevin's surprise, he felt nothing. In contrast Mark crumpled and slowly fell to the ground. Still terrified Kevin turned. Maureen was holding a gun in her hand.

"Once in the head, once in the gut just as I have been taught."

A near death experience can really confuse you. The hubbub that followed contributed further to his bafflement. At the police station, they took down his statement. While the text was being typed, Maureen sat next to him. She had already made a statement—she seemed free to move about.

"Sorry to have left you in the dark." After a few silent seconds she continued, "I suppose I owe you an apology." After more silence, "I really don't know where to start. I served my time. Actually two years. The sentence was cut short for good behavior."

They were interrupted by the policeman who brought Kevin's finished statement and Maureen waited while Kevin read and signed it.

"I couldn't get a job. I had had dealings with Mark. He was the only one to offer me a job. I didn't have much choice. I never lied to you. I was in touch with the police all along. I never expected the events to go so far. I hope you'll forgive me."

Kevin found himself changing from surprised to mellow. "There is something to forgive? You saved my life and it might plunge you into more complications."

"Actually, I'm okay. So are you. There is nothing wrong with cashing somebody else's lottery winning. You didn't even get paid for the service. Mark had another kind of payment in mind.

"I was hoping for more than gratitude from you. Do I still stand a chance with you? As shabbily as I treated you, you're the only man I've ever cared for."

"It would be very stupid not to try. I 've never loved anybody else either. It would be foolish to let it go."

They found themselves holding hands. Anything more passionate would have to wait but not for long.

******

Late, two witnesses to the original shooting in which Maureen had shot a man while on police duty, turned up and she was vindicated. It was self-defense. The gun the perp had held reappeared mysteriously. The matter was settled out of court for a few bucks—false arrest, miscarriage of justice or something like that. Kevin thought that turned out okay because one should start married life with some financial reserves and no regrets.

THE WOMAN IN BLACK

The often stated stereotype that there is less crime in a small town is frequently wrong, but quite correct in the case of Truville-on-Hudson or its closest neighbor, Orchard. Most police investigations were in fact about trivial matters. But then there is a case that can be considered strange, perhaps exotic: the case of the "Woman in Black", intriguing to some of the locals. Perhaps its roots were in the nature of the town itself.

Truville-on-Hudson was one of those towns along the river which could still be considered picturesque. True enough, Manstone's Pharmacy had been replaced by a CVS after Mr. Manstone had run off with the woman managing the cosmetic and perfume counter, leaving behind wife and kiddies. Manstone was an old-fashioned man; he had stubbornly stuck to the old ways and had refused to sell any kind of contraceptives. Despite the changes, the worn-out look of some of the houses, the recent gentrification and the appearance of an upscale café in an old building proclaimed the town's quaintness along with the subtle declaration that it was with-it.

One of the outstanding citizens of the town, Eugene Sudderson, known as Gene to his intimates, was married to a lovely woman. Martha Sudderson was shapely, dressed well and was friendly and soft spoken. Her blonde hair and regular features made her extremely attractive. Gene more often than not wore casual clothes which somehow proclaimed a not-so-casual price. Going to work he wore a well-cut dark suit and a power tie, the uniform of a well-heeled Wall Street acolyte. Anybody acquainted with the Suddersons and their two daughters Amanda and Jolie, 6 and 10 years old, knew that they constituted a contented family unit.

As part of the upper echelon of the town, Gene had to attend the performance of "Mayhem in Manhattan" by Archibald Blitz presented by the local gentry. He didn't have much patience with amateur productions but this was an obligation he could not escape. To add to the burden, his wife had insisted he take Jolie, the older of their two girls, who almost certainly would fall asleep.

This is how he first saw Gladys Rose, the only talented actress in the group. Green-eyed with reddish-gold hair, her movements were as graceful and nimble as those of a cat. She spoke clearly with a melodious voice. Gene guessed that she had had some training — a rose in an onion patch. He couldn't take his eyes away from her.

The following Monday when he went to work, by coincidence she was waiting with a throng of others for the train to the big city.

"Hey!" he said "I loved your performance. I'm Gene Sudderson."

She looked at him with a puckish smile.

"I love flattery. Tell me more. Tell me I should be on Broadway!"

That's how they came to sit next to each other on their trip to the city.

"Tell me how I'm perfect for the stage! Take me to lunch and flatter me some more."

He hesitated only for an instant.

"I'd love to if you're willing to have a late lunch."

Gene nervously checked out the restaurant as they entered trying to remember if anybody he knew lived in that part of the city. He might have to explain why he was there with a young and beautiful woman. But then, it shouldn't be too difficult to come up with an explanation. After all, he was wearing his wedding band, plain to see. Would he wear a ring so openly if he was up to something?

He was surprised to learn that she was twenty-eight. He would have guessed she was much younger. She talked about her life in the big city. She'd done some modeling and tried for some parts. Sometimes she was selected as an extra but never for a major role. Her trips to the city were only to try out for a part or when she had a specific job. Her eyes glowed with excitement. She was looking forward to a tryout that might open the door to other opportunities. This time it was a musical, somewhat tongue-in-cheek. It was tentatively called "Torquemada", based on the play by Archibald Blitz, the same author of the amateur production Gene had just seen. It was in the style of the "Producers", with a touch of Mel Brooks.

Gladys was one of the most exotic creatures he had ever met. Small breasted, she had the air of a dancer in her nimbleness.

She was pleased to hear that he sometimes stayed overnight in an apartment provided by his company for when one of the executives worked long hours. It was just a bedroom and bathroom and a living room set up for reading and relaxing. Very efficient but still not home.

"You'll have to show me sometime." She was looking at him playfully.

Gladys continued her chatter, while the thought reverberated in his mind, "You'll have to show me sometime."

He should have felt that he should get away from her. He had a lovely wife and two lovely daughters. But of course he stayed. He had been there before and found the chase and its eventual rewards delightful. True, in this case he was the pursued, but it was equally exciting.

******

Lieutenant Louis Bathos was a complex man. And that might well be the reason why his wife, Evelyn, loved him so much and why he was such a torment. Early in their marriage Bathos, she still called him that, hadn't been there when he should have. Their children had been born when he was on duty, Lord knows where. The homicides drew him away. She still remembered having to call a cab to go to the hospital for the first birth. For the second.a kind neighbor, Madame Proaska, drove her. The sign at the entrance of the neighbor's apartment, proclaimed she could foretell the future and perhaps that's why Evelyn had avoided her. But surprisingly she revealed herself to be a concerned, pleasant woman when Evelyn was in distress. She didn't even say something unkind about Evelyn's absent husband.

Doubts about his ability to fulfill his role in marriage should have surfaced before she had made her irrevocable commitment. After their two children were in high school and then in college, he still was missing half of the time with his mind elsewhere. Not that he didn't care about them — not that he wasn't attentive to their needs, physical or emotional. Finally, he had taken a job as police chief in this forgotten town along the Hudson. She hadn't expressed her opinion but her thoughts must have been transparent. It would have been so much easier if that opportunity had arisen when they were younger. But then the glamor of hiring an experienced homicide detective from the big city wouldn't have been there. In Truville, crimes and calls in the middle of the night were rare. They had more time to talk. She enjoyed hearing about his "cases", if you could glorify them with that word. True, their exchanges were completely against the rules. But then, she had been very useful more than once. Men are so dumb about some things ... particularly women!

Bathos and Evelyn had been together at the police academy. She had given up her career when they married and she became pregnant. The memory of that time was still vivid in her mind. The two of them had been casual friends. After all, they had attended the same high school and although she belonged to a different circle had shared some of those experiences. Evelyn, one of the popular, highly successful students, the valedictorian of her class —Bathos, one of those lost in the crowd. At the police academy her torrid affair with one of the instructors, a married man, Captain O'Rourke, had excluded anybody else. She had even thought she was pregnant. Sitting on a park bench a few blocks from the academy, she had let tears flow down her cheeks. The trees surrounding the bend in the path had given her a false sense of isolation. The despair from the position she had allowed herself to fall into must have been obvious. Bathos had sat next to her and taken her hand.

"Nothing is as bad as it seems."

At that moment she had been so vulnerable and he was so concerned that she had told him without naming names about her quandary — her love without hope or reason for the wrong man. Under ordinary circumstances she wouldn't have confided in anyone. She'd regretted having spoken so freely the moment the words came out of her mouth. She challenged him.

"Why did you stop? Why do you care? This is none of your business."

"That's easy to say but it's not entirely true. I have been in love with you for quite some time. I just never dared to ask you for a date."

She was doubly embarrassed and somewhat angry with him.

"Look, forget the whole thing. I shouldn't have told you. These are personal matters. Go away. Imagine that we never talked about this."

She expected anger, perhaps contempt. Instead he squeezed her hand.

"If I can ever be of help, please let me know. And you can count on me being discreet."

She tried to forget having confided in him and he didn't approach her again. The whole episode embarrassed her. She had been lucky enough not to cross his path for a long time. She wouldn't have known how to behave. Then she was again free, and it must have reached his ears. It was a year later. She had been assigned to Robberies, he to Homicides.

At a boisterous police-only impromptu party at a bar they frequented, Bathos stopped her as she was leaving alone. He offered to take her home. When he asked her shyly for a date, her first impulse was to say no. Possibly he had gotten the wrong message from her confidences — she wasn't an easy score. Besides, she was still embarrassed by the thought that he knew too much about her. But she couldn't dismiss her recollection of his kindness when she needed it most. She could always break up with him later and gently. After becoming involved with him, she had been tempted to break their relationship more than once. The two of them were so different! But the discovery of some unexpected quality in him always seemed to halt her impulse.

There was the time when a perp was using a child as a shield. Why Bathos had been at the scene wasn't clear. Bathos had walked calmly toward him.

"You don't really want to harm the little girl."

"Your fucking A! Just get too close and I'll blow both of you away."

But Bathos had continued to walk slowly toward him, without drawing his gun, talking calmly, his right hand extended to receive the weapon. And then, it was over just like that.

The men who had been present had been free with the details. It was the talk of the bar where police men and women hung out and Evelyn had been present.

"God, he's a crazy dude! He should probably be assigned to a desk before somebody wastes him!"

She had asked Bathos later how he had known that the man wouldn't shoot.

"I dunno. It didn't look to me that he would. I was afraid the sharpshooters on the roof would fuck up and hurt the little girl. And nobody should be killed if it can be avoided. I was sure my way would work."

She had realized then that there was something grand about the man that nobody else had noticed. But, had he put his life in danger like that after they had married, she would never have forgiven him, hero or no hero. In time she came to recognize that Bathos had an unexpected sweetness and sentimentality. The dark experiences in his daily life at work hadn't turned him into a cynic as many others in Homicide.

******

Gene and Gladys. Like most other encounters it started with a kiss. Their tongues searching, searching, their hands caressing. Then it exploded into a continuum of passion. They didn't seem to want to stop, didn't seem to be able to stop. Later, as he kissed her he could sense the scent of his seminal fluid on her lips.

The only other time that he had been so overwhelmed was years before. His youth had been a factor then and the woman wasn't half as interesting as Gladys. More recently, they had been what he considered "average women". If you want passion and a sexual adventure don't do your fishing in a small town or suburb. Sex has to have spice or it is dull ... dull. In his mind the men who didn't pursue were simply lazy.

******

The murder had taken place in a motel in a neighboring town.

Technically Bathos was not involved. The chief of police of Orchard, Bill Smith, beseeched him to help. His red face was even redder than usual and he was clearly suffering.

"You have experience with murders. I don't. Before I call the State Police, I would like to discuss it with you. It involves the murder of one of the citizens of your fair town, Eugene Sudderson. Surely you would know more about him than I do."

Bathos could well understand Bill's concern. The town council had been speaking of abolishing the police force for the sake of economy. The salaries of three policemen was unneeded since the State Police could be at the town's beck and call. The advantage of having policemen familiar with the community wasn't thought worthwhile. That you couldn't involve an overworked State Police in routine matters wasn't even considered by the citizenry.

The case seemed simple enough. Sudderson was having a tryst with a woman at a motel. He was killed by a single shot from a .22. The powder marks suggested that it was held close to his head. The desk clerk could only describe the woman as "a woman in black." Since there was no other visitor and the woman in black had entirely disappeared before the police had been summoned, she was the most likely suspect. The surveillance cameras in the corridor saw only one woman entering and then leaving two hours later. The fire-escape would have required passing through the corridor. The traces of semen on the bed supported the assumption that it had been a sexual encounter. But then who was the woman in black?

Evelyn exclaimed, "A black widow. First you fuck him and then you terminate him. Interesting. Maybe a profiler would have something to say. Bet you this is a case to be solved by a woman not by a man."

Bathos laughed uproariously. "The next thing you'll tell me is that the Woman in Black is a blonde because blondes look best in black."

"Laugh if you must, but put your money where your foolishness is."

"Ten bucks that she's not a blonde."

"No, that's not what I meant. Ten bucks that a major clue will come from a woman."

"Done! Bet you think you're that woman ... You're not supposed to mix into police business."

"You just want me to lose the bet. This time you're not in charge. I can meddle all I want."

"Veh is mir! Now we really are in trouble." Yet he knew how effective she could be.

In some British mysteries she had read, the first stop by an experienced investigator in a small village was to gather the gossip in a local pub. This could at least provide some knowledge of the lay of the land. Obviously a different set of circumstances applied in this case but a similar principle could be used. Evelyn didn't waste any time. She made an appointment at the beauty parlor favored by the sophisticates. It took her two visits to gather information — one to get her hair done, another to get her nails done. Obviously everything could have been accomplished in one visit, but two visits were likely to be more productive than just one. She had considered a complete make-over which would have provided a whole day of gossip. Because of the expense, however, she restrained herself at least for the moment — a whole day of ribbing from Bathos was a payback she didn't need. He'd argue that she was trying to please an admirer, at first a joke but with men you never know. Surprisingly, it was the hairdresser who came up with the first bit of information. Evelyn had the same auburn hair and heart-shaped face as another customer. The hairdresser recommended a similar hairdo. With a conspiratorial smile, she intimated that the woman with the heart-shaped face had "if you know what I mean with Sudderson ... if you know what I mean." But that wasn't all. Because of the murder there was a buzz about the dearly departed. Several rumors were bandied about. He had been seen with this or that woman. Whether every incident had any significance was hard to tell, but there was the possibility that the respectable Mr. Sudderson had been involved with several women and at least three of them Evelyn could identify.

******

Bill Smith was unable to trace the gun which had had its numbers filed off.

"All right, you came up with four names of women who are likely to have been involved with our philandering hero. And there might be more who don't live in our fair town. What can we do with that?" Bathos complained.

It was then that Evelyn felt compelled to put in her few cents worth. "As I understand it, it's possible to extract DNA corresponding to the woman from a sample containing semen."

"You've been reading again! But then you don't have anything to compare it with without inconveniencing a bunch of women who are not likely to be very cooperative and will have very uncooperative expensive lawyers. And I don't think that poor Bill would be able to get a warrant to collect the appropriate samples."

"That's nothing. It would be easy enough to collect hair from the comb of a beauty shop. These are women of means, don't forget."

"Hm! Hm! I'm not sure of the legality of that."

"Legality, shmegality! Once you know whose it is you can find a way of getting a warrant."

"First, I think Bill might be able to narrow down your list by examining whether they have an alibi."

Bill was not experienced in interrogation. His villains usually confessed in the middle of the warning about evidence, silence and the right to a lawyer. But fortunately what he had to ask was simple and through interviews, Bill found that all the women on the list had an alibi, except for Gladys Rose. She was very cooperative and quickly told them the details of her affair. She had no objection to a DNA test. After waiting two weeks for the results, they were found to be negative.

"Well, there we are. At no place at all!" Conversing with his wife, Bathos was becoming impatient. "I also don't understand what happened. Everything indicates that only one woman was involved. If we were to suppose that the motivation was jealousy, you might expect two. One for trysting and one for murder."

"Well you know what they say in fiction "cherchez la femme.""

"Isn't that what we have been doing?"

"No, not at all. What you have been doing is "cherchez les femmes" and rather clumsily at that. You haven't even considered the most logical candidate."

"What are you talking about?"

"His wife, of course. It shouldn't be hard to get a DNA sample from her."

"That's ridiculous, why would he have a tryst with his wife?"

"Well, if done right, it could give sex a taste of the illicit and the exotic, perhaps helped along by dressing in black."

"I think you're dreaming."

"Am I? Remember our vacation in the Bahamas, our only vacation in twenty years?"

"Stop harking on our rare vacations. You know we couldn't go all that often. But our stay in the Bahamas, how could I forget it?"

"That's my point. I had to stop you. I was afraid you'd have a heart attack."

"I don't remember anything like that. You're making it up."

"Not at all. I was there, wasn't I?"

"Well! His wife! That's the stupidest idea I have ever heard."

Of course it was exactly correct. The DNA samples matched exactly. Once again Bathos had lost a bet with his wife. The motive, of course, was the usual one. Eugene Sanderson 's wife had become tired of his playing around. Why she couldn't just go through a juicy divorce instead was one of those matters that have no answer.

After the case was solved, Bathos hoped that it showed to one and all how important it was to have a local police force and that the police department of Orchard should not be disbanded. He didn't have much time to grapple with that thought. The call came through from one his men. Mrs. Berenstein's cat was up a tree again. What should he do?

A RED ROSE

She couldn't ignore the intense headache and the taste of blood in her mouth from the blow. Her hands were tied behind her back and her joints ached. Yet, what hurt most was the agony of the betrayal and the sure knowledge of not having a future.

Conrad, the medicine man, and his colorful painted wagon travelling from town to town promised remedies for female complaints, ague, chills and many other diseases. It had been her shelter for two months. She had made a great contribution. People liked her. Conrad had been well pleased by her collection while she passed the bottles with the most awful looking green concoction inside. Why he had suddenly turned on her she didn't know. Couldn't even understand what might have happened.

Rose had thought of herself as having run away from home at the mature age of sixteen. In reality, she had been kicked out. First, the isolation from all that she had known, in a little room in the back of the house — day in and day out. This was after bitter vituperations from her father, a thin menacing fellow who had never shown her or her sister, Marge, any affection.

"Slut! You'll burn in hell!" His face had been twisted by what looked like intense hate.

There had been some moments of contact with the rest of the house when somebody, usually Marge, had brought her food. Few words had been exchanged. Then being barely tolerated during a painful labor which had produced a stillborn.

After recovering from her ordeal, she had no longer been tolerated and had been kicked out. While leaving in pain and fear, Marge had surreptitiously passed her some money, otherwise all she had with her were the clothes on her back, sticky and dirty.

It was eventide and the three men in front of the medicine wagon were arguing. Conrad was annoyed, insisting to the two disreputable men, "Only fifty dollars." When he wasn't announcing in stentorian tones to the gathered crowds the merits of his potions, Conrad — a middle-age man practically without teeth and with a sparse beard, lisped, mumbled and spit while he talked. With gray, stringy, dirty hair he had an expression that could look ingratiating when talking to his customers or vicious as it was during their argument. The two men were much younger, tall and gray with dirt. They were dressed in the common clothing she had first seen in the West — Stetson, denim shirts, leather pants, boots and heavy-looking Colt handguns at their sides. Rose knew that Conrad was selling her and was terrified.

"Okay, okay," one of the men affirmed.

"I got seventy-five!"

Rose hadn't heard the new player in the dreadful charade approaching. Neither had the three men who were also startled. He didn't look very different from the two arguing men. He was perhaps taller and his brown eyes were steel.

"This ain't an auction," yelled one of the men who promptly moved his hand next to his holster.

The new player laughed. His hand had already grasped the gun hand of the other and had pulled him close. "Of course not. You don't have fifty dollars."

The two men who had been negotiating with Conrad sent out malignant looks. Rose expected violence. But nothing happened. The new player laughed again. His left hand snaked into his pocket and came out with the seventy-five dollars in a pouch.

Conrad eagerly counted them and his eyes gleamed with pleasure. The two other men were clearly incensed. "We'll be seeing you. You'll be sorry to have interfered. We ain't going to forget you."

"Isn't that something! I'll try to forget you as soon as I can."

She winced when the knife cut the rope holding her wrists together. The newcomer pulled her up onto his horse, vaulted onto the saddle and they trotted away. A mule with a light load on its back, was tethered to the horse and followed. The new man was turned so that his eyes never departed for too long from the sad scene next to the medicine wagon.

Then after at least thirty minutes they moved faster in the semidarkness and among trees. They reached a clearing with as stream nearby and the man said, "This is a good spot as any." And they dismounted.

"Please mister. I got to go!" The pressure on her abdomen was unbearable.

"Go into the bushes."

She started running and his voice followed her. "Don't come back until I call you. What's your name?"

"Rose."

And then there was silence. The relief would have been more liberating if she hadn't been so troubled. She quickly rearranged her tattered clothing. She had nothing to wipe herself with — another humiliation. The fact that it wasn't that time of the month was lucky. When with Conrad she'd had the hardest time searching for suitable clean rags.

Why wasn't the man concerned about her running away? And then the answer was clear in her mind. Where could she go?

Suddenly the realization that there might be snakes among the bushes terrified her. She shuddered. Why wasn't that awful man calling her back? But she didn't have the courage to defy him. She had to wait.

There were two shots, closely spaced. Her trembling was uncontrollable.

There was silence for a while and then finally a resounding "Rose!"

She quickly scampered out of her hiding place.

The man was waiting for her — the money pouch he had given to Conrad in his hand. And then he explained. "Isn't that something. What people will do for greed. Though I guess the medicine guy had it coming."

Rose suddenly realized that the two lumps she saw several feet away were dead bodies.

"You killed them!" she said between sobs. There was an accusatory tone in her voice.

"They shouldn't have come with their guns drawn." And then he continued, "I think we should move our camp. Their horses shouldn't be too far away. Stay here. I'll be right back."

Her disgust was followed by nausea. But she collected herself. There was no reason for her companion to be any different from the other men. With an effort to control her repugnance and fear she approached the bodies. Luckily in the dark she could only see dark stains on their clothing and couldn't even distinguish their features. From the one closest to her, she wrested the gun clutched in his hand. It was as her companion had claimed, they had come with guns drawn, she decided. She walked to the mule that was peacefully feeding and hid the gun in the leather bag hanging from its load.

Her companion came back holding the reins of two horses. "They aren't too bad. Now you'll have a mount. Can you ride?"

She nodded but then figuring it was too dark to see her, she murmured, "Yes, I can."

They moved at least a hundred yards away. He fiddled with a bundle and handed her blankets. "This should be sufficient for tonight."

He started a fire after collecting dried twigs and branches. The light from the fire fluttered. The stream provided the water which he boiled in a battered pot for several minutes.

"Now we can have tea." He pulled out jerky from one of the bundles he had unloaded from the mule and warmed an open can of beans on the fire. Crackers were the only other food. The job of preparing the food had been hers when she had been with Conrad.

"This is all we have. I didn't expect company."

He placed tin plates and mugs on the blanket he had stretched out on the ground.

Rose was too exhausted to say anything. She wolfed down the food. Her companion waited for her to finish before eating. Her mind was too tired to understand what that might mean.

The following morning they started again with only crackers and tea under their belts. A few hours later a town opened far away, below the hill from where they were approaching. Her companion said it was called Harmony Falls. They dismounted.

"Let's have some food first. Then later we can have a decent meal."

Rose realized that her moment had come. It was now or never. She could get lost in the town. Railroad tracks were visible from their vantage point. The whole world would open to her if she could get hold of the seventy-five dollars for a train ticket. Suddenly, the gun was in her hand.

The man didn't even flinch. He must have faced death before. "If you're going to shoot me, you should at least know my name. I'm Andrew. Andy to you."

Rose gulped. To her, it was as if their roles were reversed and she were the one was facing a gun. Then unexpected sobs shook her.

"It's not that easy. Is it?"

Amazingly, she found herself in his arms, the gun pointing to the ground. He held her lightly, making soothing noises. She suddenly perked up.

"Please don't sell me to a whorehouse!"

"There are some things I should have explained to you. I never intended to sell you to anybody. I just happened to come by accidentally. I'll keep you until I can set you up with a job." Then after a few moments, "You know, you smell rather ripe and you need some new clothes. Will have to take care of that first."

Relief was followed by resentment. "Ripe" indeed! She hadn't had much of a choice, had she? But then she realized how foolish her resentment was.

He asked her to keep the gun. "You never know when you might need it."

They left the animals and their loads at the Harmony Stable and walked to what they thought was the only hotel in town. Clearly there was an old part and a large addition still under construction. A little bald, middle-aged man insisted that there were no rooms available.

Andrew, she couldn't think of him as Andy, suddenly became menacing.

"My niece here has had a rough time. Don't give me any more nonsense."

The man, frightened, swallowed. "I'll have to ask the owner."

The owner, a woman, introduced herself.

"I'm Myrtle Longbow. What can I do for you?"

She needed only one look to understand their quandary and grasped Rose's hand. She ignored Andy who had said, "I'm Andrew Deward."

She ignored him and directed her attention to Rose. "You poor thing! You must have had a rough time! Come with me, we'll fix you up."

Myrtle Longbow was a very attractive woman with regular features and approaching middle-age. A few white strands coursed her thick chestnut hair. Intuitively, he trusted her but he was in no mood for dallying.

"You do have rooms, I take it?"

"We'll take care of that next." And the two women disappeared up the stairs.

The hotel had a dumpy dining room. While Andy sat waiting for the steak he had ordered, he smiled as he heard a plaintive masculine voice from the kitchen. "Dammit! I wished she'd make up her mind. Hot water for showers or baths is on Wednesdays! This is going to disrupt my routine completely!"

After a while Rose and Myrtle came back. The change in Rose was astounding. She looked clean, demure and rather pretty. She was wearing a new dress which was slightly tight on her.

"We'll wait until she has eaten. Then we have a lot to talk about." Myrtle was looking at him with a serious judgmental demeanor and as if something was left unsaid.

"My God," he thought, "a do-gooder." The most difficult kind to deal with. The idea that he belonged to the same category didn't occur to him.

Rose wolfed down the food as it was brought in. Eventually, she treasured a slice of apple pie.

"You don't have to pay for her food. Just for yours," Myrtle affirmed.

Soon the three of them were in her office with the door closed.

"I'm told you're a surveyor paid by the government."

"Among other things."

"I'm told you're considered favorably."

Andy wondered how she could have obtained the information in such a short time — probably just gossip.

"So," Myrtle hadn't lost any of her severe expression, "What are your intentions?"

"What are yours?"

"Rose says you just met and you bought her for seventy five dollars."

"That's a very good price. Before slavery was abolished a dark one would have gone for at least ten times that price! "

"Let's stop kidding around. What do you intend for her?"

Andy sighed. "Whatever is good for her. I just happened to come along when she was being sold."

"Hm." Myrtle was pensive. "You certainly can't go on carting her about."

"What do you suggest?"

"She can stay here. I even have a room for her. My daughter comes only once in a while. She's in a boarding school in Pennsylvania."

"Think about it. You would be sheltering a girl of about the same age as your daughter, as I would guess from the clothing. And your daughter is not with you most of the time. Wouldn't that arouse some resentment?"

"Let me deal with that. Rose can work in the hotel."

"I don't know you. You have a good reputation. But I'll be checking up on you. If that's what we decide, Rose better write me from time to time. Otherwise, I'll have to come."

"Are you trying to tell me that after only two days you are truly concerned about her?"

"Amazing isn't it? I could even say that I'm fond of her. You can't fathom what dwells in the human mind, can you?"

Throughout the exchange Rose's feelings were swinging from elation to worry.

"Don't I have a say in all this?"

"Would staying here be okay with you?" Myrtle questioned.

Rose hesitated for a few moments. She figured it would probably be like heaven compared to what she had gone through. What did she have to lose? She slowly nodded.

She remembered that she had left home on the day of her birthday. "Today is my birthday," she lied.

That night, her lie gained her a birthday cake. Andy brought her a single perfect red rose. She wondered where Andy could possibly have found it.

CAROUSEL I

James Leviton first met Miss Clarissa at a dinner at Lord and Lady Chapell's in 1775. She eventually played an important role in his life.

A dashing young gentleman, Sir Guy Compton, perhaps at Lord Chapell's urging, had made a point of accompanying him and introducing him to other guests. He had also listened attentively to his tales, and James felt flattered since Sir Guy appeared intelligent and well informed. James considered himself lucky since Sir Guy also served as his guide on other occasions. The ways of England and London in particular were so different from his American background! He found the various accents rather difficult to deal with. Although his contact with servants and lower-class individuals had been very limited, in his mind their speech and cant sounded like a totally alien language.

Despite his mercantile activities, Lord Chapell was highly regarded and had not been barred from high society, the so-called 'ton', well represented at that dinner. After all, even in England of the second half of the eighteenth century the need to be wellborn was essential, but money was also important and the man was very rich.

The large group included many who were elegantly dressed, although James considered the fashion bizarre and exaggerated. Many of the men wore wigs or powdered their hair, and many of the women's low-cut gowns exposed more than he was accustomed to seeing. The women were frequently painted to lighten their complexions, and their cheeks and lips were rouged. Sometimes, the more foppish men followed suit, and one of the gentlemen wore high- heeled shoes as if it were the height of fashion. James wondered why any of them would bother since those devices brought such an unfavorable result. James was met at the door by Lord and Lady Chapell. He was formally introduced to Lady Chapell and bowed in the same way he had seen others do. She was a tall and thin woman who appeared as arrogant as her husband. Her complexion was sallow and her eyes hard. Her dress was of a severe gray.

"Ah!" she murmured. "Mr. Leviton from New York. A pleasure." Her lips were twisted in a moue that seemed to express the opposite.

In the conversation preceding the sumptuous meal, some of the men and women he had been introduced to were fascinated and shocked by his accounts of Indians, massacres and the religious sophistries that seemed to prevail in the New World. A man actually protested that James should be less graphic with innocent women present. James was unaccustomed to subtlety or politeness or the presence of innocent women. The ones he had known at home, such as his own sister Eloise, were blunt sometimes even to the point of being rude and didn't skirt issues or topics.

The presence of a colonial such as James Leviton at social occasions was not common. He had been invited by Lord Chapell. because he was one of a team representing a large company that had carried out negotiations with Lord Chapell for textile exports to the American colonies. His presence at social events might have had something to do with the fact that Chapell seemed to be under the mistaken impression that James Leviton was a scion of the fabulously rich New York Levitons whose Tory sympathies were well known. In fact, he was only a distant relative. James was a family name, there was a James Leviton III, a far removed middle-aged cousin who actually possessed a fortune. James didn't disabuse Chapell since the matter was never directly discussed and he enjoyed the ambiguity of his position.

Americans, rarely available, were generally socially shunned. They were considered vulgar, in part for their plain, blunt talk and outdated and coarse clothing, in part because they didn't seem to know their place. James felt that all their prejudices were confirmed by his own presence. He didn't lack insight into the state of affairs or his own makeup.

Although nobody mentioned the recent incident most of the guests had been fascinated by the gossip generated by James's two duels that had taken place in a single week. Imagine, the fool had gotten into an argument with a group of fancies who had been harassing a young Hebrew girl. He should have turned away and ignored the whole unpleasant matter like any real gentleman would. There was nothing significant about the little hussy. But, no — after vigorously voicing his objections to no avail, he had wielded his cane and meted out terrible blows before the four men could unsheathe their dress swords. James had conveyed the terrified girl to her home. The group reassembled later at their club and at first considered horsewhipping their adversary. Since he was a guest of Lord Chapell, however, the matter was reconsidered. Surely, a colonial wouldn't know the finer points of defending one's honor, but nevertheless he was visited by seconds and an uncomfortable Sir Guy and one of his friends represented James. James had chosen swords as the weapons for the first encounter and one unfortunate gentleman, Sir

Martcoss, was badly punctured in his right arm after. James had allowed his second opponent to choose pistols with the result that poor Sir Bertolow almost had to have his arm amputated. It was lucky that the skill of the attending surgeon had been able to avoid that terrible outcome. The unfortunate young men had no way of knowing that James had been intensely trained by his father since infancy in preparation for the possible consequences of exploring Indian lands and his father's recollections of the French and Indian wars.

James had been introduced briefly to Miss Clarissa. He bowed, although that display made him uncomfortable. From her last name, James assumed she was related to Lord Chapell. He was told later that she was his wayward daughter. He couldn't imagine what was meant by that. She was shapely with black hair. Her gown, although becoming and a bright purple, was very plain and she wore no makeup. Older than most of the unmarried women in the crowd, he found her regular features and her lively, mischievous eyes very attractive. She might have been in her middle twenties — an age that in England and even in the American colonies was considered to be approaching spinsterhood.

As luck or circumstances had it, he later found himself sitting at the table next to Miss Clarissa. The seating arrangement alternated men and women, didn't segregate the genders to different sides of the table as was frequently done.

Her eyes seemed amused as she commented, "Ah, the notorious Mr. Leviton. Nice to see you again. Probably ready to tell more frightful stories." And then she laughed. Most people didn't make such a remark even in jest.

"I don't know whether I'm notorious, but it has been noted that I find it difficult to stay out of trouble."

"Was it worth the trouble?" She smiled to show that she wasn't criticizing his stance.

James understood that she must have been referring to the events leading to the duels. "Violence is rarely to be condoned, but I couldn't avoid it. If you mean the fate of who I heard referred to as 'that little hussy', I would say that I'm glad I intervened. She was a shy, terrified little girl who didn't deserve the treatment."

The man across from him, whose name he had forgotten, took the initiative to change the uncomfortable subject and plunge into another even more contentious. "It's my understanding that the American colonies are in an uproar over issues of little import. What's your view?"

James was not in agreement with the man's sentiment about the importance of the issues and he hesitated for a moment. It was Miss Chapell who intervened. She might have sensed that James didn't feel like contradicting their neighbor. Women were not supposed to know or comment on political or world events. Aside from their reproductive role, their main task was to provide the entertainment of men and pleasant, charming conversations of no great significance, featuring frequently the weather and some unimportant gossip. Her social rank made her intervention even more unusual. James was surprised to hear her contribution as it unfolded.

"It's hard to predict where the current crisis will lead us, but our American colonies will sooner or later part from us. Aside from what we have in common, enormous differences separate us. They receive immigrants from many parts of the world. By and large their religions are different from ours. The absence of primogeniture will lead to the breakdown of estates and hence the decrease of the significance of the wellborn. Furthermore, they have enjoyed some degree of independence with their provincial assemblies. Dissolving them may well exacerbate the problems and lead to completely independent governments with no ties to Great Britain. Certainly, punitive measures such as the abrogation of the charter of Massachusetts and closing of the port of Boston have inflamed most, if not all, of the colonies."

The man's stern stare was disapproving and he turned studiously to his neighbor on his other side. But Miss Clarissa ignored the snub. Obviously, for her it was not a new experience.

She was ready for even more controversial topics. "Tell me, Mr. Leviton, are women mistreated in the American colonies as they are here? Are they chattel and under the thumb of their husbands or fathers?"

"Probably. The world has been very unkind to women. In America, their status differs significantly from colony to colony and depends, as it does here, on social class. I'd imagine they are more appreciated and more independent in New England than in other locales. However, they are usually banned everywhere from most and perhaps all professions."

Miss Clarissa looked at him thoughtfully. "You know this is the first time any man has spoken with me about this touchy subject as an equal. Perhaps it has happened before, but I can't remember it."

James thought she was unusually attractive once she lost her angry expression brought forth by her indignation. She had most a lovely smile which lit up her whole face.

The dinner was very pleasant and the food, served in excess by bustling maids, quite good. Conversations continued until the end of the meal. Then both the men and the women rinsed their mouths with water that had been brought in bowls by the maids, a practice a surprised James thought affected. They then wiped their lips on the edge of the tablecloth. After that, the men and women followed the separate leads of Lord and Lady Chapell to adjacent rooms — the men for brandy and cigars, the women for gossip and wine.

James found the aroma of food supplanted by that of a mixture of beeswax and wood smoke and then by the fragrance of cheroots.

His next introduction to London involved visiting the opera with Guy. He wondered whether his guide and companion attended him because he enjoyed the company of a rube, had been assigned as his guide, or just considered himself a friend. The opera had yet to begin. They had gone early at James's insistence. James carefully examined the theater ablaze with lights. He was surprised that with all the apparent conflagration the stage didn't catch fire.

He couldn't help enquiring, "Why are most of the balconies empty?"

"Most of the ton comes late. The idea is to be seen, not to see the opera itself."

"Who are those scantily dressed, elegant young women?"

"Don't you have those in the colonies? Those are fancy prostitutes, trying to attract attention.."

"My goodness! I never thought everything could be that open."

Looking around he spied the various boxes. His eyes stopped at two struggling women and a half dressed young girl. "Isn't that Miss Clarissa? And what's going on?"

Clarissa was dressed simply but exhibited a sparkling necklace and several jewels, some pinned to her gown. She had her right arm around a very young girl and was fending off the older woman with her left arm.

"God, it certainly looks like her. She must be tangling with a Covent Garden abbess while trying to rescue that child. It's best to ignore those things but our Clarissa is unable do that.."

"What are you talking about?"

"An abbess is a madam in your part of the world. She's trying to show off one of her country girls. Probably just arrived in London from the country, if she hasn't been sold by her father."

The trio had suddenly disappeared from the box.

"What's happening?"

"They probably moved to the alley where she'll get offers. That's usually how it's done."

"Let's go," James couldn't hide his impatience.

"It could get very nasty."

They arrived just as Miss Clarissa was departing with the young girl. The madam, a blowsy, rouged and outrageously dressed woman, had a satisfied look and was counting money. But that wasn't the end. There were several unpleasant looking villains who blocked Clarissa's way. One of them was very loud with his threats and looked very muscular. Whether they wanted to steal from her or attack her didn't matter to James. It seemed to be a repeat of his previous rescue, except this time he was not alone and he was dealing with ruffians and not so-called gentlemen. The two of them probably would have to face knives rather than swords. "You'd better let her go," he yelled in an angry voice.

The men turned in their direction threateningly. They seemed much amused. James lacked a weapon aside from his cane and Guy was too elegantly dressed to be a threat.

"No popinjay can tell us what to do!"

James's cane swished through the air. The man closest to him fell, hit by James's unlikely weapon. Sir Guy unsheathed his dress sword and at that point, their opponents quickly disappeared, one of them offering support to his dazed companion.

Miss Clarissa swayed. James supported her with one hand. He began thinking of her as Clarissa from that moment on. She recovered quickly.

"Please, would you be so kind as to notify my friends in the third box that I'm not staying?"

Sir Guy was quick to respond. "At your service, Miss Clarissa."

James stayed with the two women. The young girl was still scared and couldn't suppress reluctant sobs. Clarissa kept murmuring reassuring words. Following Guy's errand, James and Guy accompanied them to Guy's carriage which quickly delivered them to Clarissa's address.

A butler opened the door. "Miss Clarissa," he said as he held the door open.

"I'm most grateful for your help, gentlemen. Please come in." After they entered she said, "Please excuse me for a minute while Mr. Bowman gets my maid to take care of Dawn. Oh, gentlemen, this is Dawn." James surmised that Mr. Bowman must be the butler.

Dawn looked very young and still terrified. Clarissa held her arm and said gently, "Everything will be alright. My maid, Mary, and I will take good care of you."

Mary came in and curtsied. She was a petite woman with dark black hair and a sweet smile.

"Can you please take care of Dawn. I rescued her from bad trouble"

When Mary and Dawn left, she sighed and addressed the two men again. She didn't seem too distressed by her experience. Clearly she was a determined and courageous woman.

"Sorry to have taken you away from the opera and thank you again for your bravery. Can I offer you tea, wine or brandy?"

After they accepted the drinks brought in by Bowman, she continued, "How did you discover my plight?"

"We saw you struggling with that witch!"

"Witch is a kind term for that woman. It's lucky that I had some money in my reticule."

The incident came to an end on a pleasant note. James was much impressed by Clarissa's brave behavior.

******

The late spring day had been sunny and pleasant. A large group of young men and women had ventured forth on a picnic in the countryside. James's attendance had been encouraged by Sir Guy who was the bearer of an informal invitation. Calling the event *a fête champêtre*, as they all did, seemed most pretentious. There were so many, mostly a crowd of young men and women, they had been taken in four carriages, followed by others which conveyed the needed servants and victuals as well as drinks.

James found the outing strange. Communing with nature by sitting on enchanting blankets, with servants providing every need and every whim seemed contradictory. He soon tired of the tittering and sophistries emanating from the guests. Besides, nobody seemed very interested in exchanges with a colonial especially after earlier contacts had made his uncouthness obvious. They must have become tired of stories about America which in their minds had nothing to do with their own world.

The countryside was delightful so James detached himself from the group. Guy was bewitched by a beautiful young woman, Belinda, and James was reluctant to ask him to accompany him. He was well accustomed to being on his own and enjoyed what he was seeing. He was enchanted by a close encounter with warblers and their delightful songs. A flock of birds flew away at his approach. The display of flowers, yellow, white and blue was appealing.

The darkening of the sky found him unprepared for the change in weather. Suddenly and overwhelmingly — rain, lightening and thunder. Quickly, he searched for shelter. He had seen a structure which seemed to be an abandoned barn. On his way he found Clarissa standing under a tree, her wet dress sticking to her and emphasizing her figure.

"No! That's too dangerous. Come with me!"

He took her by the hand and they rushed to the building he had seen before. There was nothing left but to wait in the gloom, the humidity, the smell of hay and mold until the outburst subsided. The rain drummed on the roof which was leaking at several spots. Lightening and thunder occasionally broke the monotony. They were there alone for a long time. James was surprised at how comfortable he felt with her even under such unfavorable circumstances.

He felt obliged to ask, "How come you strayed so far?"

"I was looking for you, hoping to have a reasonable conversation instead of the usual meaningless prattle about the beauties of nature or the gossip about the last ball."

Left unsaid was why she had decided to participate in the event at all.

"I'm flattered! I was just admiring the tame English countryside. I'm sorry I didn't see you earlier. You wouldn't have had to drift so far and be caught by the elements."

In the dark interior they could barely see each other's faces and there was no way of sitting down, but somehow their conversation didn't languish. James didn't understand how their exchanges could quickly roam from women's rights, to whether America had responded to the deep and iconoclastic thoughts generated by French philosophers such as Voltaire, Rousseau and Montesquieu. He could assure her that they had become part of the many issues debated in the New World. He couldn't help wondering how her intellect could be so sharp and so well informed. She seemed to be curious about his life in America, but there was little of interest that he could present. Her world was much more interesting even if in his eyes very strange. She had been able to establish a refuge for abandoned young women who to avoid starvation would have otherwise drifted into prostitution. It had been a stormy path that wasn't considered respectable. But she thought she was succeeding, although many obstacles still remained. Her refuge had now three young women whom she was trying to train so that they could eventually make an honest living. Undoubtedly, the unfortunate Dawn would join them.

Finally, the angry patter of the raindrops ceased, offering them an opportunity to return to the group.

The carriages were all gone and only Sir Guy had waited for them.

"A carriage will be coming soon. But I'm shocked to find that you were alone together all this time."

James was surprised by the antagonistic tone in his friend's voice.

"We were caught in the rain. We just talked."

"I'm afraid you have compromised Miss Clarissa.."

"Don't be ridiculous! We just talked."

"I'm afraid we take these things very seriously. I'm sure you'll have to answer to Lord Chapell."

"Don't be ridiculous."

But James began to feel uncomfortable when he saw that Clarissa had turned pale.

She whispered to him, "I had nothing to do with this. Please believe me."

He still felt that the situation was absurd. "I'll be happy to talk to Lord Chapell."

In the carriage, the tension between the two men was such that Sir Guy decided to sit in front with the driver.

Clarissa addressed James in whispers. "These things can be messy. They might try to force your hand to marry me. Since you're about to leave for America, I imagine you can escape readily, although you might not be able to avoid a duel. As I understand it, based on your previous experience you wouldn't be that concerned about that. One other possibility is that we become engaged and then you leave or else I turn you down after you agree to marry me!"

"I still think this is ridiculous. Surely Lord Chapell will understand. Besides, I'm terrible marriage material. I have little money and no social prominence, I'm the wrong James Leviton." Then after a pause, "We have been talking only about my problem. But where does all of this leave you?"

"Don't worry about me. I'm considered unmarriageable, almost a spinster, because of my age, ideas and unbecoming, farouche behavior."

A few days later, facing Lord Chapell, the glacial attitude of the older man made it clear that any rationale discussion was impossible. He seemed to expect that James had to marry Clarissa.

James had had contacts with Lord Chapell when negotiating for his group. Chapell would remain expressionless and invariably presented a cold exterior — an arrogant and hard man to deal with. James had been selected by the Americans for the negotiations because he seemed to be able to deal with Chapell's antagonism. James's apparent prominence in the negotiations might have mistakenly enhanced the impression of his importance. In actual fact, the Americans had discussed their position as a group before opening negotiations and he was operating within very clearly delineated conditions. The situation concerning Clarissa was entirely different from his experience transacting business matters and James didn't understand how he could proceed.

"May I speak privately to your daughter?"

Chapell puffed indignantly but opened the door to a small library. "You can talk all you want but leave the door open."

James thought the situation had slid into absurdity but was happy to be alone with Clarissa. Remembering their previous conversation he asked, "Will you refuse me if I agree to marry you?"

"I wish to have your permission to accept. The situation has changed drastically. They closed my refuge and threw my poor women into the street. If you don't marry me I have to wed a captain who is headed to India. I can refuse of course, but then I might have only the street as an alternative or something equally degrading."

"Marriage to me might not be such an attractive option. The world is entirely different in America. It won't be easy for you to adjust to the changes. In addition, as I explained I'm quite financially limited."

"Financially, my dowry might help. For me the issue right now is what will happen if you don't marry me."

Curiously, James had never considered marriage seriously. It's not that he wasn't interested in women, but he certainly lacked experience. Aside from one or two crushes developed when he was in his teens and a brief interlude with a mature widow, he had never been seriously involved romantically.

Was this just a trap? If it was, he was almost certain Clarissa had nothing to do with it. He didn't see what advantage she would derive. If Lord Chapell had snared him to get rid of an embarrassing daughter unable to marry as required by society, it didn't really matter. What would happen to Clarissa was what was important, and besides what did he have to lose? He hadn't courted a woman for a long time. His frequent travels had made him unable to interact socially with most people. Leaving for America with her after a wedding might work well. If not it would not be necessarily a calamity. If something went wrong, there were a number of possibilities, including an annulment.

Through all his silent reflections Clarissa remained serious, looking at him without any begging or histrionics. He was struck by her dignity and her calm beauty. He couldn't imagine the well hidden turmoil going though her mind. She knew her whole future was in the balance. James was the rare man she liked, but marriage was another matter. She had no idea where it would lead emotionally, but then the alternatives seemed worse.

"James, you decide. If it's too much for you, I'll have to refuse you."

"If you came with me to America your life would be very difficult. Not only it would be a totally different environment but we live very modestly. My father and I have a scrubbing woman once a week. No butlers, maids, livery men, cooks or footmen."

"Being thrown onto the street or into a marriage to a man I don't even know would be better? Do you really think I am so useless as to need a retinue of servants?"

James was not convinced, but wasn't ready to abandon her. They quickly agreed that they would marry but their relationship would remain platonic until the events that would determine their future became clearer.

******

Later that year, it became apparent the American colonies were in open rebellion. King George III decided on a tough approach driven by his sense of duty to his empire. In contrast, many of the voices in Parliament, most notably those of Edmund Burke and John Wilke, supported the Americans and advised conciliation. However, the tougher attitude prevailed — many felt that the American colonials loyal to the crown were much more numerous than the insurgents. After the bloody encounters in Lexington and Concord in June 1775, the conflict became irrevocable.

James, who had free access to Clarissa after their engagement, felt he had to discuss the events with her.

"Look, the conflict in America is very serious. Many think that the clash will be short-lived. I know that cannot be true. It will be bloody and protracted. If you wish to stay in London after we get married, it's up to you. I have to leave. My work and my future are in America."

Clarissa was firm. "No, I'm not going to stay in London alone." She admired his resolve and felt that she could provide no less, although she knew clearly that she had no real alternative.

******

Once in America, Clarissa realized that James had not lied when he had recited the difficulty she would encounter. New York seemed small with narrow meandering streets, mostly unpaved. Except for some remarkable mansions, the houses were attached to each other. Every seventh house was required to have a light on at night.

James's mother had died many years before. White-haired, mustached, tall and formal, her father-in-law, William Leviton, was closer to her expectations. Although he lived with them, he seemed to spend his time in many activities and rarely interacted with the two of them. He had been delighted with James's marriage. He had thought his son would never take that step. He was most pleased to meet her and shook hands with her.

"I never thought it would happen! When it comes to women my poor son is gun shy!"

Clarissa felt herself blush.

"Dad, don't give all my secrets away. Besides, that was before I met Clarissa."

"I should hope so. She is charming and I'm sure very talented."

James's father studiously stayed out of their way. On certain days he played chess with his son. On other days he met with friends of the same age at a local tavern.

Keeping house was exhausting even if James had finally agreed to a washerwoman once a week and a maid besides the scrubbing woman they'd always had. James had been reluctant to use her dowry which he considered hers. Disposing of some financial instruments he had invested in before his trip to England introduced some flexibility into their finances. In a turmoil of emotions, Clarissa found herself missing what she had despised — knowing only too well its faults and that it couldn't be hers under any circumstances.

She had learned to cook a few simple dishes, and James, when in town, was always ready to take over that task, an alternative she found humiliating.

Clarissa found her social contact with James's relatives and friends puzzling when not mortifying. Hugging seemed to be required. Her experiences with her relatives in England were never so effusive. A few years older than James, his sister Eloise had even cried when they'd first met as she held Clarissa in a tight embrace. Eloise assured her that she and her brother had been very close — they had had to look out for each other. Their mother had died when they were so young! Eloise didn't live with them. She was married with two little girls. Her married name was Stewart. Eventually Clarissa met the whole family.

All their American acquaintances spoke plainly, without embellishments. Balls, gowns, fashions were not part of their conversations. Their life was equally simple. Just what Clarissa thought she'd been striving for. Nevertheless facing her new world, she found it full of emptiness.

Intruding was the menacing news of the British troops at loggerheads with the Americans, boding a violence that she was not prepared for.

She knew she was regarded as a cold, unemotional woman. Being English made her social acceptance even more difficult. It wasn't easy for her to deal with new acquaintances. As a child, it had been driven into her that a show of emotion was uncomely, although she couldn't disagree more with that sentiment. If they thought her unfeeling, they should see her weeping in bed when she tried to go to sleep at night.

James was with her sometimes. He traveled extensively for his business. When together at home, their situation imposed a distance — a forced silence in emotions, perhaps to be expected for a man and a woman living in intimate nearness, yet held together only by bonds of friendship and mutual respect, not knowing much about each other. However, at times she was very aware that he was an attractive man. Similarly, he had been aware of her comeliness even at their first meeting and it wasn't something he was likely to forget.

Although necessary, she found the platonic aspects of her relationship humiliating. Ironically, she thought she would be terrified if James tried to make love to her. She was really very inexperienced and had had very little to do with men.

Clarissa didn't know what precipitated the crisis. Her father-in-law was away visiting relatives. She had been cooking. Eloise was visiting and Clarissa took great care with a new recipe. James was coming home later and the two women were restless.

For a while they voiced pleasantries, but then the conversation took another turn. Eloise was troubled. "For the life of me, I can't understand your marriage. I have never seen either of you show much affection for the other."

Clarissa wished Eloise would stop talking about something so personal. "Well, nevertheless we're husband and wife."

"Is that why you don't share a bed? I couldn't help noticing this morning that James sleeps on the couch."

"I don't think any of this is any of your business."

"What did you do, trick him into marriage?"

Clarissa almost slapped her. The iron in her eyes made Eloise step back. But then Clarissa turned away, removed the pot from the fire and went to her room. She felt humiliated and pained. With tears in her eyes, she packed a few garments and undergarments in a small carpetbag and left the house without looking back.

"Where are you going? What's happening? I didn't really mean it. Please come back!"

Not much time had elapsed before James found her. She hadn't expected to be discovered so quickly. In her room in the inn, they found themselves face to face with tears crowding in their eyes.

"You've left for good?"

She nodded in affirmation. He had never seen her so sad and so tormented.

"It's just not working out, James."

"You didn't take anything. The life of a woman alone is hard enough. You should have some money. Your dowry and more. You worked hard. It must have been very difficult."

They looked at each other silently. She couldn't refrain from wondering and she asked, "You really want me to stay, don't you? Why?"

"I love you!"

Suddenly, they were in each other arms. In their embrace their marriage became sealed with love. They found themselves naked on the narrow bed in a passionate embrace. Clarissa, who had at one time accepted the possibility of being a spinster for the rest of her life, was amazed at how simple and how overwhelming the love between a man and a woman could be.

Much later the two of them searched for Eloise who had obviously returned to her home. She was very constrained but fortunately her husband had to be introduced to Clarissa. Eloise stared at them, first in anguish but then she saw the glow emanating from the both of them. Guilt almost overwhelmed her.

"I'm so sorry I was such a bitch. I really didn't know what I was doing! Can you both forgive me?"

Clarissa approached her shyly and hugged her. "Eloise. You can see how happy we are. Don't brood about what didn't happen. I know you were moved by love for your brother. Now we can love him together."

******

The city had quickly become an armed camp. Violent disorders were the order of the day. Many inhabitants had fled. A curfew for the military had been proclaimed by Washington who was heading the American forces in the city. In practice, it had little effect since most soldiers didn't have uniforms and couldn't be distinguished from the general population.

James knew about the rioting mobs who would attack anybody considered a Tory. Tar and feathers and railings were common. Being married to an English woman had sent the wrong signal. When the raucous crowd came, he had been ready for them. His saber was unsheathed and several loaded pistols were ready on a chair. As the crowd lumbered to his door, the catcalls and roar were deafening. James holding two pistols opened the door before they could crash through it. When a man who appeared to be ahead of the others made mincing sounds followed by the roar of the crowd, James shot him.

"If you can't see a true patriot that's what you deserve!"

There was a sudden silence and then the crowd quickly dispersed as he leveled another pistol. The unruly men took their wounded companion and disappeared. But James realized how lucky he had been. Not too long afterwards James moved his small household to a little farm with the hope of isolating them from some of the unpleasant events. Although Clarissa was speechless, James thought that the idea of leaving New York had already started to form in her mind.

******

James's father had encouraged him to read of wars and strategy when he was a boy. Among the many books, James remembered reading in Memoirs Concerning the Art of War by Marshal Maurice de Saxe, the statement that for a successful general, "the first of all qualities is courage." After his enlistment, and in midst of the fighting, James had seen Washington on horseback too close to the line of fire, examining the battleground. Courage he didn't lack. Whether Washington had the fortitude to lead in what looked from its very beginning like a lost cause, James didn't know.

Even before enlisting James had known the artillery was not sufficient, the gunpowder short, the raw and undisciplined American army at a clear disadvantage. The weapons were predominantly the flintlock musket although fowling pieces were also represented — rarely, the very accurate long-barreled frontier rifle of Pennsylvania. The clothing was varied and slipshod in contrast to the impeccable figure of Washington, who always appeared in uniform as if he were on parade. Despite the colonial's victory in seeing the British leave Boston, the march to New York had further weakened the army even though fresh recruits, mostly inexperienced, had also flocked into the city. An increase in the fortifications was deemed necessary and the men worked feverishly to complete them.

Once in the army, James had found out quickly that because of the lack of sanitation, the enemy included diseases — dysentery, typhus and typhoid fever. For brief intervals smallpox also would sometimes rear its ugly head. Furthermore, the heavy consumption of rum did little for the American preparedness. Desertions and disease cut down the number and effectiveness of the American forces.

The British with more than one hundred ships had come in overwhelming numbers. They quickly established complete control of the waterways around New York. The fortifications and American cannons couldn't touch them.

Eloise's family and father had decided to move away from the conflict. She had a good friend in Albany who had offered hospitality. James insisted that Clarissa join them.

Days later, waiting behind the stone walls partitioning the land for the inevitable attack by the Redcoats, James's mind wandered with exhaustion, leading his thoughts into forbidden territory. All arguments with Clarissa, some imagined by his unsettled mind, came to the surface.

"What do you think this warfare will accomplish? All big words. Freedom. Justice. All men are equal. Not reality. what about law and order?"

"What about the laws that perpetuate wrongs? Sure the meaning of slogans is lost often enough. The world moves forward by small steps. In this case there are gains and losses, but overall a small gain. I have to play a role in this war. I'm one of the few that has had any training."

"Don't be so sure that I will be here for you when you come back. Assuming they don't hang you."

What had it been that had played on his mind and led him to enlist? He had felt it to be an obligation. He couldn't visualize a logical alternative. The task of defeating the British was next to impossible, but it had to be done. He hoped that poor Clarissa wouldn't suffer too much and didn't mean what she had said about leaving him.

James had enlisted after the first defeat, when the colonial forces had had to withdraw from Brooklyn in a daring move under the cover of night and fog. After that he had been assigned to support the small contingent at the rearguard of the American forces headed by John Glover. Now again the main part of the American army had to withdraw to avoid annihilation. The battalion was there to delay the attackers and give a chance for the retreat to succeed. The Americans fought behind stone walls with deadly effectiveness. A British and Hessian contingent of four thousand was kept back for a full day by only seven hundred men, giving time to Washington to withdraw to White Plains. James found himself shooting as if it were a shooting gallery, and at the end of the day, he was exhausted as even his group had to withdraw.

******

After a long time, eventually, James was assigned to the forces under Gates in the vicinity of Saratoga Springs. Because of his prowess with his long rifle he was placed with Morgan's riflemen in the battle for Bemis Heights and assigned to shoot from the trees. It was a long day of uninterrupted fighting.

Then his world changed. He suddenly found himself stretched out on the ground and thought for a moment he must be dying. The pain in his right shoulder was excruciating — on the side of his head, a different kind of pain. The sound of intense shooting was all around him. Rifle shots in intense fusillades, and occasionally the roar of a cannon not too far from where he was. His head throbbed giving him a feeling of unreality. He explored with his left hand. The lack of blood either flowing out of his shoulder or sticking to the touch was puzzling. Stretched out on the ground, he knew that regardless of pain, regardless of discomfort he had to stay still, and he did so for a long time.

All he could remember was that he had been up in a tree sighting, shooting and reloading, shooting and reloading. The reverberation from his own shooting and that around him were still painful in his ears. The shooting continued around him.

He knew well that when in pain, minutes feel like hours. He must have passed out. After a long time, he was conscious of being lifted and carried. He learned later that he had been relayed to a makeshift hospital. Laying on matted leaves, out in the open, he'd been neglected for quite a while despite his moaning, his right arm twisted besides him. Then a man in an apron splattered with blood approached him. His gentle touch informed James that he was a doctor or an assistant.

"Oh! For goodness sake. They shouldn't have bothered me with this! — The man made James move to a make-shift bench and arrange himself in a prone position with his twisted arm free to move. Then he pulled James' right arm firmly. James actually heard a snap, felt an instant of even more intense pain and then nothing.

An improbable chuckle arose from the man with the splattered apron. "The treatment has been the same since the time of Caesar!"

"What about my head?"

"You were just damned lucky. A scratch — the bullet must have just grazed you. A small bandage will suffice."

The battle was over but there was more to follow. So far it had been a victory. The American lines had held. The enemy was entrenched and more would come.

James was allowed to leave on a furlough, agreeing to rejoin his regiment soon. He knew Clarissa was staying somewhere around Albany. He had forgotten the name of the farm. Only a day after his trauma, he started walking cautiously but with determination. He certainly didn't want to be shot, scalped or taken prisoner and hid as much as possible whenever he noticed other travelers. His father's teaching of the tricks acquired when he had passed through Indian territories served James well.

It was all as in a strange dream — hunger, thirst, exhaustion and the trauma of his injury. He hadn't brought any provisions and he drank from the streams he found along the way. It took him two days to get to the town. He spent a night in a barn, carefully avoiding alerting the farmer since he didn't know whether he would be a patriot or a Tory. Then in the afternoon of the second day, by the river he saw the houses and a semblance of normalcy. If the British broke through it would be all laid to waste.

He asked passersby whether they knew where he could find either the Stewarts or Mrs. Leviton. Finally an old woman knew where they were. He had to hike back some to find the farm. It was more like a plantation. Walking stiffly, dragging his feet, he approached the door of the mansion, canopied to service the discharge of passengers from coaches. After he introduced himself, a diffident maid in uniform informed him reluctantly that Mrs. Leviton was in the vegetable garden, behind the house. These were uncertain and dangerous times and James looked disreputable as did most of the Continental Army.

And there she was. He swallowed hard. He didn't know what kind of reception was awaiting him. It had been a long time. Clarissa was leaning over some vegetables. She sensed his presence, straightened and looked around. They stood looking at each other with tears in their eyes. She ran into his open arms.

Her words came in whispers. "I didn't know if you had gotten my letters. I never knew where to send them."

"I received a few. I heard you were pregnant. I heard about our daughter."

Then she held him by the hand and said, "Come and meet Honoria. I hope you like the name. It was my grandmother's name."

"A lovely name. Besides she'll be know as Honey. Very appropriate."

Many anxious thoughts flooded through her mind. James looked like a wreck. Unshaven, dirty, emaciated. Was he going to stay? What was happening in Saratoga? But all had to be held back.

A placid Honoria looked up at her father. Now two, she didn't appreciate strangers. Clarissa was relieved by the little girl's solemn but calm expression. Then hell broke loose when Eloise entered the nursery with tears coursing her face.

"Oh! My God! James. You look terrible! Are you going to stay?"

Clarissa thought that's what sisters are for. To raise the unpleasant issues that have to be faced.

"I can't stay very long. You can try to fatten me up, but in one week you can't do much."

He took Clarissa's hand and asked, "Where can we be alone for a while?"

A room he surmised was used as a library had to suffice.

"Can I conclude that you're still my wife?"

"Oh, James. There was never any question, I love you. I thought I could leave but I just couldn't even if it might have been advantageous. If it hadn't been for Eloise, I would have had a very rough time. I'm ashamed of having parted from you in such a disloyal way! I hope you can forgive me."

"I didn't know whether to believe you but I never stopped loving you. I was relieved when I found out that you stayed with Eloise but I wasn't sure what it meant." After a while, "I can't believe how beautiful Honey is. Obviously she takes after you!"

Their saga was far from over, but James felt relief and satisfaction. He had a family and knew that they were in a circle of love. He left a week later. There were tears, smiles and laughter. War introduced a painful uncertainty but James knew that they were ready for any challenge.

THE HALF-LIFE OF PASSION

Penelope had concluded that passions have a definite life span, often short. As her scientist husband, Edgar, would have put it — they have a short half-life. Sometimes they terminate in a storm of thunder and lighting. More often they trickle away over time. It's not exactly that nearness breeds contempt, it's just that passion frequently has indifference as its final state. In Penelope's mind that was the state where Edgar and she had arrived after twenty years of marriage. Facing the facts, she had confronted him. They could share what was left of the upbringing of their daughter, Jeanette, now sixteen. In her senior year in highschool she was headed for college soon anyway. But a divorce was necessary since Penny had found a man who interested her.

Edgar had stood in silence. What went through his mind wasn't clear to her. She perceived indifference, but she would have been surprised to know that his actual feelings were the result of a long held attitude — there is no point in bucking the inevitable. All you can do is to accept it without malice or anger even if it hurts. That had been the way he had lived since he had become an adult. There was no question that the break hurt, but what good would recrimination do? After that conversation, in Penolope's mind her marriage became a mere technicality.

She had served on the board of the charity, Benefactors Anonymous, with Marvin De Toux for several years. She had been flattered when she had been asked to be on the Board. Her blue-collar roots and her education, limited to four years at a community college, had obviously been disregarded in favor of her intellectual talents. Her articles had been well received nationally and there had been talk of syndicating her column. In the eyes of many, she had become a premier analyst of politics and the contemporary scene. It had been a hard road and she had to admit she had found Edgar's support essential. But that was in the past. Marvin De Toux was very attractive and she had found herself drawn to him. His male charm couldn't be denied. Handsome, always polite, always well dressed, always logical and well spoken. To her he represented all that a man should be. The pull must have been mutual because his interest in her had become obvious. She sometimes wondered what he saw in her. In her own eyes she wasn't a raving beauty and was on the wrong side of forty. A successful divorce lawyer, Marvin, himself had just undergone a divorce. Penny didn't know exactly what his long-term intentions were but at that point in their relationship she didn't really care. She accepted his invitation to spend a week in Hawaii. She quickly found that he was not only very charming but a dream on a dance floor and also very accomplished in bed. In her experiences with Edgar, she couldn't remember such abandon, such delirium.

In their hotel room, Penny and Marvin were intertwined in bed in a moment of ardor when an insistent knocking interfered with their passion. It was Marvin who swore profusely. Penny silently left the bed and covered her nakedness with a robe.

"What do you want?"

The voice of a young man intervened, "I wouldn't bother you if I didn't think it was urgent. It's apparently an emergency. I'm slipping the message under the door. The caller insisted that we give it to you personally. He said that he had trouble getting in touch with you. We didn't transfer the call to your room because you had left instructions not to."

Her cell phone, turned off, had registered many calls from Edgar. She hadn't activated them because she'd thought they were more a demonstration of peevisness at her break from him than anything of any importance. Marvin had fostered that interpretation. "A husband's last stab at being possessive. Believe you me. I have seen much of that in many of the divorces where I represented the wife."

She wondered how Edgar had traced her and quickly glanced at the sheet of paper. It had been written hastily by one of the clerks. "Jeanette has been in a serious accident. I'm doing what I can, but I thought I should tell you about it. She's presently at the Little Flower Hospital," signed Edgar. It wasn't exactly a summons but that's the way she interpreted it. Her feelings strongly denied that Edgar would send her such a message out of spite.

"Marvin," ahw said apologetically handing him the note, "I think I'll have to go." She had trouble looking him in the eye.

"Oh, God! Can't you see that it's a trick? Don't let it interfere with our plans! You can just call the hospital and verify whether she's there."

"With the time difference I would have to wait. I don't want to lose any time. I have to go."

She remembered when Jeanette, at the age of about six, and Edgar had hidden from her as she'd entered the house after a long absence. For some reason she had been overcome by anxiety at their absence until a delighted Jeanette had yelled, "Surprise! Surprise!" Edgar had sensed Penny's panic and had held her in his arms until she was able to laugh. No, he wouldn't trick her.

"I won't have you manipulated in that way. If you care for me, you'll ignore the message."

"That's not fair, Marvin. I do care for you, but she's my daughter. I don't believe Edgar would use Jeanette as a ploy to get at me."

She lifted the room phone and dialed the airline number. She made the arrangements for her return trip as Marvin seethed with impatience.

"I don't think you understand. If our love means nothing to you, go. Don't expect me to wait for you!"

"Are you saying we'd be finished?"

"Yes. It's a test."

She suddenly was overcome with anger. "In that case you can go to hell!" More forceful expressions had come to her mind, but she had repressed them. She didn't know whether she would be sorry later, but that's what she felt at that moment.

Later, calling on the phone from the airplane, she found that Jeanette was indeed a patient at the hospital. She was in critical condition but Penny wasn't given any details. The call to Edgar only activated his answering machine and his cell phone also could only take messages. Anguish took over her thoughts. What possibly could have happened?

After her arrival, Penny didn't even bother to shower or brush her teeth. Disheveled and tired as she was, she took a cab directly from the airport to the hospital. She dumped her suitcase in the lounge next to the information counter. She was guided to a private room. Although she had expected it, seeing Jeanette stretched out in bed with tubes and wires attached to her was unbearable. She choked up. For a moment she couldn't move or enunciate the words that had come to her lips.

"Oh, honey! Oh, darling!" She felt tears coursing down her face as she tried to take her in her arms.

She hadn't even noticed Edgar, a gaunt, gray Edgar, who quickly stopped her, held her hand and took her out of the room.

"She's sedated. I'm told the worse is over. She just came out of the recovery room after two hours of surgery."

"What happened?"

"She was in a car accident."

"Was she driving?"

Edgar nodded. They both knew that with a junior license she shouldn't have been driving without an adult in the car.

"Were you with her?" She couldn't hide the anger that was rising in her.

"I'm afraid not. She just took the car, with three other girls." He had warned his daughter about the restrictions on her driving. She had sneered at him, but he hadn't expected an actual rebellion. Teenagers are so unpredictable. Perhaps taking the car for a wild ride was her way of showing her disapproval of her mother's absence. But he knew better than to raise the issue.

Penny's response was unexpected. "You bastard! You let her go by herself! That's how much you care for her!"

He suppressed his rising anger. "Penny calm down. When she comes to, she'll need you. Screeching doesn't help!"

All her anger was behind her slap. The smack upset him more psychologically than physically. In all their years together nothing like that had ever happened. But then he forced himself to be objective. Her response was not exactly unprovoked. And he knew well how pain can distort thoughts and feelings.

"Let's talk about this when we are less stressed. I have lived with this for three days. I know how much it hurts. I know that it's difficult, but please try to keep yourself together."

They did calm down. There is no way a vigil can be maintained when angry. She didn't exactly apologize for the smack, but the fact that she acquiesced spoke for itself. Now composed she was able to extract from him more details about the accident.

Eventually, Jeanette emerged from her drug-induced sleep. They were both there, one on each side of the bed holding one of her hands, murmuring endearments. The drip was still attached to one of her arms.

"Oh, Mommy, Mommy!"

Penny felt tears coursing her face and made an effort not to appear upset.

They stayed like that for a while.

"What happened?"

"You're in a hospital. You were in a car accident."

Her forehead was wrinkled in concentration but she didn't seem to want to know more. Penny was relieved. There was going to be more pain when Jeanette found out that her best friend, Jane, had died and her two other friends were also in the hospital, although soon would be discharged.

Edgar insisted that Penny and himself get something to eat and some rest. They slept right in the lounge, they didn't want to be too far from Jeanette.

On the next day, Penny went home for a short while and was able to take a shower and sort herself out. Then she had a chance to speak to the surgeon. It had been a most serious state. Jeanette's chest had been brutally pushed in. One lung had collapsed and there had been damage to the pericardium. They'd thought they would lose her. Fortunately, the quick surgical intervention had saved her. It was lucky that her father had almost immediately consented since there had been no room for delay. There had also been a displacement of a vertebra and her legs had been paralyzed. Actually, another surgeon had worked on that. That's what the second operation was about. Again they were lucky. They expected the paralysis to be temporary.

Penny should have felt relief and in a way she did. Indeed, there didn't seem to be permanent physical damage aside from a long convalescence. Nevertheless, she was terrified at the possible psychological impact on the young girl when she found out the details of the tragedy.

Penny and Edgar were able to take her home with a daily visit from a nurse and an arm- long list of instructions. Jeanette had to breathe frequently through a strange device. Then three times a week she had to be taken for rehabilitation — a series of closely monitored special exercises. She soon was capable of walking with crutches, haltingly. She seemed highly motivated in her slow recovery. Fortunately her memory of the incident was still dormant. She remembered having driven a car before finding herself in the hospital, but nothing else.

With Jeanette's return home, Penny was delighted, but it did introduce an additional problem. Out of deference for what had transpired just before her Hawaiian trip, Edwin had slept on the couch. Were they prepared to confide in their daughter when she was in such a precarious state?

"Look," Penny told him, "we can share the same bed. After all we have been together for twenty years and we are not teenagers, always overwhelmed by sex and desire."

Edgar just laughed. "I certainly would love the comfort."

The arrangement seemed satisfactory. After all they were familiar with each other's presence. On the second night however for some reason she had felt suddenly terribly upset with Jeanette's problems. She was crying silently when suddenly Edgar's arms were around her and he kissed her. Penny didn't remember the exact sequence of events but they found themselves in the throngs of lovemaking. In the morning she was sufficiently concerned to ask him to sleep on an inflatable mattress that during the day could be hidden under the bed. Penny was not prepared for a complete rapprochement with Edgar, although she realized that the two of them had to work together as they had always done in the past.

A few days later, Penny was horrified to hear Edgar respond to Jeanette's questions. It's true that there is never a good time to communicate catastrophic news, but she felt that they should have waited longer.

"Jeanette, I'm sorry to have to tell you this. Jane died. Dorothy and Meg were hurt but not seriously."

There was silence for a long time. Then Jeanette broke into sobs. Standing on the doorway, Penny felt her own insides torn apart. She felt like slapping the son of a bitch. Couldn't he have left things alone?

Jeanette was now articulating her torment, "I killed her didn't I? I killed her."

Edgar was quick with the response, "You didn't kill her. It was an accident. What you did wrong was showing very bad judgment. We all do at one time or another. What counts is what we do over a lifetime — the mistakes we make and the good we do to balance them out."

Jeanette didn't seem comforted.

When Edgar left the room, Penny accosted him immediately. "You had to open that can of worms now!" She had to struggle not to be overwhelmed by anger.

"She asked me and I didn't feel I should answer with an evasion. It felt too much like a lie and then suspecting sometimes is as painful as knowing. What advantage could there be in waiting? In my experience it's best to tackle issues and crises right away or they will fester."

"You should have waited until she was stronger. And what the hell do you know about this kind of crisis?"

Edgar didn't answer, but he still remembered his torment when in Viet Nam he had shot down and killed a man who turned out to be not only an American but also an acquaintance. The man's crime had been not to identify himself as required, although in the confusion that followed Edgar wasn't sure of what had really happened. His pain had been unbearable and he had found no solace a year later when he had talked to the widow to explain how sorry he was. She was entirely hostile and even rejected the financial help he had offered, the little that his modest means would allow. "Conscience money! You can stick it you know where!" He must have felt the pain for a long time because not wishing to upset her, he'd never told the story to his wife.

A few days later after an exhausting excursion on crutches in the park, Jeanette after swallowing repeatedly asked, "Have they had a funeral for Jane?"

"That was some time ago. They'll have a memorial service when school starts so that all her school friends can attend."

"Shouldn't I?"

Penny responded, "That's up to you honey ... If it won't distress you too much

"I'll send them a note now to tell her family how sorry I am: 'I'm terribly sorry about what happened' ... No, that's too cold. 'I'm terribly sorry about what happened. I love her'... I mean, 'I loved her.'" "That sounds like a good idea."

Edgar was proud to see that the two women in his life were recuperating from their ordeal showing courage and sensitivity.

With the three of them in the kitchen, after breakfast Penny was puttering with some dishes at the sink when Jeanette asked her father, "After all this, do you still love me?"

"Honey, I'll always love you no matter what. Your mom also loves you no matter what. She also worries as part of her love for you. It's the way of all mothers."

The conversation suddenly went on a tangent, as he had frequently noted happened with his daughter. "Do you love Mom?"

"Certainly!"

"I mean love like being in love."

"That' s a funny question. Yes!"

Penny dropped the dish she was wiping onto the sink. Her heart lurched. Had the poor girl sensed something more that would worry her? She was relieved to see that Jeanette had a pleased expression on her cute face and her question didn't reveal some hidden concern.

Did he still love his wife? Edgar felt the woman he had loved had gone through a strange period, but her intensity on Jeanette's behalf convinced him that she was the same woman. Yes, he still loved her.

The start of school presented an entirely new routine. Jeanette insisted on being driven and she lurched on the sidewalk on her crutches. They had to pick her up after lunch for her rehab routine. Mother and father shared all those duties as they had earlier in her recovery. She seemed to be reasonably carefree, although at times her eyes would cloud with regret and tears.

Both Penny and Edgar were concerned about the memorial service, which was held in the school auditorium crowded with students and some parents. Jeanette cried silently when Jane's accomplishments and short life were described by the speaker, the Superintendent of Schools, but she seemed to hold together better than they'd expected.

There was a small reception after the service. Jeanette found herself facing Jane's mother.

"I'm so sorry for what happened. I loved her."

Jane's mother's face became contorted with fury. "You have the gall to show your face here, you bitch."

Jeanette was visibly trembling under the onslaught and Penny tried to intervene, but Edgar held her back.

Jeanette looked up at the crying mother and simply said, "I also loved her."

Jane's mother suddenly hugged her.

"I'm sorry. I know you were friends. Something happened inside me. Please forgive me."

"Pain can distort everything. You don't have to apologize."

Penny had never expected her daughter to show so much strength and good sense.

And the words, she recognized, could have come from her father. She couldn't help feeling immense pride and joy.

Penny was puzzled by the fact that Edgar seemed to be home an awful lot. "Don't you have to go to work?"

"That's something we'll have to talk about. I quit. They insisted that I return to work immediately. It's a very busy time for them. It was after they knew about Jeanette's accident. They didn't seem to care as long as I went back to work. It was clear to me what the choice had to be. But don't worry, I can find another job soon despite approaching middle age."

She found herself saying, "That's terrible," but wasn't really worried. He had never failed before.

Another crisis was approaching, she felt. Hadn't she given Edgar his marching orders? She had behaved abominably when she had left him to pursue her affair with Marvin. She was also aware of how unkind she had been after returning from Hawaii. Every inconsiderate and judgmental utterance came back to haunt her. And except for their mutual effort on behalf of Jeanette and the unfortunate incident when they'd shared the same bed, they had been very circumspect with each other. They had avoided discussing their plans for the future. She had been happy during the last few weeks. Jeanette's recovery was proceeding as expected. She had been proud of her daughter's courage in facing what had happened. She wished her daughter had had a less traumatic path to growing up. There was no question that Jeanette was no longer a rudderless teenager. But everything has a cloud. Did Edgar really love her? He must have declared his love for Jeanette's sake. Penny was suddenly aware that fear of rejection had something to do with her aloofness toward Edgar during the past few weeks. What did she actually feel?

Her situation was brought to a head when Marvin phoned and asked to see her. The conclusion that he was a contemptible man had slowly formed in her mind, but she felt that seeing him again would provide an opportunity to close that episode in her life. She felt very uncomfortable at the thought of seeing him again. In line with the openness she had held to throughout her marriage, she told Edgar that she had agreed to talk to Marvin. There was little doubt that Edgar understood who he was and was also filled with unease.

Marvin seemed to be somebody from her remote past. She couldn't even understand what she had seen in him. The thought of breaking up her marriage also had been troubling her. Edgar had shown himself to be all that she could want in a man. Did she still love him? She wasn't sure.

Edgar suspected that he was about to witness a repeat of their previous encounter when Penny had left for Hawaii. There was much to regret. The experience of the past few weeks had at least reinforced their friendship if not their marriage. If they really split up, and he felt that was what would happen, again Jeanette would have to face an emotional disruption. He'd have to explain to her what had happened very carefully. But these days the breaking up of marriages is a common occurrence. She should be able to understand. While musing, he had sat down, waiting for the time when he was supposed to pick up Jeanette from school. It was his turn.

Surprisingly, after Penny's meeting with Marvin, everything fell into place and she returned early, noisily. She seemed to be in high spirits. "Well, that's that!"

"Are you going to keep me in the dark?"

"Of course not. Marvin said that he would forgive me and proposed marriage. I told him I couldn't accept. I love my husband — love like being in love."

He felt like laughing and crying. But above all he felt joy as he held her in his arms. They went together to pick up Jeanette at school. They were late. Their daughter wondered why they seemed so cheerful and affectionate.

THE TRYST

An elegant dinner among friends — that's all it had been set up to be. Josh Elwood, with all of his five years at the Embassy, had not had very many opportunities to dine with a socially prominent Argentine family, such as the Alvarados, with all the accolade that it implied. He had met them at Embassy functions, and they had always been a friendly and interesting addition to his small circle of acquaintances. The elegant tablecloth and napkins provided an air of formality he wasn't accustomed to. His host was polished — dressed elegantly, as were the guests and family, as if the dinner were a formal function. The women, Alvarado's wife and daughter had a charm that spoke of generations of intellectual and social prominence. There were two other guests, a married couple who felt at home in the surroundings. The meal was sumptuous. The conversation flowed easily. The amount of gentility and knowledge in the discussion was exciting. For the first time, Josh heard of Juan Gelman. He remembered vaguely having read one of his poems in an anthology of Argentine poetry he owned. His host recited an exciting poem authored by Gelman — the words had just stuck in his mind without any effort to memorize them, he assured his guests. Josh could well believe him. The rhythm and the visual images the poem gave rise to were captivating. He found it powerful, moving. However, he was surprised to hear the subsequent discussion of Gelman and his poems. The military government regarded him as radical.

Josh didn't remember when he'd first become distracted and noticed the maid who was serving the dishes. He probably never would have been aware of her if he hadn't been psychologically isolated for months, rejecting all that he had been doing in his work. His resignation from his job at the Embassy would become effective in another month. And to think he had wanted the job so badly! It had seemed ideal considering his command of Spanish and his understanding of Latin America. He had held an ambiguous position, half diplomatic, half intelligence. The profusion of data he had collected clearly indicated a series of bloody outrages committed by the military government.

He had grown to resent the passivity of his own government. By default, by its lack of diplomatic pressure, it could be considered an accomplice. The stories of cruel murder had just started to unfold and had been a subject of his reports. He might have not been the only one at the Embassy who felt like he did. In fact, George Michaelis, who Josh had known since he had first come to Argentina, was silently sympathetic to his position.

To his eyes, the servant in uniform wasn't pretty. Attractive maybe, with a certain gracefulness in her movements. Noticing servants was a no-no as he had learned early in his career. You were supposed to think of them as automatons. He hoped that with his years of practice he had perfected the art of appearing not to realize the obvious — in this case that he had noticed her and she was well put together. Yet, she had no makeup or lipstick and obviously was trying to look as unobtrusive as possible as is expected from a servant. Nonetheless she had sustained his glance intently — a contradiction.

It was past midnight when they adjourned. The maid had reappeared and helped the guests with their coats. It had been a blustering evening outside. The polite good-bys had delayed Josh. He was surprised when the maid helped him with his coat. Unaccustomed to such attention, he was startled when her hand placed a note in his. What was it about? Political intrigue? Perhaps she didn't know that he was a has-been as far as his embassy was concerned and no longer able to carry out intrigues. He had blown his effectiveness. Somehow he felt that the surreptitious note had more to do with an amorous advance. Regardless of what it was, he should immediately chuck out the missive. But curiosity had always been his weakness. A sense of freedom and readiness for any challenge, no matter how irresponsible, had resulted from his lack of an official capacity that had restrained him in the past.

The cab had showed up as originally contracted. I should make sure that I give him a hefty tip, he mused. In the car, he glanced at the note just before closing the door. All it said was "2 AM, service entrance." Despite the fact that he didn't particularly consider himself attractive to women, it seemed to be an invitation to an assignation — it was about sex after all. He let the taxi drop him at his apartment. Why did the note bother him? Perhaps it was his abstention of several months. Perhaps it was the tension he had been under that had him searching for a possible distraction from his personal woes — or more easily understood, the excess consumption of the excellent wine. Perhaps he had been invited into a trap that would put his life in danger. Perhaps it just indicated the willingness of the woman to engage in a trashy affair. Whatever the reason, after a long wait he caught one of the rare cabs cruising at that hour and asked to be dropped a few blocks away from the Alvarado's house. He was sure that on the following day he would regret his impulse and consider his behavior not only dangerous but also idiotic.

What is a service entrance? He wondered as he viewed the house. Then he saw a small door right next to the closed garage door. Sure enough the little door gave way, but he didn't get a chance to think. She grasped his arm, pulled him in and closed the door, at least he surmised it was her. It was lucky, he realized, that she hadn't a nefarious intent because in his state of confusion, he wouldn't have been able to defend himself. But her aim was entirely different. She took him by the hand and pulled him into a small bedroom.

"My name is Paloma," she said and then kissed him and hugged him until he felt himself responding enthusiastically. It was very early in the morning when she pushed him out of bed. "You'd better be going. Sunday is my day off. I'll meet you at your house in the afternoon. Write out your address." It seemed strange, but he followed her instructions.

Josh found the interlude very baffling. There was no question that Paloma had known how to make love and it had been one of the most passionate encounters of his life.

Sunday came before he had reached some sort of idea of how to behave with her. He felt that there was more to the story than his own charm. He had mulled the question over in his mind without any resolution. He didn't doubt for a moment that she would show up and his time was filled with impatience, concern and indecision about what to do.

Reading a book seemed a way to ease his suspense. His bookcase was filled with good books, besides some somber looking bound reports which he despised. In both Spanish and English his collection constituted an interesting world he could plunge into to relieve his daily stresses. He chose *Speech and People*, a discussion of how language reflects the psychology of a culture. In the early afternoon, his bell rang interrupting his reading. He went to open the door with a pounding heart, not doubting for a moment that it would be Paloma.

Although her dress was very modest, the woman at the door didn't look like the maid he had first encountered. Perhaps it was the marvel of makeup and lipstick. With all his indecision, he had not expected the behavior that automatically took over. He took her by the hand much as she had done. They kissed briefly, but then he led her to his living room. She quickly looked around as if pleased with her surroundings. He couldn't avoid what was on his mind.

"We have to talk." He felt her sudden stiffness and distancing. "Who are you exactly?"

Very serious, she took a few steps past him and pulled a book out of his bookcase. To his surprise she leafed through it quickly and gave it to him, open at a specific page in the anthology of Argentine poets. The poem was by a Paloma Gutierrez. Paloma started, "En el mundo hay dolor de ayer y de mañana, luz de las nieblas ..."

Surprised he interrupted, "You're Paloma Gutierrez?"

She nodded.

"Do the Alvarados know about it?"

"Yes and no. I have to be their maid in every respect."

"Why are you there?"

"I was spending a night with a friend. A boyfriend if you want to know. The army raided our apartment while I was gone. I lived with a group, possibly slightly radical, but mostly all talk. They were all taken. I couldn't go back.

Josh knew that it wasn't an uncommon story. The taken were usually never seen again. He nodded silently — he wished to express some sympathy but couldn't find the right words.

"What's the secret of my charm?"

"Does it need to be discussed? You're cute and I needed to be hugged. It hadn't happened in a long time."

"I don't buy that."

"Well, it's partially true. By the way, my English is not bad if you prefer. My mother's name was Callahan. I also know about you and your job at the Embassy."

"How is that?"

"El señor Alvarado used to be in government before the last upheaval. He has followed the political scene very carefully. Probably out of old habits, he keeps a diary, not a personal account, but observations about the current state of affairs, with a wealth of detail. I looked through it. You were mentioned, including your efforts to collect information about the recent outrages. I thought you would be sympathetic to the victims."

"And how! You don't know the half of it," he thought. "You got hold of his diary?" he asked.

"When your life is precarious, you are allowed some infractions of good behavior."

He hadn't meant to sound disapproving. It wasn't what he felt.

Their exchange gave their relationship a different tenor which he didn't understand. In a way, he regretted the change since he was still strongly attracted to her, perhaps even more so after her revelations.

"I don't know if I can be of any help. I have resigned my job at the American Embassy. I'll think about it. I might come up with some ideas."

She visibly relaxed. "You know I don't trade sex for favors. I didn't mean what happened to be an exchange. But I do need help. I have to get out of the country before I'm discovered. And then I found that I was attracted to you."

They spoke softly, formally, as if they were old friends in an earlier era. They sat close together on a couch but without touching. He noticed later that they intermixed Spanish and English switching from one to the other without hesitation.

She had lived in a group, not for ideological reasons but for its cheapness. Notoriety came by itself without any effort on her part. The café she frequented offered poetry readings by various authors. One of them didn't show up one evening. After an uproar, the organizer, an older man, had selected her as a substitute, probably because she had just raised her hand without making the fuss the others had created. The poem she had conceived was engraved in her memory —in her soul. It was the story of the death of a country that she loved, step by step into blood, suffering and ignominy. She could have recited it even in her sleep, emotionally, and even theatrically.

A Mexican publisher had contacted her later and asked to see all her poems. He quickly warned her that there was absolutely no money in poetry. Nevertheless, she saw her thoughts and feelings in print with her name proudly displayed: Paloma Gutierrez! On the back of the cover, a photograph that was just too attractive to be hers. After that, the concern of not being able to duplicate the feat, although her mind kept churning and she kept writing.

Josh's path had been tortuous. Serving his country and perhaps the world had been his naive youthful thoughts. Surely in diplomacy, sincere and earnest negotiations could keep to a minimum wars and conflicts between nations. He had served faithfully. His collection of information, sometimes from statistics, sometimes from cleverly planned interviews, not so much from official sources but with cunningly selected individuals, had born fruit. In his mind it had at least helped bring down one dictator and certainly had made a small contribution to government policies. When later he was assigned to Argentina, he felt he could contribute as well. His Spanish was good and he soon found ways of collecting information. When he had concluded that he had no real effect or role, he decided to pursue other endeavors.

They ate at a corner café and then upon returning to his apartment they made love. The encounter was gentle, loving and didn't have the unbridled passion of their first meeting.

How do you get a wanted individual out of the country? He imagined that upon discovering her prominence, the powers that be would actually focus on her capture. Were he able to enlist the help of the CIA and come up with a good reason for the action, it would have been simple. But he knew that avenue was no longer open to him.

He assumed that the main forms of transportation were being watched intently. His first impulse to find a *cédula de identitad* of another woman that would take Paloma to Uruguay was too risky. Once in Uruguay, of course, something could be arranged from the American Consulate. After all she was a bona fide refugee.

He was not without friends, but except for Michaelis, he was reluctant to discuss the matter with them. His intimate thoughts had always been kept from them because of his diplomatic status. Francesco Labello might be an exception. Labello was a cultural attaché in the Italian embassy, who had befriended him. He had a clear vision and had never forgotten his involvement in Italy with the partisans during the war when he had been just a child. Josh had discussed with him the Argentine situation and thought that he could at least present his problem without equivocation. He was right. They met at a café. Labello was silent for a few moments.

"I think maybe I can help her. Shall we say some of my acquaintances at Alitalia might be useful?"

The acquaintance was called Bettina and she could manage to get Paloma on board as a flight attendant as far as Montevideo. Josh had names of friends of long standing at the American Consulate. They could help her apply for a visa to the United States as a refugee. After a few days, he passed on the information to Paloma.

They had been meeting at least once a week and had become good friends besides being lovers. One of their intellectual disagreements was on the subject of love. Neither of them were contemplating marriage, but Josh thought he was ready for a permanent bond with a woman. Paloma thought that this just showed how innocent he really was. On her part she had never found a man she could trust entirely. Beneath their charm and attractiveness, they were all quite incapable of a long term relationship, much less one that would last a lifetime.

In a sense, their relationship was as close to an idyll as they had ever experienced. But Josh soon found out they could no longer meet safely. He was being followed. Somebody must have seen them together and recognized Paloma. They were trying to discover her refuge. He called the Alvarado's house to alert her of the changed circumstance. The woman who answered the phone indicated that in the Alvarado household servants could not come to the phone. Josh had to invent a family tragedy to get to talk to Paloma. Their conversation was terse, but he was sure she understood the danger.

He had hoped to be able to keep track of her flight via Labello or a direct call from her once she arrived in Montevideo. But it was not to be.

Josh was indeed being followed even when he went to the Embassy. He'd thought that he was at least partially safe because of his diplomatic status. But he had been wrong. Returning home one day he was surrounded by a group of men. He spoke to them politely, exhibiting an outrageous gringo accent.

He mentioned his diplomatic status. When they grabbed him, he kicked the one closest to him in the testicles hoping it would disable him from any carnal pleasure for the rest of his life. It was all to no avail. They pushed him into a car and he was spirited away.

Somehow he knew what they wanted. Paloma was the only secret he knew that would interest them. Obviously, the Alvarados would be implicated also. There would be no trial, judge or jury. Some of the stories Labello had told of World War II came to mind. How Labello had had a hand in moving by train and with false documents British pilots who had been shot down. If they were too blond, the proper amount of shoe polish served to make them look Italian. If accosted, they would say in Italian with the proper hesitation, the one word they had practiced for hours and answer any query, "Ma?" which could mean, "how would I know?", "it all depends," "I really don't understand you." and "Can't you see I'm retarded?" Apparently it had worked well.

And then the terrible tale of Ignazio Umino that Labello had heard. How he had been tortured for hours to find out where their arms and explosives were kept. Ah! But Umino knew how to handle himself. First he delayed everything. He could only speak well Venetian dialect, his Italian was too limited to understand their questions. When the appropriate Venetian black shirt was found, they had obviously misunderstood him, he had meant Veronese. And then they kicked him, slowly slashed him, pretended to drown him, pulled his nails, used electric shock on his genitals. He found a way of fainting, either by surreptitiously pressing on his carotids, or insulting them so badly that they couldn't resist hitting him wildly until he passed out. It was a macabre game of chess. He'd won out because he died before they could extract anything useful.

Josh didn't think he would be able to stand up to anything like that, but at least Umino had provided him with a script to follow. Please speak in English. He had little knowledge of castellano. No, can't they find somebody that really speaks English? Don't they understand his diplomatic status? He kept yelling, "Yo Embajada Norteamericana!" But eventually they forced their methods on him. He found his most effective, and in a sense satisfactory trick, was shouting insults about their manhood, sexual orientation, their impotence, the degrading sexual practices of their mothers or girlfriend. This gained him some periods of unconsciousness, but they always revived him with cold water and once by injection. Once, he had fainted from the intense pain of the electric shock and when slowly coming out, he'd heard a voice in Spanish, "Are you out of your mind?" And without orders from superior officers." "We don't need an international incident over this." After that, half conscious he was relayed to the hospital.

He found out later that one of his neighbors had observed his abduction and contacted the Embassy. Michaelis had taken it from there. After all, despite his resignation Josh was still a bona fide member of the group. In fact, the event had produced an international incident with the American government protesting the treatment and the Argentine government denying any involvement, as reported by the newspapers.

Josh recovered slowly. He had ached all over and there had been some damage. However, the psychological wounds were the more serious. He doubted he could feel safe ever again. Yet, he had a certain amount of pride in having been able to keep his own counsel. Perhaps he really loved that crazy woman. Perhaps he was just a stubborn son of a bitch.

Finally, there was no reason to remain in Buenos Aires. Aside from the people he knew from the Embassy, he felt he would constitute a danger to his other friends. Leaving, however, didn't mean that he wouldn't be tormented by inexplicable terror or suddenly sweat and tremble when he'd least expected it.

Josh wondered what had happened to Paloma. Labello had assured him in a hasty telephone call that she had left Argentina without difficulty. But where was she now? He yearned to see her again, but he would do anything to avoid having her see him in his present state: afraid of his own shadow.

Paloma wondered exactly what had happened to Josh. In Uruguay, she had read about the fuss and diplomatic maneuvering that had taken place. His "disappearance" had happened when she was still in the Alvarado's household. She could well imagine, however, what had happened. Josh's argument about a lifetime commitment between a man and a woman suddenly made sense. Would she ever see him again? Would he reject her now that he had undergone so much suffering on her behalf? Anyway, it seemed almost impossible that they's meet again. But then you never know. After all, they had many interests in common.

After a few weeks in New York City she made friends who showed common interests. A group of poets treated her with more respect than she deserved, she thought. She'd been asked to read some of her poems in a Greenwich Village nightclub. She protested that they'd be in Spanish, but she accepted. Paloma was pleased that there was a contingent from Spain and Latin America among the audience who would at least understand her poems. Perhaps at some point in her life she would translate them — a forbidding task that she dreaded.

In the nightclub, close to midnight, just before her turn, she saw Josh hiding in the back. Surprised that she had recognized him despite the gloom, she quickly walked over to him. They looked deeply into each other's eyes.

The first words she was able to blurt out were, "Do you still want me? For a lifetime, I mean."

"Paloma, I'm not the same man. I'm beaten, afraid of everything. You need somebody with some strength left."

"I need you, and a lifetime commitment means I would take care of you if I have to. Please come with me." She took him by the hand, much as she had so long ago when she had guided him to her bed. At the podium, still holding him by the hand she said, "Ladies and gentlemen, if I don't insult you by calling you that." She was interrupted by some jeering in line with their bohemian personae. But she continued, "I'm Paloma Gutierrez and I'm going to read to you in Spanish some of my humble contributions, but first I want to introduce to you the love of my life, Josh Elwood. We'll get married as soon as we get a chance." They were greeted by pandemonium, but it was clear that they welcomed them. Paloma began her poems from memory, still holding Josh's hand. Josh's sense of loss and insecurity evaporated at least for that night.

THE WALLFLOWER

Federica knew that she shouldn't have come. When Charlie Lowler had asked her to go with him to the dance, he had seemed in earnest. The school encouraged a dance once a month — possibly to civilize the students in the upper classes. Federica felt it might do the exact opposite. The attendance was open to couples. Single boys were thought to be too disruptive.

The invitation had pleased her. She wasn't accustomed to being singled out by boys, except perhaps as the butt of jokes. He was in her class and had all the awkwardness of a boy in his teens, and perhaps that's why she hadn't felt intimidated. Tall, with wildly disorganized strands of brown hair and a prominent nose on a lightly freckled face, he hadn't shown any interest in her before. She hadn't expected Charlie, supposedly her date, to disappear after talking to some of the school crowd. His image, gyrating wildly with his hair in even more disarray than usual, appeared intermittently before her eyes — at some distance, in the middle of the dancing throng. To leave by herself to avoid any further humiliation was not simple, since Charlie with his brand new driver's license had driven her to the school. So, she was stuck being a notable wallflower, decorating the wall.

The gymnasium had been converted into a suitable dance hall. The loud rhythms and the psychedelic and rotating beams of multicolored lights provided the proper environment for the frenetic frolicking. The chaperones were unobtrusive, sitting on the side where Federica had found herself. Some couples were nuzzling and embracing and some going even farther. Federica wondered whether the chaperones were ever going to intervene.

She considered stepping out. The weather was still mild and she would be by herself. Not that being ignored was new to her. Attending an exclusive private school as a scholarship student and coming, so to speak, from the wrong side of the tracks presented many disadvantages. Her appearance wasn't particularly noteworthy. Her breasts were small, causing her some self-consciousness and no joy. She didn't speak pretentiously or in the latest cool slang. Her two dresses were humdrum. In contrast to hers, the jeans of the other girls were usually designer jeans. Fortunately, except for special occasions, the cutesy school uniform, blue and with a tartan skirt, avoided her sartorial inadequacies. Other factors solidified her reputation as a weirdo. She challenged teachers in class presenting cogent arguments — her voice becoming shrill when she became excited.

Perhaps her exact opposite was Patricia McBay. Blonde in extreme in contrast with Federica's drab brown hair, she had a perfect figure even at the age of sixteen. Always ready with the right word for her peers. Her laugh was a controlled trill. She rarely showed any emotion, possibly to show her sophistication — she was the ice princess. The only time Federica noticed Patricia to get excited was when she announced to all within hearing that she was to be brought to the monthly dance by Captain Horace McBay, a decorated Air Force hero, who was her cousin. She had hoped he would come in uniform with all the shiny medals. Tired of all Patricia's preening and posturing, Federica's vindictive imagination concluded that he probably was only Captain Horrible McGoo, who during the latest war had never left the parade grounds.

The chaotic rhythms in front of her made her feel even more isolated. But then, interrupting her mind's meandering, somebody stopped in front of her and surprisingly sat next to her. Intrigued and intimidated, she quickly glanced to her side. To her mind, he was clearly an older man, in his late twenties — well dressed — not unattractive. Adults rarely were allowed to be present at a teens' party. Federica sensed that he must be Captain Horrible, not in uniform. Of course, she concluded, there was no way to stop a first cousin of a fashionable student from attending. What he was doing next to her, she couldn't imagine.

"Nobody should be alone in the midst of all the merriment!"

"Do you think I had a choice?"

"What I was saying is that you don't seem to be having much fun."

"Did Patricia send you to torment me?"

"I don't know about any secret motivations. She said you were the most interesting student in the class and even suggested that I might enjoy talking to you. She seems to like you."

"That must be a very sudden development."

"Don't be so cynical. Sometimes it's easier to detect enemies than friends."

"Shall we discuss the Reformation or Evolution versus Intelligent Design?"

"Ooh! You are bad, aren't you?"

She found herself laughing along with him. The amusement on his face was hard to miss and a smile played on her lips.

Federica's smile confirmed his cousin Patricia's judgement.

"Believe it or not, you have a very attractive personality, if you just smiled more often."

"Lah, lah! The next thing you'll say is I'm beautiful!" She had simply tried to make his remarks sound ridiculous. She was embarrassed to think that the way she had said it seemed to fish for a compliment which she definitely did not deserve.

"No, I wouldn't go that far. Just very attractive if you tried. You could stand losing a few pounds. For first, for a party, I would advise a different kind of dress."

"Oh! How rude. And now comes the lecture from the fashion expert. And don't you think that lack of money might come into play?"

"Maybe you're right about that. But let me show you."

He'd gotten hold of a leaflet announcing the dance. On its back he quickly sketched a few lines. Federica was amazed to see the outline of a dress that somehow conveyed elegance.

"You really think I have the figure for that? And where did you learn to draw like that?"

"I can't speak for your figure. You'll have to decide about that. As for my drawing, my mom is a fashion designer and I must have gotten something by osmosis."

"Dress right and everything will be alright. Is that your message? At least it makes a fine slogan that even rhymes!"

"No, I was just carried away. But every difficulty can be easily remedied. Patricia feels you are frequently ribbed by the boys and snubbed by the girls."

"You have a remedy for all that? Are you Dr. Phil?"

"Oh, far from it. If you want to neutralize the boys when they are making fun of you or even insulting you, just give them your magnificent smile. That kind of approach confuses most macho villains into silence. I don't know why."

"Ah! Isn't life simple! What do I do with the girls?"

"All you can do is ignore them. The chances are that they are just jealous."

"Jealous of what?"

"Apparently, you are very accomplished in school."

"Oh! I have a better solution to all these difficulties. I'll quit school. It would delight my parents. They feel I'm drifting away from them and would like me to bring in a paycheck every week."

"Have you ever been bored?"

"Are you changing the subject? I have been bored more times than you can imagine."

"Then think how it would feel to be bored every moment of your life. Gray and more gray. Nothing really new for even a second of your life! A mind needs to be used, otherwise life will be deadly."

"Maybe you're right. I was just teasing anyway."

"Let's just dance for a while. You might be able to show me a few moves. Old fuddy-duddies like me are not only ignorant of the latest but also very rusty."

"I really don't feel like it."

"Come on!"

Pulled out of the chair, Federica was overcome by the force of his pull and the rhythm of the music.

The interlude had been pleasant and even flattering. She had even felt that it might have had some effect on her image — like having attracted the attention of a prince at a royal ball. But she knew it might all be in her imagination and could just be that her self-image had improved.

How to deal with Patricia was a new factor. Could they be friends? Federica didn't dare approach her. Wouldn't she be exposing herself to an unnecessary rejection? But it was Patricia who made the first move.

"How did you like talking to my cousin?"

Federica felt herself blushing. She was embarrassed. But that kind of response just wouldn't do.

"I think he's super. Thank you for pointing him in my direction."

"He's the only relative I can count on. I thought you needed some cheer. He's been providing it for me. I would be lost without him. He even answered my letters during the war!"

Horace, Federica now thought of him as Horace, had been right. Patricia turned out to be a lonesome girl. Under a protective layer of studied indifference and coldness she turned out to be quite a person and Federica found her to be a good and loyal friend.

Visiting her house, Federica acquired some understanding of her new friend. There were cars in the driveway of models she had never seen before. She read "mercedes" spelled on one of them, BMW on another and then one of them was an Italian model that started with an L. She couldn't figure out why they had so many.

To Federica, the house looked like a museum. The furniture, sofa and chairs were impeccable and in good taste. Patricia's mother was flawlessly dressed and elegantly coiffed and made up, and was eminently standoffish. She exuded an air of disapproval, possibly accentuated by her displeasure at Patricia's choice of friends. And that's where some of Patricia's character showed through. She obviously didn't care what her mother thought of Federica. And that was that.

On her part, Patricia was overwhelmed by Federica's household particularly because she had no siblings. So much movement, so much noise in Federica's. She had two little brothers who seemed to be all over the place in perpetual motion. The warnings from Mama or Federica were frequent. Laughter and jokes in bad taste seemed to be the order of the day. Federica's mother was a large, cheerful and affectionate woman — usually wearing an apron. Her father was a serious, conservative presence who at times was quite ready to laugh, particularly at his sons' antics. He had some manual job in town. Meals were a social occasion, with all of them, including guests, sitting at the table. There was food upon food, redolent with spices. Each dish was served with pride by either Mama or Federica.

For reasons neither girl could understand, their differences seem to have cemented their friendship. After thawing, Patricia knew how to behave in a group. Federica was a whizz in academic matters.

Two years passed rapidly. They both even had minor roles in school plays. One was a Sheridan frolic with malapropisms in abundance. The boys in the class had surreptitiously come up with some of their own with sexual or scatological implications. Boys will be boys, reflected the two girlfriends.

At graduation, it was nobody's surprise to find that Federica was the valedictorian. Apart from her nervousness at having to make a public presentation, she was excited about meeting Horace and his new wife. Both girls had maintained a lively e-mail correspondence with Patricia's cousin. Upon getting news of his marriage, Federica first had felt a pang of jealousy. But that went away quickly. Meeting Nina she couldn't help liking her. Nina was attractive in a lively way — full of laughter and insight. She had immediately appreciated Horace's role in the lives of the two girls.

Yet again Patricia's parents were absent. They had some unbreakable commitment. Federica's parents were there, very proud. They had forgotten their resentment of her accomplishments. They were even ready to accept her next phase when she'd start college. The two brothers, much more subdued than when Patricia had seen them before, were also present

Federica's speech was not at all the version she had submitted to the principal. Studded with low-keyed jokes, it was about the role of a school aside from instruction in scholarly subjects. What one learned from human interactions was as precious as what they studied. Somehow her eyes kept drifting toward Horace and Nina or Patricia. At the end she thanked all her teachers and fellow students for her experiences. She hoped she hadn't bored the assembly and apparently she hadn't, although the applause was polite, perhaps more puzzled than enthusiastic.

Federica was very proud of her accomplishments. And no less proud of the dress she was wearing.

"That looks awfully familiar, " Horace teased.

"It should. My mom and I made it from some weird drawing I rescued at the first dance I attended. And then I had to lose some weight for it to fit right."

Both Federica and Horace laughed and so did Nina when she heard the story. It seems not everybody needs a fairy godmother.

THE CAROUSEL II

"Human nature does not change ... What happened yesterday,
will happen today, will happen tomorrow."
in "Shadows," Long and Short Stories, by Henry Tedeschi

There is no way of predicting the future. Who would have thought that his marriage of only two years would dissolve into nothing? His wife, Isabel, was a most attractive woman, not just physically but in her bearing, her thoughts, her vitality, her mental agility. Yet Adam Cotrell had lost her without knowing why. In his imagination he still saw her lovely face, when she had still loved him.

"It's just been a huge mistake," she had intoned, her face stern. "We are just not suited."

He hadn't been suitable for her parties, her special activities, her understanding of culture. Adam knew there was another man, but he thought that wasn't why she had rejected him rather cruelly. She hadn't wanted to discuss the matter with him. She had just left and started divorce proceedings. He had agreed to a Reno divorce.

His parents had been incensed and his mother's reaction was clear. "How could you have let something like this happen? She's such a suitable woman." There was little he could explain since he didn't know the reason himself. He had expected some support, some concern for him from his parents but those hadn't materialized. Isabel's social standing and her charm seemed to be what they had cared about.

His previous involvement had had a much more rapid denouement. Just out of West Point, he had met a charming girl, June. No great beauty — no dazzling intellect — but he'd cared for her. In his naiveté he had taken her home to meet his parents. They had been clearly disapproving and expressed it in very nasty, sneering ways. After that, June had refused to have anything to do with him. That had been his first love, many years before.

In the middle of his emotional crisis, it became clear that he'd have to serve in the army. After West Point and having taken care of his obligations, he had immersed himself in reorganizing his father's engineering and architecture firm. Fred Cotrell, his father, had founded the firm which had acquired a solid reputation. Adam, who was well qualified in engineering and well informed about architecture had taken over because of his father's faltering health. Then it was time to serve in a most vicious war. He had never expected that to be the case. For a long time a war looked to be in a remote future if at all, although he had always been in full agreement with Roosevelt's support of wounded Great Britain. He had learned long ago that bullies can only be dealt with by force.

For his divorce, Adam had left everything in the hands of his lawyer, without really caring about the details of the settlement. His money, some of it inherited, had always been a concept to him rather than reality. It had been very helpful in reorganizing his firm, but in his mind had no special significance.

The tragedy of Pearl Harbor had determined his future. He had become even eager to have a role in the war. There was nothing more important, as cruel and disruptive as it might be. After delegating the proceedings to his lawyers, he'd dedicated himself to the enjoyment of life for the short time of freedom that remained in front of him.

Adam had no real friends left to frolic with. The ones acquired during his marriage, he felt stood clearly in Isabel's corner. Some neglected acquaintances — out of his past —a freewheeling, boisterous bunch were easy to contact. One night they cruised several night clubs. He had no idea of how he'd found himself in a workingman's bar. He remembered later that he'd entered as part of a group.

The bartender kept harassing one of the waitresses. That's how Adam first noticed her. After drinking a good deal, his companions were gone and he found himself alone, flirting outrageously with the waitress, a honey-blonde with a fine smile. Her name was Joanna. In part, he started his courting with flirtatious compliments and double entendres to irritate the bartender whom he found cruel and unpleasant. Somewhat attractive, Joanne didn't have any of Isabel's qualities. Dressed carelessly, with too much cleavage, her attire was too tight on her, although he wouldn't have considered her fat. She became a challenge. Suddenly in earnest, his every effort, all his wiles were to get her into bed. They arranged to meet when her work was over. He thought later that both of them must have been operating with only a small part of their brains functioning.

He picked her up in the parking lot. It was well past midnight. The fancy Lincoln he drove impressed her as he thought it would.

"Haven't you had a bit too much drink to drive?"

Adam ignored her concern. It didn't take long for the two of them to tumble into bed at the apartment he had rented after Isabel had left him. There had been no useless prattle about love or romance. For both of them it was a case of naked desire. Despite the effect of his drinking, the encounter was intense, passionate — different from any love-making he had known before. In the morning, they looked at each other sheepishly. They exchanged phone numbers but he never called her. He imagined that she felt the same way about him. What had happened, must have been from the convergence of a number of factors, just for that once.

Two months later, after a stint at Fort Dix, he was back for a short while and in civilian clothes. The doorbell rang and after a brief delay while he was yelling "I'm coming, I'm coming," he opened the door. She was in the doorway. He had never expected to see her again. Joanna looked demure and much younger than he remembered. He had not noticed before that her eyes were a dark gray-violet. She smiled shyly.

"Can we please talk?"

Adam stood aside and let her in. He was surprised that she had remembered where to find him and curious about what she might want.

After they sat down on the couch, it took her a few moments to speak.

"I'm sorry to have to tell you this. I'm pregnant."

Nobody could possibly realize how much it had cost her to come and confide in him. Their encounter was something she couldn't even understand. She wouldn't have come to him if her need hadn't been desperate. She had lived hand to mouth for some time. She had no idea how to cope with an added burden. Although she appeared calm, thoughts and worries were churning inside her.

When Adam had been much younger and had just discovered the joys of sex, his parents had been very concerned about the ploy women use to trap men into hefty financial settlements or marriage. What made it plausible was the fact that the family was financially very comfortable and the depression had not yet abated. Adam had never believed in the reality of their warnings. But at that moment it occurred to him that he might be facing such a ruse.

"Are you sure you're pregnant?"

She nodded.

"Are you sure it's mine?"

She was blushing, "Adam, I'm not a whore. I might have given you the wrong impression when we first met. I'm not after much, but if you can, I would appreciate a helping hand."

"Help for what?"

"Children take money to raise."

Adam was amused. This seemed to be a game if he didn't take her too seriously.

"I'll think about it."

She took it for the rebuff it was. "Sorry to have bothered you. I'll be on my way."

Why did she feel abandoned and betrayed? She hadn't expected anything else, but somehow she had hoped this man was a bit better than all the others she had met. But then, the two of them hardly knew each other and why would he really be different or more caring than all the men she'd known before?

Somehow Adam was taken aback by her quick decision. He offered her a ride home.

"No, thank you. I won't bother you again"

Her attitude seemed to affirm her claim.

At first he chose to forget her although he admitted to himself that she probably needed help and that he bore some responsibility for her plight. Then many thoughts started tormenting him. He was going away to the wars. Whatever conventional future he'd had, it had been wiped out. He regretted his terseness with her. In the evening, an idea formed in his mind. Why not combine helping her as he really should, with an ultimate vengeance against his fate, against his parents' lack of sympathy?

It took him a while to identify where Joanna worked. There, he was able to obtain her address. She worked only evenings. The bartender and owner was not friendly.

"That slut! I wouldn't give you her address if I had it!"

Adam was overwhelmed by anger. "Watch your tongue if you want to keep your teeth."

That's when he discovered that somehow, unconsciously, he had acquired loyalty and concern for Joanna and the unborn child.

The bartender glared at him. Adam held his eyes for a silent moment and then left. Just outside the door a waitress gave him a piece of paper. He learned later that she was Joanna's friend, Dawn.

"He can be a first-rate bastard and he's been trying to screw her ever since she started here. Didn't manage it."

When he arrived at her address, after a long delay, Joanna opened her door in disarray, with red eyes and wearing a frayed robe. She probably had been sleeping. They didn't greet each other and Joanna spoke first.

"I thought you had expressed yourself clearly. You aren't interested."

"Look, very few people can respond rationally when faced with such a big surprise. I thought about it. I believe you and perhaps I can help."

After a few moments of silence she responded, "Yes. All I need is a few bucks a month for about a year. Maybe a thousand for the year, maybe a bit more."

"I'm going away in the army. It will be a long stretch. You need something more solid. Why don't we just get married?

She was visibly shocked. Then she decided he was teasing her and laughed. "Please, this is too important to joke."

"I'm not joking. I have given it some thought. I'm perfectly serious."

"That's not logical. There is no future in a shotgun wedding," and then blushing, "even in the absence of a shotgun."

"Isn't there? I don't want to have fathered a bastard."

"You won't go through with it. You're reputed to be well-to-do. As I understand it, if we get married I could really collect a small fortune in a divorce settlement. Not that I would do that, but after you talk with your lawyers you won't go through with the wedding."

"That can be taken care by a prenuptial agreement. Look, you owe it to the child. A single mother is very vulnerable. If I get killed in the war, as improbable as it sounds, you would get nothing for the future. The easiest way of solving the problem is for us to get married."

She paused for a few moments. "Adam, I don't think so. Marriage without love can be a trap. I appreciate your concern but I don't think it would work. I'll settle for a small payment, perhaps a thousand dollars, just to tide me over when the baby comes."

Her response had dispelled any doubts about her honesty. Sadness joined his disorientation. Imagine, he was now rejected even by a woman who needed him and was in desperate straits. He went quickly back home and stayed there to make arrangements for what he expected would be a long absence —a few phone calls. Instructions for the manager of his business. Talking to his architect partners. Some instructions for his lawyer to alert him to Joanna's possible future needs.

In the evening, he was wondering what else he might have neglected when the shrill trill of the telephone brought him out of his thoughts. Joanna's voice, now familiar, sounded very hesitant.

"Would you ... would you allow me to change my mind?"

Adam didn't know whether he was pleased by her words or was ready to rethink his whole offer. She sounded in distress. And then an impulse resolved the problem for him. "Yes, of course! Did something happen?"

"Yes, I'll tell you when I see you."

At his door Joanna appeared flustered and unsure of herself. Her face was flushed and tears were crowding her eyes. Her story was very short. She had felt rather sick and had left work for half an hour. She had thought that her morning sickness would be gone at her stage of pregnancy, but that was not the case. And it wasn't even morning! She had been fired by her boss, the same man who had been trying to bed her for the past few weeks.

Adam took care of the necessary hasty arrangements — the blood tests, the license, the appointment at city hall. He brought her the papers for the financial settlement if they ever got divorced. Joanna signed it without even reading it. What choice did she have? Dawn and another waitress who had worked with Joanna were the witnesses at the wedding. Nobody else had been invited.

Joanna was actually trembling through it all. She couldn't understand why under ordinary circumstances brides and grooms could have the jitters. Her case was special. She didn't know whether she was making a terrible mistake or not. She hardly knew Adam and his apparent concern might simply turn out to be an idiosyncrasy, an aberration which had nothing to do with his real character. Perhaps to him it was all a joke — the situation appealed to his sense of humor.

The token kiss after the very brief ceremony was perfunctory. But then at his apartment, he grabbed her and kissed her passionately, with his hands wandering under her clothes. She held his hands.

"Do you really think we should?"

"Isn't that what most married couples do?"

"Yes, but it seems to be too much like an exchange. You give me this and I'll give you that!"

He silenced her with kisses and then she was reassured by his tenderness and gentleness — nothing like their impetuous encounter when they had first met. The single bed was too small for the two of them but it didn't seem to matter even when later they slept easily.

In the morning, he announced. "I'll be gone in about a week. We are going to have a six-day honeymoon."

What followed was a whirlwind. Although they didn't travel, they stayed in a fancy hotel she had only admired at a distance. She couldn't believe how every little whim of theirs was quickly catered to. Every evening, the bedding was turned down and two pieces of chocolate were placed on their pillow. She was as delighted as if she were a child. The bed was so large, she thought they might get lost in it, although Adam always managed to find her.

Adam had insisted that they buy her some fancy designer dresses and they only ate at the fanciest restaurants. They went to a play and a concert. She skipped the sumptuous breakfasts in favor of staying in their room. She felt that she was experiencing what a fancy call girl or mistress of a rich millionaire would go through. The thought made her very uncomfortable, but then she decided to enjoy herself as much as Adam seemed to. She still had an upset stomach, fortunately only in the morning. Adam was very understanding and patient. At all times he was the perfect gentleman. Their afternoons and evenings were dedicated mostly to sex. She knew that reality would soon set in and then all would be gone.

Adam made sure that she meet his lawyer, Rutman, of Margolis, Margolis and Rutman. Rutman was a sour looking short gentleman in a gray suit and a fancy red tie. His sparse hair was dark gray and a small narrow gray mustache adorned his round face. He spelled out the financial arrangement Adam had devised. She couldn't see how she could even spend half of her monthly allowance. They also went through the prenuptial agreement she had signed before the wedding. She couldn't understand why Adam was adamant in making sure she knew every little detail. He even signed a document giving her powers of attorney.

She had the uncomfortable feeling that he was preparing to die, a thought that upset her. What could possibly be going through his mind? At first, he had seemed so indifferent to her problems and fate. Then everything had changed. Taking care of her was something that came naturally. Why shouldn't he? He was beginning to think of her as a real wife. She was considerate, thoughtful, friendly. What more would he want in a woman?

The fateful day arrived when he had to leave. He suggested that she move into what had been his apartment. He had jotted on a piece of paper how he could be reached and that was only by snail-paced mail. On his side the mail would be censored and there would be much he couldn't discuss.

******

Over four years they exchanged many letters. For some reason they'd found nobody else they could confide in. They could tell of their pains, feelings and thoughts without fabrication or pretense. The correspondence left in their minds a collage of intimate memories and confidences.

******

It didn't take long before there was an encounter between Joanna and Adam's family. Adam's mother, Lucille Cotrell, made an appearance accompanied by her daughter, Sophia Mathews. Lucille Cotrell introduced herself with hauteur as Mrs. Cotrell and then she let forth with an acrimonious tirade.

"This is a falsehood, a sheer fabrication. You have no right to be here. You must have tricked him. We'll have you thrown out."

Somehow, Joanna was not surprised or helpless. Something had happened since she had met Adam, something that she couldn't define.

"Thrown out from my house? How would you manage to throw out your son's wife?"

"Wife? A masquerade. We'll expose you and have it annulled."

"Really? On the grounds that the marriage was not consummated?" Joanna laughed and caressed her belly that was beginning to show.

"Bitch! Bitch!"

A dignified, calm Joanna asked them firmly to leave and they did, Mrs. Cotrell murmuring threats. Joanna lost no time and called Mr. Rutman of Rutman, Margolis and Margolis. Rutman promised to wave at Mrs. Cotrell the threat of a court order to keep the unpleasant woman at bay. Joanna wasn't bothered again.

When Adam had a chance to respond to her story a few weeks later, he seemed much amused, although in some ways he'd been surprised at Joanna's strong backbone. He wished he could have been there to witness the exchange.

Sophia came back the following day after a brief phone call and gave her a friendly smile. "Don't think that I was a party to that unforgivable display. You handled yourself beautifully. I don't think I could have done it that well myself."

Unexpectedly, Joanna had returned the smile and waited for more.

And Sophia had more to say. "Adam and I were never very close, but he is my younger brother and I understand why he proceeded the way he did. You know, he didn't tell us about the wedding. Imagine what a melee our mother would have created! But that's not why I came. Perhaps I can be of help. With Adam gone you seem to be alone. I have three children of various ages. The least I can do is share some of my experiences. And perhaps I can do more. "

Joanna nodded.

"No mother, father or siblings?"

"Mother and siblings, yes. They weren't invited to the wedding either. I expect them to call at any moment to try to borrow money. For psychological or any meaningful support, I'd have to look elsewhere."

"You can count on me if you wish. I'll be glad to do whatever is needed."

They chatted for a while. Sophia shared some of her experiences with her children. Some stories were funny. Others very serious.

On parting, Sophia asked, "Do you think I can hug you? Or would that be too presumptuous? After all we just met."

Joanna held out her arms and they embraced. Sophia's parting words were, "You seem to be so sensible. I think finally Adam has been lucky. I'm glad he married you."

******

A soldier's training isn't so much to learn how to fight, but more how to die! What a terrible equation. After a stint of organizing the continued training of soldiers, Adam was transferred overseas and had to interact with his British counterparts. Besides his military contacts, as an officer, he had met a number of individuals socially — some of them charming women. He couldn't resist writing that he hadn't found any who measured up to Joanna. What could he possibly mean? Joanna was conscious that she'd had only a high school education and had never been considered a beauty. She felt a stab of jealousy despite the good intention of his comment. She suddenly realized that if he strayed, and he had every right to do that, her heart would break. Nobody ever knows where their hearts will lead them. But then perhaps it was just her pride that would suffer.

For Adam, the contacts with his British counterparts required a good deal of tact he didn't think he had. He felt he should be with his soldiers — their light moments, their laughter, their fears mostly hidden by bravado, their suffering and their death.

Joanna hadn't really thought that Adam's death in the war was possible. She hadn't faced that eventuality. Suddenly, learning how he felt, she became tormented by the possibility.

******

There was the day when Sophia invited Joanna to dinner. She had led her into the living room. Two little boys and one very young girl were playing on the rug, and a man was right there playing with them, sitting on the floor.

Sophia made the introductions. "Guys, this is Joanna-auntie and I hope occasional babysitter. That's Calvin and the children: Dawn, John and Robert. Calvin is a regular guy as you can see. He passed muster with Mama because he can be polished and charming when he wants to be — the hypocrite!"

Calvin was laughing at the introduction. "I only had to be a hypocrite when I was introduced to Mama. After that, once a year for a few minutes. Sophia had to dissemble several years through her childhood and teens!"

Dinner was pleasant. The children had to be asked to behave a few times. One of the boys, Joanna thought Robert, had to be asked to stop running and sit down. With each dish, Sophia would absent herself from the table for a few moments to go into the kitchen.

After the children went back to their games, the grownups sat leisurely chatting over coffee or tea. Sophia confessed how relieved she was that Calvin did not have to serve in the armed forces. He was forty and involved in the defense industry.

It suddenly occurred to Joanna that she had found the family she never had. With a pang she also realized how tenuous her position really was.

******

Adam mused that it was unfortunate that the Luftwaffe was still dangerous despite the air superiority of the allies. Sometimes the swift roar of engines could be heard overhead. The airplanes had Swastika markings and would fly low, almost at roof height. The staccato sound of anti-aircraft guns and then the grave tones of the pom-pom were followed by the terrifying explosions of the bombs which shook the ground. The Germans used aerial torpedoes and the strange glider-bombs released from the parent aircraft at a distance and guided by a radio beam. And then dive-bombers followed.

It took a while for the Allied Air Force to exert its superiority with heavy bombardment of the German forces. An endless stream of aircrafts unloaded their bombs, throughout the day.

******

Joanna had had prenatal care from an obstetrician. It had been one of the conditions Adam had insisted on. In her limited experience this concept was new to her. Her worries were more about what would happen when her contractions started. She had only Sophia or Calvin as possible support. Would they be available when they were needed? For some reason the delivery itself didn't worry her. But first she had to get to the hospital.

The contractions started in the early morning before her due date. Joanna considered calling the Mathews, but for some reason didn't think the birth was imminent. When her water broke, and inundated her bed, she knew she needed help. It was Calvin who came and drove her making soothing talk. After all, he had had experience.

In the hospital the pain became excruciating. The initial hubbub around her, she didn't even notice. She was relieved to see her own obstetrician present for the delivery. She had heard that it didn't always work out that way.

Laura came into the world not without some difficulty. When Joanna held the little creature, love, tenderness and pride almost immediately overwhelmed her. The baby was so perfect and so lovely even when her little face was distorted by her weak cry.

Joanna wished Adam had been with her. Fancifully, she imagined him delighted with Laura.

She was lucky that Sophia was with her to soften the changes in Joanna's life that came with a new baby.

******

Small streams ran at the bottom of the valleys. Winding, they had cut deeply into the earth and acted as anti-tank booby-traps stranding armor and supplied perfect cover for the Germans. In rainy darkness the men with Adam waited for an attack on a February night. When the attack finally came shells burst all around them, Then the enemy soldiers followed with shouts of "Sieg Heil! Gott mit Uns!" inherited from the Germans of World War I. It was bloody. Machine-guns cut them down but yet they came. The Germans seemed to appear out of nowhere. Rifle shots, the thumping of the Bren-guns and the ripping sounds if the German spandaus, the bursting of hand-grenades, the tanks, and then hand-to-hand combat became the rule. A terrifying, noisy scenario.

In the confusion, Adam felt the fear of an imagined impact on his body by the metal pieces exploding and disintegrating around them. Artillery and tanks did their best to contribute ear-shattering din and mayhem. His battalion was in the middle of it all, with machine-guns stuttering and hand-grenades exploding around them in an intensity of sound and destruction. He wasn't sure he would survive. Only few did. At the end, only a small fraction of the men remained but the battalion had held its ground. Adam was proud of their performance, saddened by the deaths. Everything had an air of unreality and the dulled hearing only increased the disorientation.

Later he realized that he'd been lucky to have provided for Joanna. One less matter to worry about. Most of the men had dreams of sweethearts, wives — real or imagined. Frequently they were just pin-up images they were ready to hang on the tents that sheltered them during rare quiet moments. Adam didn't have to hang pictures of women. For some reason, the image of Joanna, his wife, was always in his mind. In those moments he realized how fortunate he was to have Joanna to get back to. At other times, exhausted almost at the edge of hallucination, he wasn't even sure she really existed.

After their retreat, the allied forces had to be ready for more as there were no reinforcements. Adam and his men were exhausted, hungry and cautious. But it all had to go on. The war had gone on for a long time and Adam knew that some of the fiercest fighting had still to take place. But the end would eventually come.

******

After Laura's birth, Joanna was filled with contentment. Breast feeding isolated the two of them in loving intimacy. After that, the care of her daughter and the worrying about her well-being filled her days. Having Sophia as a support was a godsend, Joanna couldn't be more grateful. Interacting with Sophia's children was a delight.

All her life Joanna had worked and as Laura became a toddler, she started thinking that she had accepted the role of a parasite. In her mind, the money Adam had provided was excessive.

Besides, a war was going on. There was an acute need for workers. Impatient with herself, Joanna still knew that she couldn't take a full-time job without neglecting Laura.

Almost by chance, she discovered what to do. One day, her friend Dawn, with whom she had been a waitress, phoned her frantically. Her brother was one of the casualties of the fighting. Joanna accompanied by Laura, now two, went to Dawn's apartment to see what assistance she could provide. Dawn was hysterical. Joanna had to hug her to calm her down. A torrent of tears followed. Joanna felt helpless.

Fortunately the bell rang. Two women entered — sober and soberly dressed Joanna judged them to be in their late forties. They smiled and asked,

'Dawn Ferguson?'

After Joanna answered, and pointed to her friend, they addressed Dawn. "We are from the Association of War Widows. We try to support and if necessary offer material assistance to the families of GIs killed in the war. In our case, we are widows of military personnel killed during World War I, but we welcome anybody interested in our activities."

Joanne observed how carefully they consoled Dawn and offered their help. Apparently, they also were part of a support group where families met to discuss the emotional and physical problems they had encountered. Suddenly she saw she had to join them. She also realized that in extreme cases she could offer some of the money she really didn't need. Adam had left her too well provided! She found that her sensitivity and affectionate concern went far to console the bereaved families.

******

The wounded couldn't be removed from danger quickly. The hospital was too close to the fighting and had been sprayed with bombs. Basically the physicians, medical personnel and nurses were in the line of fire.

The wounded in dirty coats, pullovers and battle dress sodden in mud and blood were placed in rows. Sometimes they couldn't be attended to for hours. The nurses more than anybody else contributed to raising the morale of the wounded. In their minds they represented a step toward normalcy.

Often the wounds were in the form of gashes or multiple injuries. Adam had been hit and had a rifle bullet in him. It hurt but his wound didn't bleed much. He chose to ignore it. Seeing the wounded men around him, he considered himself in good shape and returned to the fighting. It was later when there was a temporary lull that he could be attended to.

******

When Laura was two years old, Sophia's agitated tones on the telephone couldn't be missed. "Have you heard anything from Adam about selling his business? It seems to me absolutely the wrong move."

Joanna wished she could reassure her. "No, he hasn't said anything. But you know, I don't always get his mail and sometimes it's really delayed."

"I can't believe that he would do it. Right now they couldn't possibly get much unless the company is getting a military contract. In peacetime, in Calvin's opinion, it's going to be worth a mint!"

"I can look into it if you can baby-sit for Laura.

"When could you go?"

"Tomorrow, PM, seems a possible time. That's when the board meets." That much she knew.

"Okay. I'll pick up Laura in the late morning. Laura seems to have gotten accustomed to me and my domestic turmoil."

What was happening was a strange development that worried Joanna. In all his correspondence, Adam seemed to be troubled only about the war. She didn't feel he would be contemplating such an enormous step. Would he want her, a mere woman he hardly knew, to stop the transaction? And how could she possibly do that? Although she had gained much self-confidence, she couldn't see herself facing seasoned businessmen and architects. And would that be what Adam would want? She read her powers of attorney through and through. Perhaps there was a mistake. Without spelling out the details, Adam had given her the power to manage the house and finances. His business wasn't even mentioned. Nevertheless, the powers he had delegated were general — encompassing everything as far as she could see.

Rutman, the lawyer, was the only person who could explain to her the intricacies of the situation. How could they speak of selling the firm without explicit permission from Adam?

According to Rutman, everyone on the governing board was a partner, although Adam was the main shareholder. The manager, a Mr. Seymour Coosick, could sell or dispose of the firm alright, but only if Adam was unavailable. The idea was that Adam might become incapacitated by disease, an accident or such eventuality. The documents had been formulated during peacetime. The possibility of Adam being in the army hadn't been contemplated.

Joanna thanked him and for a while was totally confused. What could she possibly do? It occurred to her that in a way she had pledged to intervene simply by having accepted Sophia's offer to take care of Laura.

Joanna had never had any contact with Adam's business. The building was modern. After she reached the door labelled Cotrell, Inc., she felt totally unequal to the task and perhaps a foolish interloper. What did she really know?

The secretary was a well dressed, attractive woman.

"What can I do for you?" Her voice was musical, in harmony with the surroundings.

"I would like to talk to Mr. Coosick."

"At the moment he is in a conference and cannot be disturbed." Joanna noted that the secretary had unconsciously tipped her head almost imperceptibly in the direction of a door. "Would you like to make an appointment?"

Joanna decided it was time to use her credentials. "I'm Mrs. Cotrell."

"I'm so sorry not to realize that. I'm Susan Smith. I don't think we ever met."

"I want to see Mr. Coosick now."

Joanna didn't give Susan a chance to respond. She quickly went to the door and opened it.

A man jumped up from the conference table. "This is a private business meeting. Please leave." And he glared at Susan who had run behind her. There were several other men present. She assumed they were discussing the conditions of the sale.

"I'm Mrs. Adam Cotrell." Joanna thought the man who had addressed her must be Coosick and she assumed the same tone as Adam's mother had when she had come to chastise her.

Coosick was clearly flustered. "Oh, Mrs. Cotrell. I'm so sorry. We never met. What can I do for you?"

"I would like to hear what is being discussed."

"Oh, Mrs. Cotrell, this is a business matter. No reason to involve you. A complicated matter."

That sounded too much like, "the little woman wouldn't understand." It was enough to toughen her resolve.

Joanna pulled out a chair and sat down at the table. She extracted a copy of her power of attorney from her purse and handed it to him. "I'm sorry, but there are plenty of reasons for me to be involved."

Coosick briefly perused the document and then opined firmly, "I don't see how this gives you the power to intervene. We are doing what best for the company."

"I've been in contact with Adam. I really don't think this is what he wants. I suggest that we discuss this before you go any further."

Coosick only saw a young woman, practically of college age facing him. How could she possibly take a stand against him, a seasoned businessman?

"Mr. Belfour of Otto Corporation is negotiating with us to purchase Cotrell Inc. now. We can't waste the opportunity."

"I don't think Mr. Belfour can take the chance." And then turning to the group, "What Mr. Coosick has in his hands is a powers of attorney given to me by my husband Adam Cotrell. on his behalf, I oppose this move. I'm having my lawyer send Mr. Coosick such instructions in a certified letter. If you wish to ignore me, I'll see you in court."

Joanna had no idea if her move would do the job, but she felt that even if Coosick ignored her position, Belfour definitely couldn't. She turned around and at the doorway she heard only silence. And then suddenly several heated voices intermingled.

Once she was back home everything looked different. In the heat of the moment one may have a certain perspective. But then the doubts begin. Perhaps she had been entirely wrong and what Coosik was trying to do really was in Adam's interest. Why else would he want to carry out the sale? Coosik had been an able administrator for Adam for some time. Since she had to see Rutman anyway, she would put the conundrum in his court. She called Sophia and asked her to keep Laura a while longer. Luckily Rutman agreed to see her for a few minutes.

From her previous contacts, Joanna had thought that Rutman had no sense of humor. But upon hearing of her maneuver he couldn't contain his laughter, which contorted his round face. Joanna was taken aback. "Mrs. Joan of Arc Cotrell," then he laughed again. And then seriously, "Well you sure did it. I will ask my secretary to type the letter."

Joanna was not finished. "What bothers me is what his motivation might be."

"He might just need his share of the money. Business must have been awful with the war blocking all civilian enterprises. He might simply need his share of the cash for himself now."

"I'm not sure I want to lose him as a manager. He might resign. Adam thought highly of him. I don't think I could extract the truth from him by myself. Could you try, please?"

"What's on your mind?"

"Well, perhaps a loan."

"I doubt if you could extract money from Cotrell, Inc. They must be strapped for cash.

"As you know, Adam set up a very generous fund for my upkeep. Some of it might be lent to him in some mysterious way you lawyers can figure out."

"Let me have a go at it. I'll phone you when I have some news."

Joanna really had blocked the sale and she was pleased to find that Coosick had accepted her offer of a loan.

After several weeks Adam's letters caught up with the events and Joanna was pleased to find that Adam approved of her stance.

******

Demobilization eventually brought Adam back. He no less than Joanna had been looking forward to their reunion. They had been corresponding all along and had been very frank with each other. Somehow the new situation had given rise to new worries.

Did Adam really love her? The letters seemed affectionate. But how much of his affection was an illusion? In a sense their marriage had been forced on Adam by circumstances — perhaps his conscience and sense of duty. Would he see it now as a trap? Could Joanna and Laura lose him now?

Adam was terrified that Joanna would just suffer him out of gratitude. Hadn't it all been a huge mistake? Perhaps with his return she wouldn't really want him.

As he disembarked he looked around trying to find a woman he hardly knew and a little girl he'd never met. Much was happening in the cacophony and confusion around him. Emotions coming to the surface. People hugging, crying. Children in distress. Some couples, the man in uniform, were hugging and kissing with tears in their eyes. The soldiers had been gone for so long!

Adam suddenly saw the demure familiar figure of an attractive young woman holding the hand of a little blonde girl. The reunion was entirely driven by their emotions. The man and the woman were hugging and crying. Then Joanna picked up the girl and introduced the man to her. Laura was looking at both of them very seriously.

"Why you crying?"

Adam allowed Joanna to answer. "Because we are so happy!"

Later at home after Laura had been put to bed, they sat on the couch, holding each other. Their embrace provided a calm spot away from the rest of the world. They were man and wife in every sense of the word.

WHAT COUNTS

In a way, it was Nicholas, known as Nick, who started it all. He was Jenny's older brother and a junior at the exclusive Wilmington Academy, class of 1907. The whole family, Nick, Jenny, Grandma, Sothern father and mother, were sitting around the living-room as they usually did after their Saturday dinner. The grown-ups were drinking coffee or an after-dinner liqueur. It was a family tradition. It went back to when great-grandfather Sothern was alive. Sometimes the two children were quickly excused particularly if they had some activity of their own which was considered important.

In a jocular mood Nick said, "There is a Jewish boy in my class."

An agitated Grandma, was the first to respond, "My God! What are things coming to!"

A comment from Father followed, "I heard about that. The Levintons are very wealthy, they bought him a place in the school with a sizable donation. Very regrettable. These days, money is everything. He doesn't belong in Wilmington. And of course it lowers the status of the academy." Nicholas Sr. was a judge and very proud of his position.

Jenny, a vivacious irrepressible fourteen year old, three years younger than Nicholas, had no such thoughts in her mind. "What is he like? I have never met a Jew."

"He's like everybody else!"

Jenny continued. "It's such a snobbish place. Do they tease him?"

"They used to, but they don't now. He's very bright and has a way of looking at you that makes you feel very foolish when you pick on him."

"Let's talk about something more pleasant." Mother interrupted the flow of the exchanges before it led to something even more objectionable.

But of course, Jenny was not finished. She interrogated Nick when they were alone. "What does he look like?"

"I told you, like everybody else"

"That's not what I meant. Is he tall? Short? Blond? Dark? Does he have a hooked nose? Doris says all Jews have a hooked nose."

"That's what your dumb girlfriends would say. He's got a very ordinary nose. He's pretty tall, dark haired and somewhat dark. What is that to you?"

"Does he have an accent."

"He's like everybody else."

And that was pretty much the tenor of her inquiries for the moment. She always was very inquisitive. She always wanted to know everything about everything an everybody.

A few days later she returned to the topic. She couldn't leave it alone. "I'd like to meet your friend."

"What friend?"

"The Jewish boy."

"First of all, Joshua is not my friend. He happens to be in my class. And why would you want to meet him?"

"I'm curious. The only Jews I know about are in the Old Testament."

"You know you're pretty stupid."

"I'm just curious."

"Curiosity killed the cat."

"Those are only boy cats. Girl cats are too clever."

"Sure! Sure!" Nick looked at her indulgently. After all she was just his foolish little sister.

Time went by. Nick got to know Joshua a little bit more. They had been assigned for a project they had conceived together for a school science fair.

Although science was a male sphere, Mother Sothern was elected to represent the family for the allotted evening fair since Father had an unbreakable engagement that had to do with his judgeship. Jenny wanted to go too and met her mother's opposition.

"You have homework to do. Besides it's all science stuff — man stuff. You wouldn't be interested."

Silencing the irrepressible Jenny was not possible, particularly with that argument. So mother and daughter went to the fair.

Nick's and Joshua's display showed electricity chemically produced in a galvanic cell — a zinc rod and a copper rod in copper sulfate solutions, with a salt solution bridge connecting them. They had also built contraptions with carbon filaments that produced light when connected to the cell. Unfortunately they would self-destruct almost immediately, but luckily they had replacements ready. Another weird looking device produced electricity by rubbing a rubber band moved by a crank against a glass rod so that the sparking was most impressive.

Jenny spent some time at the electrical display of her brother and Joshua, after she was introduced by her brother.

"This is my bratty sister, Jenny, who thinks she wants to know everything!"

Jenny kicked her brother but not hard enough to create a major diversion. Joshua, who also had sisters, was vastly amused. He knew how annoying they could be. The explanation of the display kept her there for a while. She mostly understood Joshua's calm and thorough account. She found Joshua very attractive. He wasn't particularly handsome. Perhaps she liked his serenity or the merriment shining in his eyes.

When Nick was gone for a while to look at other displays, Jenny had Joshua all to herself, but she knew that sooner or later they would be interrupted.

"Could I talk to you later on another day?"

"What about?"

"Jewish people. Jewish things."

Joshua examined diffidently her eager cute little face. But there was only fervor and interest with no trace of malice. He wasn't dealing with an ill considered jest such as those he had experienced from his peers.

"What you need is to go to a library."

"I'd rather talk to you."

"What's going on?"

"You are the only Jewish person I have met and I'd like to ask you some questions."

"Why?"

" In part curiosity. There are many things I'm wondering about."

"Would your parent approve."

She smiled her big smile. "Of course not!" She would have been surprised to know that the matter was settled by her smile.

He was doubtful that she would actually come, but he arranged a meeting at a park bench, third on the left from Robin Street.

But she did show up, just as cheerful and interested as before.

He found that he was strangely attracted by her, although she was just a slip of a girl, not even a woman yet, with a big warm smile.

"This must be your office, Joshua."

"Unfortunately some people think they have they right to sit here and disrupt my day! Sometimes I like to read here, away from everybody. What do you really want to talk about?"

Later, he couldn't believe that the conversation had actually taken place.

"I want to find out about Jews. All the religious ideas of the Western world seem to have originated from the Jews in ancient times. Than why then are Jews so badly regarded?"

Joshua laughed out loudly and for a moment afraid of having offended, Jenny was miserable.

"I didn't mean."

"... to make me feel like shit?"

Jenny acquired a crafty look. "You don't feel like shit. You just think I'm silly."

"Not at all. I'm not even insulted. But it is what has been considered by many an age-old mystery. The way I see it, it has nothing to do with religion. People dislike whomever is different. Perhaps because it can too easily be imagined as a threat. Others always like to feel superior to somebody else. That's easiest when you're dealing with somebody who's unlike you or new in the scene. Look how the Irish or Negroes are treated, and they are totally harmless. "

"I'd like to witness a service in one of your churches."

"They are not called churches but most often synagogues. I can ask one of my sisters to take you on a Friday night. You know in most synagogues, the men and the women are separated. Some of us haven't become entirely civilized yet!"

"That's no way of speaking of a service! And why Friday night?"

"The Jewish Sabbath starts on the evening before Saturday!"

******

Jenny did attend a service with Deborah, Joshua's sister who had agreed to take her. Deborah had no idea why Jenny wanted to be there. Joshua himself went to a service only when accompanying their father or in the High Holidays.

When Deborah first met Jenny she was suspicious and very tense. Jenny had come to her house. In the synagogue, in a short while, before the service actually started they were talking about girlie things and they found that they liked each other.

For Jenny the whole experience was bewildering. All the chanting in Hebrew, the opening of the large Torah scrolls. Were all the men actually fluent in Hebrew? Deborah laughed at her question. Most of them probably understood some of the blessings, but little else. After the service, Deborah explained to her the major Jewish holidays and their bases. They were so different from the Christian ones. Jenny was particularly taken by Passover. She felt that it was a universal challenge to tyranny and slavery.

After her fateful visit to the synagogue, Jenny kept in contact with Deborah and they became friends. Jenny still met with Joshua, weather permitting. She found that he had the most unorthodox thoughts.

All religions, he said once stripped of their mythology were very similar and worthwhile. By mythology he meant the stories, icons, legends and rituals accompanying the core values. With their mythology still attached they were responsible not just for unhappiness, but for a tremendous amount of bloodshed.

"Think of the Crusades, the Saint Bartholomew's Day Massacre of Protestants in France, the persecution of Jews over centuries, Cromwell's slaughter of Irish Catholics and many other bloodbaths I can't remember now." And he was most emphatic he had mentioned just a sample of the horrors that had taken place through the centuries.

Jenny was surprised by his thoughts. She hadn't heard about some of those events and inspired by their discussions she read intensively about them. She had to conclude that there was a lot of truth in what Joshua had said.

One time understanding his feelings about religion she commented, "You are really not Jewish then."

"On the contrary, that's what makes me Jewish. I'm upset by all the inequities in this world."

"What are inequities? You use such big words!"

"Sorry! Inequities are injustices."

"All Jews are like that?"

"No, of course not. For most, religion is a tradition that is followed without any thinking. But certainly my thinking is in the Jewish tradition. Jesus Christ challenged the ancient world with his ideas and that kind of challenge is very Jewish."

"You are just trying to confuse me!"

He suddenly saw a puzzled, attractive young girl looking at him and felt guilty.

"I'm just a conceited ass making speeches. Please forgive me."

But Joshua had started her in more thinking.

Jenny really enjoyed their exchanges and even loved to provoke a discussion. "Do you really think that 'all men are created equal'?"

"I believe all humans, men and women, are created equal. Like Abraham Lincoln liked to say, they are equal in their rights and in their pursuit of happiness."

She was dazzled by his knowledge. Discussions such as they were having never took place at her home.

"Of all the inequities you were talking about, you left out women. They cannot work at a profession, most of them can't get a decent education. They have no rights at all. To survive they have to marry somebody who can support them."

"You're quite right. They might fare better after they get the vote. But perhaps not."

*****

115

With the weather turning cold it was much more difficult for them to meet and Jenny was distressed to see how rarely they were together.

On a weekend she had suggested they go for a walk possibly out in the country. Joshua had come to her house to pick her up. Her parents were away and they couldn't object to their keeping company, as they would have if aware of their meetings.

The sky was leaden and Josh wondered whether it wouldn't have been wiser to postpone their intended outing. They walked a few blocks to take a trolley.

Joshua, inured to pranks that boys frequently engage in, had noticed they were being followed by two men that looked rather disreputable. What should he do? Was it his imagination? But everything happened too fast. The men were suddenly in motion. A horse drawn van was next to the sidewalk and Joshua and Jenny found themselves thrown into the van, locked in while the carriage was quickly moving.

Joshua's shouts were to no avail. In the semidarkness he could hardly see but could interpret Jenny's faint sobs only too well. He reached in her direction and touched her arm.

"Don't worry, we'll figure out something." He knew that he could hardly console her or reassure her with those words, but he didn't know what else he could do. His heart was hammering but after a while his mind calmed down sufficiently to allow thinking. If he was the target of the abduction, they must be after a ransom. His family was known to be wealthy. Why then include Jenny? If Jenny was the target the meaning of what had happened could be more ominous since her father was a judge. But then why involve him? Joshua didn't have to wait long for the answer.

After about twenty minutes who seemed to be an infinity, the clop-clop of the horse ceased as the van came to a sudden stop. The door of the van opened after a clinging of a key against the lock. Joshua had prepared to rush his captors but the man he first saw was holding a revolver.

The man was leering at them. He was bald and had very bad teeth as shown by his sickly smile. "Well, well, well! I got both Sothern youngsters! Ain't that a hoot! Now let's see if Judge Son-of-a-bitch will hit Dormut with a long time inside!"

They were pulled out by rough hands. There were a total of three men and the two youngsters were conveyed upstairs to a ruin of a house. Joshua's mind had been at work. The captors hadn't done their homework well. They thought he was Nick. In almost an instant a plan had formed in his mind.

"Hay! Hay! You don't want to get the chair do you?"

Joshua was dropped on the steps.

"What the fuck are you talking about. Don't play games with me ass hole!"

"My sister has diabetes. If she doesn't get an injection within an hour she'll just die."

"Don't try to fuck with me!"

"No! No! She goes into convulsions. She almost died once when she was small." And then, "What do you want her for anyway. You only need one of us."

Joshua had no idea whether his ploy would work.

They were taken up the stairs and the door slammed shut. The room was a garret, with sloping ceiling. It was dusty and entirely bare except for a chair and a pail. The latter, he imagined for their bodily functions.

In the semidarkness, Jenny was crying. "I want to stay with you!"

"I don't know whether my trick will work but if you're let go, I think I know how to proceed!"

"Sooner or later they will figure you're not Nick and kill you!"

A sobering thought, he realized. "Be brave! I have other good ideas." Of course he didn't.

Joshua explored the room where they had been thrown. The door was solid. The lock seemed to be on the outside. The window was missing from its frame, but it was right under the roof, at least three floors up. He couldn't possibly jump or climb down the wall or along a drain pipe. There was no way of getting hold of something solid. Thoughts of being able to flee in that way left him.

The door was suddenly unlocked and opened. They hadn't heard his steps on the stairs. The man was there with the gun on his side. An old harridan was accompanying him. Dressed in dark clothes and with gray hair in disarray — in Joshua's mind she was more of a witch than and old woman. The man with the gun instructed her.

"Take her downtown and lose her in the crowd. We'll blindfold her, then when she is away from here remove it."

Joshua was relieved. Not only was Jenny to be let go but the presence of a woman, a new character in the drama, seemed to signify that there wouldn't be any funny business.

Alone, the situation seemed hopeless for Joshua. Certainly when Judge Sothern would let them know that they didn't have Nick or simply rejected their deal, his life would be in danger. For some reason despite the fear he wasn't paralyzed by despair. A thought eventually crystallized in his mind. No, obviously he couldn't climb down. But could he be able to go up? There might even be a way to exit from the roof. Intuitively, that seemed improbable, but he had to try. Possibly, if he could climb onto the roof, his adversaries would conclude that he had found some strange way of escaping.

The room seemed to be directly under the sloping roof. The window opening was under the inclined section. He climbed on the chair he had moved to the opening. Leaning backwards, he allowed his fingers to sense the edge of roof. There was what must have been a decaying rain gutter. Certainly that wouldn't do. It crumbled as he was touching it. Exploring with his fingers he found struts holding the drains in place. They seemed solid enough. He found two that were not too far apart. He had always been good in gymnastics. Could his arms and fingers allow him to lift himself over to the roof? If he was careful, what did he have to lose? He first tested to see if they would support his whole weight before. They held. Of course once he engaged in any shenanigans it might behave differently. He couldn't test them from every possible angle.

With considerable effort he was able to lift himself and stretch his body on the sloping roof.

It was a tenuous advantage. For how long could he hold himself in that position? Where could he go from there? He couldn't see any possible opening that would let him enter the house from the roof. He stayed stretched virtually motionless for a long time. A silent drizzle made his life even more miserable. He was wet and freezing and he couldn't really move without fearing that he might roll out of control down the roof.

Exhaustion created a new danger. Then men's voices reached him, not distinct enough to be understood. They sounded angry. They must have discovered his disappearance. Then Joshua heard a yell of somebody in pain and then a bark from a firearm.

Could it be that one of them had been accused of letting Joshua out and then got shot? That was an eventuality he couldn't have predicted. Joshua stayed motionless on the roof. There was only silence after the shot. But of course somebody might still be there. Sounds didn't carry well to where he was.

There was no great advantage staying on the roof. He seemed less fit as time went by. He was trembling from the cold and his fingers lacked sensation. He couldn't count on anybody seeing him on the roof and rescuing him. He had to risk reentering the room. He rubbed his fingers against each other in an attempt to keep them warm and pliable but it was clear that it wasn't working. He could leave the roof only if he could count on their effectiveness. But it was then or never. It was strange to realize that it would be harder to reenter the room than it had been to climb out of it. Holding as tightly as he could to the struts, he lowered himself. He missed the opening on a first attempt, but on a second he fell to the floor of the room. At least he was out of the rain. But was it worth it?

Examining the room in the poor light he saw a mound at one end. The smell of blood and gore was recognizable. Terrified as he was, he perceived that the door was open. Still trembling from the cold, he hastened through the doorway. He almost fell down the stairs — his legs stiff and unresponsive, but he quickly regained his balance. In the street he had to walk several blocks and finally saw a policeman who was hard to convince about what happened. But finally, the police took action and Joshua was allowed to return to his family.

The next day he was summoned to Judge Sothern presence. Joshua's father accompanied him but was silent most of the time.

"I understand you were seeing my daughter secretly. And it put her safety in danger."

"I wouldn't say that we met secretly. We always met in a public place."

"Nevertheless it was without Mrs. Sothern or my permission. The girl is only fourteen. It seems to me that she was subject to undue influence. I forbid you meeting with her from now on and as soon a possible she will start in a boarding school."

Joshua thought, "What exactly are you afraid of? And you seem to forget that I saved her life." But remembered the saying that silence was golden, at least on certain occasions and didn't open his mouth throughout the tirade. To his relief his father didn't break his silence either.

******

Years went by. Joshua heard about Jenny from his sister, Debbie, who had kept in touch with her. Jenny had attended college and graduated.

Joshua was visiting his family to introduce his fiancée, Allison. It had been a delicate endeavor. Although Jewish, Allison belonged to the group that was practicing religion only marginally. As he had expected, that introduced some tension, although it must have been apparent to his parents that Allison was a delightful woman and the two of them were well suited to each other.

To have some privacy the couple went for a walk. The weather was pleasant and they proceeded holding hands. Joshua was surprised to see Jenny strolling along the Esplanade in the opposite direction.

"My God! After all these years. Jenny!" He exclaimed. They kissed and hugged perhaps more enthusiastically than it was called for.

Allison had just gone through a trying period. Joshua's parents had received her well but she had been quite nervous for a while. Then suddenly there was another test. A very pretty woman, a friend from Joshua's past was kissing and hugging him. It wasn't that she hadn't heard about Jenny but nevertheless the effusive greeting upset her. Was she feeling a sudden stab of jealousy?

Jenny was in perfect control of the situation. "Debbie told me you would be here!" Looking at Allison she continued. "And you must be Allison. Glad to met you. Joshua and I are good friends from practically childhood. To be specific, I love him but without romancing. He saved my life once. He's blushing now, but that's the truth!"

"Aren't you exaggerating a bit?"

"He also managed to save his own skin rather cleverly. But let's talk about something happier."

After a few short exchanges, Joshua was surprised that he, Jenny and Allison shared the same relaxed and analytical view of life. He was pleased that the three of them could converse as old friends.

There are events in life that influence the whole future. He and Jenny had been changed for ever by their short-lived friendly association.

REGRET

Mrs. Adelaide Carterhouse, the widow of Gustav Carterhouse, had not only been the last of the line of the Moshers with all their money and accruements, but she had also married well. The Carterhouses had been more than wealthy. Her wealth, severe countenance, elegant but sober dresses and her ramrod posture did much to enhance her reputation as an uncompromising, old-fashioned old woman. She suspected that her image was a fraud and the result of years of artifice.

At that moment she was facing her niece, Elmira, who was trying to break away from her stultifying background. She was a pretty girl whose cutesy appearance hid a first rate mind. Her dark blue eyes, heart-shaped face and lovely complexion made her very attractive. Elmira certainly was one of the few who was not intimidated by Adelaide's age or social background. Adelaide, herself childless, loved her without reservation, the way a mother would. She had followed her progress since Elmira had been a baby. A child in perpetual motion — then a woman full of energy, a sharp sense of humor and common sense. Nevertheless, her parents had intervened and expected her aunt to discourage her plans, following the clearly delineated arguments that had been used so many years before to ruin Adelaide's life.

Elmira, no doubt, was to be warned about the terrible mistake she was contemplating. A rebel who had attended a community college rather than Smith or Bryn Mawr, Elmira was about to embark on an independent life in the big city with a boyfriend considered entirely unsuitable. He was from a questionable family, supposedly with no prospects and no future. Although a graduate of Princeton, he was an English major for goodness sake! Neither of them had a gainful occupation. As Mrs.Carterhouse had heard, there was a surplus of waitresses and waiters even in the big city. To top off their unsuitable relationship there were no announced plans of a marriage.

Months before, Elmira had introduced her aunt to her young man. Adelaide knew from the aura surrounding them that their attachment was a strong love match, even if marriage vows hadn't been exchanged.

But what happened when she faced her niece surprised Mrs. Carterhouse. She didn't feel like assuming the role assigned to her and found herself in a pixieish and rebellious mood.

"My dear, I should admonish you against your ill-advised plans. But I was in a similar situation once. Love and adventure had beckoned. I regret not having followed my heart."

Elmira couldn't have been more surprised. "I'm sorry if you regret anything in your past. And I never suspected that you were concealing such a romantic soul!" Her eyes were bright and her smile sweet. Her aunt realized once more why she had always loved her niece.

"You can't know what's inside a person — even an old lady. I wish you good luck with your plans and please say hello to your young man for me."

She accompanied her niece to the door and hugged her heartily.

Alone, she was left with reminiscences of the past which had acquired prominence with the passage of time. Why, Adelaide, still only seventy, could remember more persons who had passed away than were still alive.

Her first and last true love had been Jim Cavendish. He had been a sweet boy. Not exactly handsome, but Adelaide had felt strongly attracted to him — to his sense of adventure and humor. At that time she could have said that they were truly soul mates. She had given herself to him body and soul. But marriage was another matter. Her parents were strongly against the match and at that time she had concluded she couldn't possibly live hand-to-mouth, the picture she had been warned about. Even so many years later, she remembered the pain on his face when she turned him down — the brown warm eyes showing overpowering sorrow. After all the years, her decision still felt like a betrayal.

With the passage of time she had not known what became of him until the short obituary in the Goltown Express had updated her. Goltown was where she had grown up and lived until marrying Gustav Carterhouse. The item explained that Jim had died after a short illness. Adelaide imagined that it meant either a heart attack or a stroke. He had been married to Josephine Teyt, who had died a few years before. They had had a son, James Jr. James Sr. had founded Cavendish Enterprises, which in due time had become a very successful business. It was currently run by James Jr., now in his early thirties.

Adelaide had heard about Cavendish Enterprises but hadn't realized that Jim had founded it and nursed it along. It had become a very large international enterprise and she felt the very young Jim Jr. would have some trouble running it.

When reviewing her investments with Joseph Roundbow, she couldn't resist satisfying her curiosity.

"Joe, what can you tell me about Cavendish Enterprises?"

"Ah, Cavendish! I would have said a promising investment when old James Cavendish was alive, but it's underfunded and young Cavendish will have a problem with that. He needs to renew much of their machinery. He's unproven and will have problems raising the money. Lots of sharks in the waters. They would love to buy it to close down such a determined competitor!"

******

Jim Cavendish Jr. felt overwhelmed with worry and guilt. He couldn't share his worries with Anne. The new baby, their first, had fully occupied her emotionally. In his mind, he had betrayed baby and mother by his bad judgement. Perhaps it was the arrogance of youth that had made him decide he could take over from his father. He had chosen to borrow in order to continue with Cavendish Enterprises — he hadn't considered that without his father at the helm the enterprise might be considered a risk. New money had become hard to find.

Selling the business at the very beginning probably would have been a good move. Later it became too hard. All that really remained was an excellent staff, a name with a good reputation and a mountain of debts that would eat up whatever he could obtain from the sale. The employees had always been considered by his father as part of his family and the thought that they would join the army of the unemployed hurt Jim as much as knowing that he and his small family would be deeply in trouble. The thought of the hardships that his failures would cause his wife and child was agonizing.

Jim forced himself to follow his usual routine as if nothing was happening. What else could he do?

Evan Evans was the manager who had been there when Jim's father was in charge. Jim was just taking his jacket off when Evans knocked on the door of Jim's office.

"Jim, we have to talk. Something new came up."

"Please pull up a chair and sit down." Jim sat next to him and braced himself for another disaster. "What's happening?"

Evan Evans was a middle-aged, partly bald man. Always dressed conservatively in a dark suit, in Jim's mind he represented all the virtues needed to run the business.

Evan sat down bearing a deep frown. "I have no idea. You'll have to figure it out. We have an offer. If we form a corporation, we have an offer to purchase forty-nine percent of the shares. These are valued to cover almost exactly our shortfall."

"Does that mean we would be finished?"

"Hardly. The enterprise would not only stay afloat but you would still control it. That's what's so strange. They also specify that you should be the CEO at a perfectly reasonable salary, probably negotiable."

"Should we take it seriously?"

"Definitely. The offer is being handled by Joseph Roundbow and he represents only serious investors."

******

Talking to Adelaide, Roundbow was most disturbed. "Why did you decide to do something so silly?"

"You question my judgment, when I just made a three million dollar killing in Google stock in just two days!"

Roundbow laughed. "I guess this new investment is peanuts to you, even if you were to lose all of your Cavendish investment."

"I wouldn't call it peanuts," she said as her mind was thinking — "Silly man! It's the least I can do. I could have been Jim's mother."

THE UNEXPECTED

What could be more unexpected than becoming in short order the owner of an old townhouse in Greenwich Village? mused Martin Elfort. His friend Milton, who had owned the house, had found himself in a tangle. Allegations of sexual harassment or worse had forced him to abandon his lucrative high-pressure job on Wall Street and leave town in a hurry. The details of the event had been kept from Martin. However, he couldn't pass up the opportunity to take the house off his friend's hands. Milt just didn't want to go through the hallowed procedure of contracting an agent or advertising. For his part, Martin had offered a fair price and seized a good opportunity. After all, real estate in New York City could almost always be counted as a good investment. His own now abandoned Wall Street experience had left him at age thirty-two, free and with a tidy capital. The house dating from the middle of the nineteenth century had been converted to three apartments a long time ago. To some extent its simple straight lines belied its age. He found the house charming even if in some need of repairs. However, moving to the vacant apartment wasn't attractive. The apartment he currently occupied was from his better days and very comfortable.

Martin thought of himself as very ordinary-looking and a thoroughly ordinary man. With most of his dark hair intact, he had a nice smile and imagined from friends' responses that he was moderately charming. Very few people had had the opportunity to note that he was a determined person with ironclad ethics, but still with a sense of humor which often expressed itself unexpectedly. He was single but couldn't really be called a confirmed bachelor since he was far from considering his state permanent. Women he liked, but found the ordinary ritual of dating uninteresting. It reminded him of the colorful but grotesque courtship dances of birds. In earlier times he 'd had very warm relationships with girls in high school and college, but then he had been full of illusions and daydreams.

After leaving the world of finance, Martin had kept busy dabbling in writing, an enterprise that magazines and literary journals had received with indifference. He tended to favor stories where the unusual moral strength of common people emerged in the face of challenges. In his articles he liked to take to task common shibboleths, such as the remarkable preconceptions regarding same sex marriage, contraception, women's choices and ignorance in relation to the dictates of the Constitution, which led to it being disregarded when inconvenient. Somehow as expressed in the printed rejection slips, his article or story never seemed to fulfill editors' needs. Occasionally, the scribbled note on the printed slip would say "a good read" or "keep trying", which delighted him and raised his hopes for a short time, but certainly couldn't replace an acceptance. His volunteer work with abandoned or abused children provided him with more satisfaction. Cruelty toward children was something that raised his hackles. This and violence against women were the only reasons that might provoke him to violence.

The third floor had been occupied by Milton, and Martin had eventually rented it to a couple, George Merrison and Emilie Prospect, with Merrison signing the lease. Whether they were married he had no idea nor did he care. Before signing the lease, Martin had ascertained that Merrison was the successful nightclub owner of the Golden Parrot. The other two floors, rent stabilized through the bizarre New York City canon, were not a source of any great revenue. But eventually they would be vacated due to ill health or death, since the renters were in their eighties. How cynical he had become! he mused.

Mrs. Rosenblatt on the first floor, a widow, was the guardian of this small universe. She would stop Martin for a chat whenever he entered the house. Her knowledge of the neighborhood went back at least fifty years, and she would impart interesting stories laced with current gossip. Not incapable of flirting like a young girl batting her eyelashes, she was a small plump woman dressed in somber clothing with an occasional splash of color in the form of a scarf or a kerchief. Her hair was a darker gray than it should have been, by deliberate subterfuge, he guessed. She referred to the new tenants as "them" or "the two of them."

Martin had never intended to be a landlord, a sub-species he had regarded with indifference if not some disapproval. Nevertheless, it was all routine and not unpleasant. But then unfortunately it was payback time. On the phone, the woman on the top floor, Emilie Prospect said she wanted to talk to him urgently, in person. Most probably something had gone wrong with the plumbing — something possibly unpleasant destined to consume some of his time and money.

The door to her apartment opened almost immediately after he'd pressed the bell. She couldn't have used the spy hole. He was surprised to see Emilie's animated face. When he had met her before she'd looked plain and expressionless. This time, he found her rather comely — small without being petite, with chestnut hair and fine features. And once more he realized he had never understood what made a woman attractive. Not just looks but perhaps vivacity, the allure of a smile or something else that escaped him.

After a cheerful greeting she guided him to the living room, not the kitchen or bathroom as he had expected. She moved gracefully, he noted. The room was plain with unattractive modern furniture which probably, he judged, reflected a masculine taste. Large framed photographs of women singers of yesteryear adorned the walls, perhaps George Merrison's contribution. Martin recognized the likeness of Peggy Lee, Eartha Kitt and Nancy Sinatra.

"Please sit down," she said. Martin was intrigued. When the two of them were sitting on the couch, she continued, "Bet you expected a problem with the plumbing!" And then with an amused yet shy smile, "All these old houses have problems with their plumbing. But I have something else in mind. George and I are splitting up."

She certainly didn't look heartbroken. In fact, her cheerful face indicated quite the opposite. However, Martin's mind was immediately distracted by the fact that he would have to find new tenants. The lease would protect his interests, possibly after some unpleasant legal maneuvering. But then she continued, "I would like to stay. If you can reduce the rent just a bit, I'll assume responsibility for the lease." So the problem might be solving itself.

His position as landlord put him on a role he would have loved to disregard, but nobody likes to be taken for an inept fool. "What do you do for a living?"

"I'm afraid I can't reassure you. I haven't worked for a while, George has spoiled me. Fortunately, I have some money put aside that should suffice until I get a new job."

Later George had contacted Martin and confirmed he had accepted the lease transfer putting finality on his involvement.

It was Mrs. Rosenblatt who stopped him on the stairs one day and elaborated on what had happened. "I hear 'they' are splitting up. That girl has no luck with men."

"What are you talking about?"

"She's been married a number of times. She's a professional wife, ideal for a wealthy social climber or a successful businessman. With the proper makeup and clothing she looks fabulous. I have heard she can be very gracious — an ideal hostess. She knows what is fashionable and what isn't and she's widely read — preposterous but true."

Martin was not particularly interested although somewhat intrigued. A professional wife, indeed! He knew that the proper wife was essential for some men in business or in the search of social status. But making it a profession seemed rather far fetched.

Martin never expected the house he owned to affect his life. Certainly, it would require upkeep, so in that sense would change his routine somewhat. That was acceptable if it didn't interfere with the hours he set aside every day for his writing or for some of his volunteering. But other matters began to intrude as well. The older tenants, Mrs. Rosenblatt and the couple in the apartment on the second floor, were engaged in a verbal feud that had roots in the distant past. Martin had regarded the couple as two very quiet tenants. But apparently when riled they were capable of a good deal of vituperation, which he couldn't even understand. Mrs. Rosenblatt had tried to enmesh him in the oral conflagration, and it was only with extreme tact and diplomacy which he didn't know he had, he was able to extricate himself.

One Saturday, he saw a disreputable looking man knocking Mrs. Rosenblatt to the ground, in front of the house. The fellow grabbed her purse while the old woman resisted. Martin had no time to think or consider what was happening. Skills acquired in the past seemed to resurface. He found himself immobilizing the man by forcefully holding his arm behind his back. Several neighbors appeared responding to Mrs. Rosenblatt's cries. Martin surmised that somebody must have called the police. He let the man struggle free so that he could attend to the old woman. Aside from the frightful experience she was okay and refused medical attention when the ambulance arrived. The incident was broadcast far and wide by Mrs. Rosenblatt. Somehow in her account, Martin had been transformed into a heroic figure. A knife was mentioned in one of the versions circulating. He had even been contacted by a reporter whom he was able to discourage by pointing out the banality of the encounter. There must have been hundreds of similar events on the same day.

In the neighborhood, the attack with all its worrisome implications was not forgotten quickly. One day Emilie smiled at him amusedly and stopped to talk as he was treading up the stairs while she was going down.

"I hear you're a hero!"

"I'm sure Mrs. Rosenblatt would propose a canonization if she weren't Jewish! Or whatever they do to heroes."

"Perhaps a fanfare with trumpets followed by a tribute from a whole orchestra!"

Life has a way of proceeding along with unexpected results. Emilie couldn't have been farther from his mind when he'd accepted an invitation from the Winns, friends from his Wall Street days. But there she was in the elegant living room with a drink in her hand.

"No need for introductions, we know each other," he was able to say to Elizabeth Winn as Jonathan Winn was bringing him a glass of white wine. Emilie and Martin smiled as if they were old friends, although Martin for no particular reason felt embarrassed. Their paths crossing via common friends was indeed unexpected.

It was a small party. Perhaps six or seven couples. Besides effecting introductions, Elizabeth dedicated herself to carrying out her other duties as a hostess, not only providing the victuals but also stopping for short conversations. Without hired help, Elizabeth herself or even Jonathan were offering the hors d'oeuvres warm from the oven. After a while Emilie parted from a group of friends and helped her hostess. Her familiarity with the rituals of the house suggested that she knew her hosts well. For his part, Martin couldn't help noticing her presence as a charming and witty woman. She occasionally addressed, warmly, a serious man, Howard Percell .Martin assumed that he was her escort. He couldn't help remembering Mrs. Rosenblatt's catty comments about her role in life as a professional wife.

It didn't take long for Martin and Emilie to exchange words again, with Emilie sporting a teasing smile. "Martin, what do you do with your life besides being a slumlord."

"Ooh! That hurts. You're so unkind. A double whammy! Not only do I take advantage of poor desolate tenants but I'm also totally indolent. Or wasn't that what you were saying?"

Emilie laughed. "Oh! You're just misreading my meaning on purpose. I was just implying that a man with your energy and talent is probably involved in many other activities."

Martin could only chuckle at her verbal dexterity. At his point he could introduce his writing efforts, but he didn't feel like dwelling on his failures. "What's wrong with being retired?"

"Nothing at all. For some people it's their favorite occupation. But you're funning me no doubt. You're too young for that!"

"Why would I tease you? As far as my moneymaking, I'm mostly retired. I do some volunteer work although I'm not very good at it."

"Very intriguing. Do you mean to keep it a secret?"

"I'll tell you if you don't conclude that I'm a do-gooder. I prefer the image of a rapacious landlord — has more pizzazz."

"Stop being so coy! You're just trying to wet my curiosity."

"I couldn't be doing anything less impressive. I'm involved with mistreated children who have been removed from their families or abandoned children. I read to them. I hold them. I hug them. I hope it does some good." There was no reason to mention that he financed some of the activities.

Emilie was suddenly silent and after that they only exchanged pleasantries.

Another time as Martin was entering the house, Emilie was exiting holding a colored leaflet meant to encourage voting for Jason Umlaut for Congress. Many had been left strewn at the entrance along with menus of Chinese eateries.

After the restrained greetings, pointing to the brochure, Martin couldn't resist an admonition, "You're not considering voting for him, are you? He'd bring back prehistory!"

"Oh! I wouldn't do that, but I have been invited to an event intended as a fund-raiser for him next week. Since somebody else is paying for it, I intend to take advantage of the occasion. I'm sure the food will be good. I've never been to one of those. I thought I'd have some fun. All it requires is a fancy gown and some patience. I imagine if there are going to be any speeches they will be very boring."

"Nothing is free, except of course my incomparable opinions and wise advice. I would urge you not to ruin your reputation."

Emilie laughed, "Oh, I lost that a long time ago."

For some reason Martin was embarrassed and blushed, but fortunately Emilie didn't seem to notice.

Martin found that he was intrigued and attracted to her and didn't know why. The young women he had been dating lately seemed humdrum compared to her. Unfortunately, he didn't know how to proceed with Emilie. He suspected that being her landlord would invite a charming and witty rejection.

Of course, he wouldn't have any trouble obtaining a ticket to the Jason Umlaut event. The Wall Street firm he had worked for would be awash with them. After all, Umlaut was after money. Martin collected an invitation, perhaps to share a few fleeting moments with Emilie.

There was a major jam of fancy cars, rented limousines and yellow cabs in front of the fancy hotel, The Primrose, where Jason Umlaut was being feted. Martin, uncomfortable in his formal suit, dress shirt and tie, was pleased to have selected the subway and the short walk. The feeling that he was about to mix with a crowd he despised embarrassed him. He found strength in the realization that none of his good friends were likely to be counted among Umlaut's supporters.

The ballroom was awash with fancy gowns, jewels and fatuous conversations. Buffet tables held shrimp, smoked salmon, caviar, tiny lamb chops grilled to perfection, and pastries. The speeches had yet to come. At the moment through the microphones at a head table, comments mimicking a conventional, so-called 'roast' of the candidate were supposed to be funny, but were too kind to resemble the outrageous utterances of a real roast

Martin appropriated a glass of champagne from one of the roving waiters to hold as a first line of defense. On the lookout for Emilie, he was relieved not to see her. After all, what could he say to her?

His was ready to leave when his boredom was broken by the sight of a woman in a lovely gown treading resolutely through the crowd heading for an exit. For an instant he didn't recognize Emilie. When he did, alarm coursed through him — an infuriated man was hurrying after her. Without thinking, he put down his drink and followed the pair. The exit door slammed next to his face. Martin didn't hesitate to push it open. The man with his fists raised towered over the woman prone on the floor.

His words directed to Martin seemed to confirm his conclusion that the man had attacked her. "Take a hike asshole!"

Martin's eyes were steel and he raised his fists. But the man wasn't finished.

"Whaddya, fuckin' deaf?"

Again Martin's response was reflexive. He interposed himself between the two and when the man took a swipe at him, his own fists pounded the stranger.

Fortunately, at that point two burly security men broke up the encounter. They probably had been instructed to always proceed with discretion. After all, there were very many important people present. The man, red-faced, lifted himself from the ground muttering and then exited. Martin helped Emilie up. Her mouth was twisted in pain but she seemed to be spry enough.

"Are you okay?"

Emilie's sense of humor wasn't easily dowsed. She was laughing. "My hero!"

He took her home in a cab. At the door of her apartment she asked him in. "It's the least I can do!"

They sat silently in her living room after she poured drinks.

"How did you happen to be there? I thought you were dead set against Umlaut."

"It was all very sophomoric. I wanted to be with you and I haven't figured out how to go about it."

Emilie laughed affectionately without derision. "All you had to do was ask. I like you too." They were silent for a while, and then she continued, "I suppose you deserve an explanation about what happened."

"Look, there is no reason why I should know."

"It's no secret. I don't know exactly what triggered his ire. I was with Howie. It might be something he said. The man, Eugene Gorman, was my boss many years ago and I discouraged his advances. Actually, I took him to court because after that he'd fired me. He didn't know to leave well enough alone. It's something about you guys, you don't take rejection kindly." They were silent for a few moments. "I'm very tired. Why don't we have lunch or dinner together tomorrow so I can thank you properly."

"Dinner will do. I'll call you."

At the door they were standing close to each other. Martin kissed her gently barely caressing her lips with his, but then she held his face with both hands in a passionate kiss. Responding in kind, he slowly detached himself from her. "Let's talk tomorrow!"

They dated a few times. He was surprised when eventually they found themselves together in bed. She definitely was accomplished and skillful. Martin had never experienced anything like it. Passion, lust and camaraderie intermixed. For her part Emilie was struck by his tenderness. She had never experienced that from men. As much as she loved every minute of it, the experience sounded an alarm. She was getting involved emotionally more than she wished to. She dreaded the crash when the affair would be over. When they were together or she thought about him, her heart somersaulted like a teenager's. She kept telling herself that he was nothing special — just an ordinary guy. His calm, logical approach to life and his lack of male guile might have had something to do with the attraction. Her heart had been broken twice before at various times in her life when she could least deal with it. After her last experience, she had vowed never to find herself alone and deeply hurt again. On those occasions she had been left with the feeling that she had been manipulated cynically. No, it was best to avoid all that suffering by breaking the relationship before it went any farther.

Martin was surprised to find himself facing her with the bad news.

"You're a great guy but it won't work You're too intense. You want more than I want to give you. It's been great but it's time that we went our separate ways."

What it all meant was a mystery to him. He did care for her and suspected that with time he might have fallen in love with her. He hadn't acted possessively and all their commitments had been vague. He respected her wish. After some time passed without seeing her, he realized the break may have come too late for him. He was already in love with her.

Although Emilie had paid her month's rent Mrs. Rosenblatt insisted that she had moved out. A letter from her confirmed the old woman's opinion. It was addressed to him but only explained the facts coldly. She was gone. If he were unable to rent the apartment, she would eventually get in touch with him and cover any losses he might have. The envelope bore the post office stamp of a place in Maine.

******

Even in the state of Maine, Martin never would have expected to find a boarding house of yesteryear, intact and with a mature woman, Mrs. Evelyn Rostuff, in charge. Of course, it was called a 'Bed and Breakfast Lodge'.

The trip had been uneventful. The views of woods and mountains spectacular. He was too nervous about his visit to appreciate the scenery. He had timed the last leg of the trip with the hope of finding Emilie still at home. Mrs. Rostuff had taken on herself the task of knocking on Emilie's door so that she was not taken by surprise by his visit. After a few minutes Emilie came down the stairs sedately. He recognized the graceful movements. He wasn't surprised that she didn't smile or even greet him. After all, their last encounter hadn't left him with any hope. He couldn't read her expression when her eyes locked on his but she didn't seem angry.

"You found me. I don't know how. It couldn't have been easy. Let's go for a walk so we can talk. I also will show you something that is important to me."

From the road they followed a primitive path and arrived at a pasture with a most marvelous view of the sea, its immensity interrupted by rocks, the whispering waves in motion without menace, a sailboat clearly visible — the singing of birds in the background. They sat on a large rock.

"I inherited some money and this is where I'll build a house little by little. I'll get some help but I'll do some with my own hands. My father worked in construction and some of his skills rubbed on me."

She let silence follow her words and then she spoke again more forthrightly. "I don't want to hurt your feelings. It's not that I don't like you. You're a nice man. We are just not suited. You're too emotional, too fiery. You don't say so but you demand a strong emotional commitment. A long time ago I fell in love with a man. It broke my heart and it still hurts."

When he took her hand in his she visibly flinched. A strange response since they had been lovers. "Don't worry. This is the only intimacy I want for the moment." After she visibly relaxed he continued, "I don't know why I love you. I just do. I'm not interested in a fleeting affair — what passes these days as 'a relationship.' I want something for a lifetime. I wouldn't break your heart. Though of course you might break mine. And yes, it would mean children. I can't do without them. Despite everything you say I'm sure you'd make a good mother. You'll know all the mistakes not to make. Think about it carefully, it might be a cliché, but in life there is only love —romantic love, love of children — love of whomever you can hold in your heart."

They stayed side by side without talking. Releasing her hand he spoke again, "You can at least have dinner with me. We'll talk about nothing important. Tomorrow, I'll come and see you in the morning. If you still don't think it will work, I'll leave you alone from then on."

******

Emilie remembered well her visit with her grandfather when she was in college. That might have been the reason why in distress she had come to Maine again. Many years before an impulse had taken her to see him. After all Colby College where she was attending school wasn't very far from his home. He had been detached from the rest of the family for some time. Emilie had only met him once when he'd come for her sister's wedding. Before her visit she just remembered him as reserved, almost shy. Her uncle had visited him at various times a long time ago, but he was mostly a stranger to his grandchildren. His birthday gifts that never failed to appear reminded his grandchildren of his existence and converted him into a mysterious legend. When she'd finally met him in Maine, she had found his affectionate glances unexpected and at times the amused look in his eyes encouraging. Troubled after a questionable romance, she had many questions that perhaps many young girls would have on their minds but couldn't easily ask. Her grandfather was in a way a benevolent stranger and that made her confidences and queries easier.

"Grandpa," she had noticed that he loved the appellation, "do you feel that a romance can last a lifetime?"

"That's not something that can be answered easily. There are many which have. Many which haven't. As you must know, grandmother Betty, left me after thirty years of marriage. She never told me why. But the years we had together for me were my happiest. I think she also was happy for most of them. They made the suffering that followed worth it. I loved her without reservation. I still love the woman I had met and married and with whom I shared the children. The woman who left me, I simply don't know. I can't resent her. She is a stranger. So you can say that in my case my love affair never stopped and it was the most significant part of my life. If I had to do it all over again I would. Don't forget that the capacity to love was God's greatest gift to humanity. "

Later he continued, "A woman's married life is very hard. At least then, Betty could only be a housewife and abandon any intellectual ambition. With only housework and children she was isolated. Eventually the resentment piled up and she found her unsatisfactory life unbearable, and that included me. At least that's how I see it."

Emilie had sensed his emotions and had grasped his hand.

Years later, sitting alone on the stone she had shared with Martin, these exchanges came to life as thoughts and memories swirled in her mind. It was as if she could hear her grandfather's voice.

His leaving her a legacy with enough money for her independence at least for some time and the possibility of building the house of her dreams was unexpected. Building the house in Maine was in her mind a thank you to the old man.

Emilie and Martin had an uneventful dinner. They exchanged words as if they were mere acquaintances. Before parting, she said, "Give me one or two weeks. Then I'll give you a final definitive answer."

Days later, after being convinced that he would never hear from her, his heart fluttered as he read the e-mail message on his computer. It was strong and unequivocal.

"I have added a nursery to my plans for the house. It is also designed so that we can make additions when necessary. Love." It was signed, "Emilie, slow but certain."

FANFARE FOR AN UNCOMMON WOMAN

Adelaide Morsing was a good-looking woman although well past her prime as testified by her well-coiffed gray hair. Her dark dress was from a noted designer, and she wore an impressive necklace, a diamond pin and diamond earrings. She had retained a well-formed shape that didn't require any compromises or adjustments and she exuded wealth and privilege. To younger people her appearance might have seemed severe except for the mischievous light in her eyes. Sitting at her table at the fancy hotel restaurant, she was trying to attract the attention of Andrew Finelin.

Andrew Finelin, at the moment on his feet, clearly had not yet recovered from the angry outburst with which he had dismissed a very attractive young woman who had been sitting with him. Still angry, it showed in his irate expression. His appearance was that of a rich man accustomed to giving commands and always having his way. He wore a very expensive, well cut suit. With a full head of white hair, he was handsome in a rugged and mature way.

From a nearby table, Adelaide had clearly heard the words "slut", "go back to the sewer I saved you from," "I already had the lock of the room changed " and "you won't be able to get your stuff." The young woman had left the table was walking out of the dining room. Although she was holding her head high, her eyes were awash with bitter tears.

"Andrew Finelin! May I have a word with you?"

Finelin stopped abruptly, surprised. On seeing Adelaide his eyes softened. Clearly he recognized quality and a woman of similar age, status and wealth to his own.

"Do I know you?"

"When you were at Harvard and I was at Radcliffe you knew me well, though you never managed to know me in the biblical sense as much as you tried!"

First taken aback, Finelin burst into laughter. "You must be the incomparable Adelaide. used to be Clarkson. Better known as Mitzie! Still outrageous and feisty, I see!"

"The same, but now Adelaide Morsing," she informed him.

"You're still outrageous, and attractive I might add."

"Tut, tut. I have to work hard to keep myself together."

"Like all of us, I guess."

"Let me cut to the chase! You were giving that young woman a very hard time. I think undeservedly."

"God! After all these years you're still in your Joan of Arc guise! Let me point out that it's none of your business. She was my trophy girlfriend." With a sardonic expression on his face, he sat down across from her.

"Your trophy mistress! And what does Susan think about that?" She knew from the pained expression on his face, which showed infinite sadness that what she had said was entirely wrong and uncalled for.

There was silence for a few seconds. "I'm afraid you haven't heard. I lost her three years ago. Breast cancer."

Adelaide was frozen for a moment. "I hadn't heard. Please forgive me for raising painful memories." After a good deal of silence, "She was such a plucky lady!"

"That she was till the day she died! I imagine you're still married to ... what's his name? George? George, yes"

"Not really. I lost him to a young trophy second wife."

"I'm sorry to hear that."

"Well, at the time it hurt a lot. But now it looks to me that he was no longer the man I married. Therefore it wasn't a real loss." After a pause she continued. "That doesn't change what I said."

"As you said, she was my mistress. I gave her everything I could and as you might imagine I was very generous with money, clothing and jewelry. We were about to embark on a luxury trip around the world. Yet she betrayed me with a young fellow."

"Now come on! Your situation was far from being a marriage. In this case one gives something and the other something else — perhaps not an even exchange but isn't that the nature of things? Why is the woman always impugned and never the man? Aren't the two equally guilty? Where is the betrayal? What's her crime, really? She fell in love with somebody else. It wasn't planned or underhanded."

"Ah! I guess you have information that I'm not privy to. Isn't that like cheating?"

Adelaide blushed and swallowed her pride. "Sorry, that's true. I'm here with my nephew, Roger, who took the place in my heart of my three lovely daughters who absconded first to college and then marriage. He's very dear to me and doesn't have a penny to his name but has a job with good prospects. He loves Eleanor, knows everything about her including her relationship with you and asked me to meet her. I think it's a good match despite the inauspicious aspects — despite her past."

"I think you're kidding yourself."

"We'll have to wait and see. But you shouldn't be so cruel. She was open with you. It didn't make it easier for you but she was hoping not to hurt you. The way I read it your pride is what was mostly hurt."

"Ah, it must be a blessing to know everything. Well, this is a good moment to part. It was nice to renew a friendship even if it was under such goofy circumstances!"

Adelaide felt terribly foolish and embarrassed, as he turned and left. She should have handled it better. Her tendency to get to the point without niceties had always been her weakness and had lost her many arguments. In some ways she was sorry she had intervened. Obviously, it had done no good. Despite the absurd scenario, she had found that Andrew was likeable and she had been alone for too long.

....

Adelaide in her sumptuous hotel room had in mind packing to get an early start in the morning, but was just too lazy to get going. She had been left with a bitter-sweet sensation from her stay. She was too old to identify with the young and feel that she had to fight their battles.

The telephone rang and she expected to hear Roger's voice, but instead it was Andrew's.

"Could you come down for a minute?"

Driven by curiosity and prudence she agreed to come down to the lounge. It was lucky she was still dressed or it would have taken much longer. Andrew was waiting when the elevator door opened, dressed in informal clothing — cotton slacks and a knitted shirt. She couldn't read his demeanor, although he suddenly smiled. He took her hand and led her to one of the comfortable sofas hidden in a corner of the lounge.

"I looked for Eleanor. I'm glad I found her alone. I gave her the new electronic card for our room (in a moment of indignation I'd had the hotel change the formula) and told her she could keep all my gifts and wished her and her young man good luck." With a loony smile he continued, "She even kissed me good-by! Are you happy now?"

She nodded, but he continued, "I want something from you now. Something like reparations."

"Reparations for what?"

"For making me forgo the pleasure of being the injured party."

"Tut, tut! Some reparation. What do you have in mind?"

"I told you that I was going around the world with Eleanor. I'll have to cancel the reservations unless you come with me to keep me company."

She laughed, "I can say emphatically no, but if you want to go to one place and one place only (perhaps Paris or London), I will accompany you for a few days, always understanding that you'll reserve two separate rooms."

It was his turn to laugh, "Yes, of course at our age ...."

"Speak for yourself. You're the one that needs young flesh. I'm still in pretty good shape."

"Seriously, Mitzie, I need the company. I can't stand being alone in search of a good time."

"Me neither."

And that's how it all got started.

MISS PRIMROSE

Miss Alice Primrose knew that at the school where she was principal she was called "Miss Prim" behind her back, meaning "prudish" and conservative in leanings and demeanor. She was lucky that it wasn't a vile nickname. For the principal of a girls' boarding school it was not a bad appellation or even a bad example to follow. But at the moment she was all but prim. She was dressed in skimpy but still modest clothing and reveled in the morning breeze and sun. Alone, she was enjoying her holiday on the Mediterranean for which she had saved for years. Below her the beach was punctuated by sunbathers and some large umbrellas. "Alone in a crowd" she remembered the quotation whose source she had forgotten.

Her past had been determined by the Depression still rampant in the year 1935. She'd had to support her parents and a younger brother and sister. Jobs had been scarce and Alice had had a steady one, first as school teacher and then as principal of a fancy private school. Along the way, she had abandoned the idea of romance. She neither had had the time for such things nor were the prospects good. In addition, she would have had to give up her job. Married ladies were generally not allowed to reach such professional heights. She remembered a girlfriend admitted to a prestigious medical school on the condition that she pledge not to marry. But now, while at the seaside she felt totally free with no obligations and no need to maintain an image. Furthermore, the little luxuries she allowed herself were for her unusual —.an occasional brandy, a second helping of a creamy dessert. She didn't dare try cigarettes, although now fashionable —. in her mind still the mark of a fast woman.

Her tranquility and self-satisfaction were suddenly interrupted by what she was seeing. From the height of the esplanade where she was sitting, she saw a man swimming in the sea, obviously exhausted as shown by his listless strokes, and still not very close to shore. Any minute he could be overcome and disappear into the waves. She alerted the hotel's personnel. After calming down as much as possible, her French proved adequate. A boat was commandeered and two men were able to pull out the swimmer and row him ashore. Her fright was abated as the man was helped to his feet. Despite her old-maid inclinations, she found his prominent musculature and youth attractive even though the man was limp and drooping.

It turned out that he was American and she was the natural person to interpret what he was saying. He spoke haltingly but he wasn't hard to understand. He had fallen off a yacht, the *Pelican*. The response from the ship had been too slow and when the swimmer saw the ship's image fading in the distance, he decided to try for shore.

The hotel allocated a room for him and search boats that had been alerted by the yacht's crew terminated their quest. The swimmer, Francis Bolton, favored the name Frank. A few hours later, after resting and changing to ill-fitting clothes, he reappeared in the dining room for dinner. He had insisted on eating. Still obviously tired, he had regained some of what must have been his normal composure. Two hotel employees kept him company. Several of the guests had surrounded his table, but once informed of the details of his adventure had quickly dispersed to their own tables. Miss Primrose was also fascinated and approached his table after Frank Bolton had finished eating.

"May I sit down?" she asked.

"Please do."

She had found the whole sequence of events, although fascinating, almost incomprehensible.

"How can somebody fall off a boat?"

Frank laughed. "Not easy, but I managed it."

"Your yacht?"

"That would be the day! No, it belongs to friends and I was a guest."

"Was it supposed to be a pleasure trip?"

Frank nodded.

The hotel employees excused themselves. They had already heard all they wanted to hear and their understanding of English was limited. Miss Primrose was surprised that she was not embarrassed or uncomfortable being left alone with him. Although she did have some good male friends, men were not frequently part of her world and she was well aware that her angular lines were not suited to attract the opposite sex. Frank was young enough to sometimes remind her of her brother and had the distinction of being a captive audience. Miss Primrose, however, didn't feel comfortable under the eyes of the dining room spectators.

"Let's drink our coffee outside," she suggested.

At first Frank was obviously uncomfortable. But, after exchanging a few words with Miss Primrose, some of the discomfort seemed to abate. Her profession was acknowledged and perhaps her calm homeliness translated into psychological comfort. She had no hidden agenda. Just curiosity and kindness. Having spoken with students for so many years might have taught her how to approach a person who she felt was in trouble.

"Actually it's a long story, Please don't feel sorry for me," he said.

"I'm here listen if you wish to talk, but you don't have to say anything."

It was like a dam breaking. "I didn't really fall off the ship. I was pushed. No, I don't mean pushed off the ship on purpose. Just an expression of indignation. First a slap and then a push. What happened was well deserved. I'm not a nice man." After a few seconds he continued, "Actually, if you want to know the truth I'm a total prick. Susan Treadwell pushed me. Her father owns the yacht. She probably misjudged her strength and didn't expect me to fall into the sea." After another pause, "I had been bedding her for two weeks. My first victim. Despite her age Susan is very innocent. There was no problem getting her into bed. I even got her to agree to live with me in the future. I'm sure she would have agreed to marry me had I asked. That was my financial future. The Treadwells are very wealthy and she is their only child. She thought she was in love with me. Stupidly, what I was doing didn't feel right so I told her frankly what had happened. I had just been playing with her. I liked the luxuries. She slapped me and then pushed me."

Of course, none of that explained why he was telling Alice in the first place. Feelings of guilt? Or perhaps, was he really in love with Susan Treadwell? Alice had heard that men can be very confused about their actual feelings for a woman.

Once the ice was broken other confidences surfaced. He was from a large family and hadn't gotten much attention most of his life. For some reason his performance in school had shined. A scholarship allowed him to complete college at Columbia, despite strained circumstances and living at home. Along with the university experience he had learned to enjoy mixing with the rich and admire their easy life. His behavior with Susan might have been a continuation of that pattern.

For her part Alice contributed accounts of her early struggles and her present world. In fact, she thought, there wasn't much worth telling.

The night had descended without their noticing it, their coffee cups long forgotten, when she had a perception of the moment that she normally would have ignored. "You know, I have little to regret. Except for one unsatisfied curiosity. I've never had sex and it's something that remains a mystery to me."

"Oh! That should be easy enough to fix!"

"For the principal of a fancy girls school under the scrutiny of parents, administrators and students? They expect perfection — an old maid behaving like Caesar's wife!"

"You're on your own now. After all this is France!"

"I wouldn't mind going to my room — you and I taking care of that right now!"

As she was laughing, she didn't know whether she had meant it as a jest or not.

"Oh, please. Not that!"

"It would be just for this once. No obligations or regrets. Am I that unattractive?"

"No, but you could be my mother."

"True enough, but I'm not. Let's try!"

It was the sort of thing that never would have happened but for the strange mood they both were in.

Alice was reluctant to undress in front of him. They compromised by having her undress under the bed sheets. She found his weight on her and his fumbling not unpleasant. Then a stab of discomfort. After that she participated fully and understood well why humans made such a fuss about such things. It was like being at a party, all inhibitions gone after drinking too much.

They kept their commitment, that it was just for that one time. He had been right. Continuing together just wouldn't have worked.

The following afternoon, Alice had the satisfaction of seeing a young woman, who she guessed was Susan, entering the hotel lobby. She gave a surprised exclamation on seeing Frank. With tears coursing her cheeks, she ran to him. His arms enveloped her and they held to each other for a long time.

Alice was pleased that story had a happy ending. In her own case, after the two weeks of her planned vacation, she had to go back to her life of routine and more routine. Not exactly unpleasant but devoid of fire or surprises, although leading girls to a meaningful womanhood was not exactly dull. Trying to make them use their minds and striving toward independence did not lack challenges.

The next chapter in Alice's life didn't follow the usual pattern. The chairman of the school's board had insisted that she attend a late afternoon lecture at the university presented by a Dr. Douglass Clement. The talk was entitled "Coeducation and Single Sex Schools: A Comparison." Alice was sure the presentation would only emphasize some male-centered point of view that was completely without validity. Because it was scheduled for late afternoon when most of her duties were over, she was unable to evoke an excuse

She had some trouble finding the lecture room. She wasn't familiar with the campus and the signs were few. As she entered the lecture room she noted that a sign touted Clement as a professor at Norwall University, another distinguished institution. The speaker was already at the podium being introduced by a professorial-looking host. Apparently, Clement had an international reputation. The accolades piled on the guest were delivered with great pomposity. They seemed to confirm Alice's view that she should have stayed home. Clement himself was a short, well-dressed unpretentious man who seemed embarrassed by the introduction. Soft-spoken he made no effort toward drama. The material was interesting by itself. He proceeded with a good deal of data. He compared different countries, different socioeconomic statuses and histories of the families. Some of the time was dedicated to the shortcomings of such data. By necessity some of the information was anecdotal. Although he did conclude that the two kinds of programs had different results, he didn't reach firm conclusions. There were arguments supporting either form. Some students flowered under one and some under the other. It probably was a question of matching the student with the school. Nothing revolutionary there, Alice thought.

After the customary applause, the man who had introduced the speaker reappeared on the podium. Professor Clement, he said, would be happy to answer questions. The questions seemed to be only vaguely related to the talk. Some were about his most recent book on the history of public education. A student was intrigued by a description of obligatory education until the age of sixteen in some of the Italian Ghetto Jewish communities of the eighteenth century. The education provided by as many as three teachers was entirely free and paid by the community. Clement answered each question quickly in short sentences until the discussion was called to a halt.

The professor who had introduced Clement, Alice still hadn't caught his name, thanked him profusely. As the two left the podium, a group had formed around them flashing some individual questions. Alice tried to congratulate the speaker but didn't succeed. The group quickly dispersed before she'd had a chance to say anything. The official host shook hands with Professor Clement. As the three of them walked toward the exit, Alice heard him ascertaining that Clement had come with his own transportation. Then Clement and Alice were left alone. Alice couldn't contain herself. "Is that the University's hospitality? They don't even offer you dinner?"

Clement chuckled much amused by her spontaneous indignation. "Well, an official committee took me to lunch."

She felt personally offended. A man had made a magnificent presentation and his hosts didn't see their obvious obligation of taking care him.

Alice couldn't let the matter rest. "I'm Alice Primrose. Why don't I take you to dinner? It's the least I can do. I found your presentation enlightening and entertaining without the usual academic trappings, frequently referred to as bullshit, if you'll forgive my frankness."

Clement chuckled again. "Is that frankness?" And then after a pause, "Are you with the University?"

Alice felt herself relaxing. "No, I'm with a fancy girls school if you really want to know."

"I'll have to accept your invitation, but on the condition that we'll go Dutch."

The dinner was pleasant. Clement, who she now called Douglass or even Doug when one of his comments made her laugh, had a good deal of knowledge on a smattering of topics all accompanied by amusing anecdotes. He listened carefully when she expounded her opinions and never tried to impose his notions. He was just good company.

When it was time to part Alice asked, "Can we do this again?"

Doug was enthusiastic. "I'd love to, and for now let me drive you home."

After that they met every weekend and their friendship firmed.

Alice didn't know what gave her the courage to speak out. "Would you consider spending a night with me?"

Doug seemed confused for a moment, but then responded without subterfuge or vacillation. "My dear Alice! I have to confess that you're the most exceptional woman I have met in a long time and I care for you. But you might be in for a disappointment. I haven't been with a woman since my dear wife, Martha, died a good ten years ago. You're taking a chance."

A chance she was willing to take. In his apartment, she took him into her arms, onto the bed and inside herself. She felt jubilation as she had never felt before and realized that for the first and probably last time in her life, she was in love. Until then she had been totally unprepared for the experience. What is worthwhile in life if not the few delightful occurrences?

ONE PLUS ONE

Bernard and Judy were brother and sister, or so they said. Bernard's mother, Alice Winston, a few years after a contentious divorce had married Judy's father, Mark Rynook, a widower. The new family unit lived in what had been Alice and Bernard's house. That made Bernie and Judy brother and sister, or so they said. At that time Bernie was fourteen and Judy twelve. Bernie had another sibling but he was in college and made only a rare appearance. His father was a workaholic and Bernie rarely spent time with him. Bernie was not comfortable with him and felt that he had mistreated his mother.

The two parents were readily accepted by the two children. Mr. Reynook was very warm and had a fine sense of humor in contrast to Bernie's own father who had always kept a distance from his boys. Alice Winston, now Rynook, was an affectionate mother; besides, she had always wanted a daughter and had been denied that joy. Judy's image of her own mother had receded with time and Judy appreciated the affection and dedication of a woman. The two parents always acted in unison, and if there were arguments, these were held in private.

Nevertheless, Judy wasn't happy. She thought her father, if he'd had to get married at all, should have married a childless woman or one with a child who wasn't as gross or unpleasant as Bernie. As an only child, the apple of her father's eye, Judy had been the belle of the ball even when her mother had been alive. Although a tomboy, her delicate prettiness, blonde hair and big brown eyes conferred on her the little princess role. With Bernie, she had just gained an unseemly, annoying sibling. Together to give her a feeling of uncertainty, were her loss not only a familiar world but also playmates of long standing. The new environment was not unpleasant, but it was in a part of town unfamiliar to her. She didn't keep in touch with the few casual girlfriends she'd had, so everything was very strange. For a long time it was, if not menacing, uncomfortable. She had her own bedroom, as she'd always had, but it wasn't the same as her old familiar one.

Bernie didn't care about their changed status — he didn't care whom he teased. However, there were many reasons to resent his new sister. She could outrun and out-swim every boy he knew. Having a sister like that wasn't a way to make friends with other boys. Very bright, she was difficult to argue with, and eventually started as an exercise in logic, a discussion would deteriorate into name calling at which she was also very good. Whenever angry with him, she would regal him her "basilisk look," that of the legendary reptile with deadly breath and gaze. Bernie could well understand why the boys who used to come unannounced in and out of his home stopped doing so. Furthermore, his popularity decreased even more when his mother insisted that he spend some time with Judy as well as walking her to school. She had to find her way around the new students and teachers.

Other grounds for disagreement also emerged from every day living. Why do girls stay in the bathroom forever? Bernie hated not only the wait but the smell of what passed for perfume, along with natural odors. And this happened almost every morning. He had tried to get up earlier but that never seemed to help.

Judy couldn't stand his frequent pronouncement of the f-word. Boys, she figured, couldn't help themselves — just part of their repellent personality. In contrast, of course, Bernie was always polite and charming when adults were present.

Judy was despairing in her bedroom, sobbing. She had made no new friends. Within her hearing, some of the girls in her class had made some very disparaging remarks about her.

But somehow, it turned out that it wasn't all dark for her. Bernie passing by her door heard her muted weeping and remembered he had said something nasty to her not long before. Although she had just responded with her basilisk look, the remark might have hurt her. Not in any mood for apologizing, he was nevertheless upset, well aware of the social problems she had to face in school. Knocking on her door brought the expected response.

"Go away!"

Despite her interdiction Bernie opened the door.

"When you're new it's always hard. Besides many of the girls are jealous. You're smart, excellent in sports and possibly pretty."

"Why don't you get lost, jerk? Possibly pretty, indeed!"

"Just smile and talk to them. If anybody gets nasty just laugh at what they say as if it were funny. I've found it works for me."

It was lucky he had stepped out and was closing the door or he would have been at the receiving end of the shoe Judy had hurled at him. What boys' nonsense! As mad as she was, the exchange encouraged her. At least he cared, although like most boys he didn't understand anything. An armistice was the best the two of them could hope for and it was mainly to sooth their parents.

Time went by and something subtle must have changed because one day in school, out of sight in a corner of the hallway, she heard Bernie's voice at its threatening best.

"If you talk about my sister that way you'll be missing some teeth soon."

Another voice responded, defiant but unexpectedly almost conciliatory. "Oh, yeah?"

She thought she recognized the voice of the hallway bully, twice Bernie's size. Amused, she noted why Bernie had won the round. The door of the vice-principal was ajar and then it had suddenly opened to reveal the bulky vice-principal, Mr. Elmoos, who seemed entirely oblivious to the exchange.

Judy thought nothing of the incident until days later. Bernie had actually taken her side! Her having witnessed the scene and the presence of Mr. Elmoos was never discussed by the two of them.

It took a snowstorm a year later to change entirely the tone of their relationship. They had been on a mountain excursion with some other students under the supervision of Mr. Morris. They were exploring the mountain on skis. This was done every year by the adventurous members of the school's Outing Club. Bernard, a novice on skis, had fallen and Mr. Morris thought the boy might have broken his leg. A heavy snowfall started — an unpleasant surprise — big, wet flakes. Mr. Morris took Judy aside. They didn't think Bernie would hear, the wind and the falling snow seemed to snatch the sounds away. "I'll call the rescue squad on my radio. But then we better leave. There is danger of an avalanche. I just got a warning on my hand radio."

"You mean leave without Bernie?"

"It can't be helped. What else can we do?"

Her eyes hardened, "I thought you were supposed to take care of us."

"I'm doing my best. What would you do?"

"I think you're a total fuckhead. Go, go, before you wet your pants. I'm staying."

"Don't be stupid. The rescue squad will be here soon. I can't endanger the whole group," he shouted and then left with the other students.

Judy calmed down and sat next to Bernie's prone body. "Here, hug me. We might be able to keep warm until they come for us." She had wrapped a blanket around them, part of the load they carried, in case they decided to stay at the refuge not far from the summit— a single room log cabin with an outhouse.

"Does it hurt a lot?" she asked. He nodded.

After a while she realized they couldn't possibly survive the cold by remaining where they were. The storm still raged around them. Could she drag Bernie to the refuge? Would he have enough strength to help her while she hauled him up the mountain? She felt they had no choice. She slid backwards on her skis once, but was able to control her ascent. Bernie's skis seemed to be an encumbrance and for a moment she considered ditching them. Throughout their unfortunate trek, he leaned on her and must have been in considerable pain. She was grateful for his silence. Had he moaned or complained, she wouldn't have had the determination to continue. She hoped his leg wouldn't be damaged more than it was.

With snow swirling around them, the visibility was poor, but eventually they did arrive at the refuge. The door opened readily after she pushed away the snow that had accumulated. It was not supposed to ever be locked. She helped Bernie stretch out on one of the cots. There were four and she chose the one the farthest from the door. She covered him with the blanket after shaking off most of the snow sticking to it. It was cold and she hoped she could fire the stove, the only possible heating available. With no electricity and Judy's unfamiliarity with kerosene lamps she was forced to work in the semidarkness. Fortunately, there was wood in the stove and with great difficulty she started a fire with kitchen matches. The newspapers and kindling she used might have been moist or perhaps she didn't have the proper knack. But the fire finally took and provided warmth and some phantasmagoric illumination.

She had a cell phone tucked away in her clothing but as she suspected it didn't function — not as powerful as Mr. Morris's instrument.

She examined what else was in the room. Some crackers were in a metal can and there were several water bottles. Eventually, she found a first aid kit on a shelf. She opened it with difficulty. Her fingers were still stiff from the cold even after she had warmed them up next to the stove. She found codeine and carefully read the instructions attached to the container. She helped Bernie swallow one pill followed by water from a tin cup. She hoped it would relieve at least some of his pain.

They spent the night sleeping next to each other. Judy had to get up to refresh the fire but it was fairly comfortable for most of the night. But then she woke up with an intense need to pee. Intuitively, she felt it would be a terrible mistake to step out in the middle of a storm to reach the outhouse. After some hesitation, she urinated away from the cots. What choice did she have? Later in the night Bernie woke up with the same need. She helped him on his feet and he leaned on her while she moved him close to the spot she had already used. Judy was worried that he would wet himself and be most uncomfortable. He was too woozy to object to her intervention. She held his penis until he was finished. There was no other way of solving the problem!

She remembered the joke she had heard where a little girl had said, "What a convenient thing to bring to a picnic!"

In the morning Bernie was more cheerful and apparently not in pain — only uncomfortable. If he resented her intimate help during the night he didn't mention it. His cheery voice brought her to attention as she was waking up. "Sis, do you know you snore?" Followed be her indignant, "I do not!" and his obligatory chuckle.

The snowstorm seemed to have abated but still no rescue. She presumed the rescuers would check the refuge. The crackers she had found, together with some freshly brewed tea, served as a meager snack for them both. In the meantime, her mind started working on how to get back. She could produce a makeshift sled with their two sets of skis and some rope she had found. It would help in conveying Bernie down the slope.

The sound of a helicopter rotor brought her suddenly out of her reverie. She ran out of the refuge, waving with both arms as much as she could. The new snow crunched under her feet. She had expected her legs to sink in the snow cover, but the snow must have mixed with rain and then frozen. She was able to run a good distance, but despaired as the helicopter seemed to go past her. But soon the sound of the rotor came back.

There was enough excitement about the episode to make the newspapers and the TV news. Poor Mr. Morris was excoriated, although Judy realized that he really didn't have any satisfactory choice. She even defended him. Fortunately the accounts died down quickly.

Bernie's leg healed nicely although the cast made for a significant distraction. Everybody in school insisted on writing something on it, some comments approached the indecent, others derided his skiing ability. The crutches that he learned to use proficiently didn't slow him down and they also provided him with a handy defensive and offensive weapon.

To their parents surprise Bernie and Judy no longer got into silly arguments. Except for the rare outburst, they always behaved with circumspection toward each other. They never discussed their misadventure on the mountain although it had changed the quality of their interactions. Bernie started helping Judy with her math problems and she checked his writings for grammar and spelling, which tended to the deficient. When he was finished with some complex mathematical explanation, he would say — bordering on jest and sarcasm — "One plus one is two!" The first few times his utterance gained him a frosty look. Eventually she found his teasing funny and chuckled. If he forgot to say it, possibly because he was in a hurry to go outside with his friends, she would say it for him — it became a cheerful coda to their sessions.

All was well until Judy began to develop into a woman. It had taken time, but to them it seemed to occur suddenly. It changed her interaction with boys. She even began go on dates with some of them. Bernie didn't know what to make of it. His feelings contained a combination of regret and jealousy. He felt their relationship was taking second place to her popularity. He was also concerned about her. Some of the boys she attracted weren't what he would consider reliable and he became aware of a girl's vulnerability.

The situation came to a head when in high school she started dating Buster Beacon. Bernie was apprehensive. It wasn't just the jokes he had heard in school about Buster's name and its possible sexual connotation. He thought that Buster, handsome football star and all, was a bit of a bastard. He had a reputation of dating girls only when he wanted something from them, such as coaching for exams or sex. Then when he didn't need them anymore he'd drop them.

Eventually the inevitable happened. Bernie had been in bed for a while. Half asleep he had heard Judy's movements in her bedroom across the hallway from his —then the subdued but discernible sounds of sobbing. He knocked on her door and went in without waiting for an answer.

Even with only the hallway's light, the signs of a beating were clear on her face and her clothing was in disarray.

"What happened?"

Between sobs she told him. "I wanted to ... make love ... he wanted to fuck."

"I'll beat the shit out of him!" As if he would have had a chance!

"Don't bother. It wasn't exactly rape. He's just a brute!" Then more firmly, "Just hold me. I have to feel like a human being again."

And that's what he did until her anxiety seemed to subside. When he was back in his room stretched on the bed, she came in and crawled in next to him. "Please kiss me," she said. After he did, "Kiss me as if you meant it."

He was lost in the kisses and felt sensations that were entirely new to him. She murmured, "Do you have a condom?"

It so happened that he had one in his wallet put there to gain him bragging rights with the boys in school. That's how they had gotten started. It marked one of the happiest periods of his life. Of course, it had to end.

He didn't know how their parents had found out. The two youngsters had to face the two serious adults. Their father seemed to have the floor although both parents looked in earnest.

"You're too young for this sort of thing. Particularly Judy. I want you to stop. First, you have to promise not to do it again. Bernie will go to a boarding school of my choice to simplify matters. He can come home for vacations and the like. But you have to promise to desist at least until Judy is eighteen. After that it's your problem. If you don't agree, since you're both minors, we'll separate you so you never meet again while you are under our supervision."

Their mother intervened. "It's just a terrible idea. It isn't just the danger of pregnancy, but you're making an emotional commitment before you know the world around you, or even the possible alternatives. Promise me that you'll accept our proposal."

What else could they possibly do? After that their intimacy was entirely gone.

******

Back from college for a short visit, Bernie noted that something was wrong the moment he entered the house. Mark Rynook was in the living room sitting in the gloom. His hello was dejected. Bernie had a worrisome premonition.

"Where is Mom?"

"I don't know. She left last night and I haven't heard from her. I hope she's alright."

Bernie didn't need an explanation, he had gone through the divorce of his mother and father. The difference was that he loved both Mark and his mom. His biological father had been abusive and unkind.

"That doesn't sound like her! Did you try to find her?"

"Yes, she at the Floriton Hotel."

"Did you try to talk to her?"

"She may not want to talk to me. She's the one who left."

It occurred to Bernie that the two of them were in a situation that could easily lead to misunderstandings. Mark had lost his mate suddenly and painfully. Bernie had witnessed how Alice had been abused by her previous husband. Yet he was sure the couple was well matched and any problem could only be temporary.

While he was considering what to do, the door bell rang. Reluctantly, Bernie went to the door. Judy was standing there with a boyfriend by her side.

"Yes, you guessed it. I forgot my keys again."

"This is not the time for socializing. Mom is gone." His expression must have shown his concern. "Ask your friend in and I'll go to talk to her if I can find her."

"I'm coming with you. Harold, please come inside. I'll introduce you to Dad."

"Look! I'll come back later. No problem. I know how to entertain myself."

Judy insisted on talking to her father and gave him a hug. He brightened visibly

"I'm sure it will all be straightened out!" she said.

Although registered at the Floriton Hotel, Alice wasn't there. They both sat down in the lounge while Bernie tried to sort out his thoughts. He remembered that in the past when his mother had a crisis, often a humiliation or an unpleasant encounter with her first husband, she would sit for hours on end next to the Hudson. Bernie knew the spot she favored — having found her there before. For some reason her solitude offered her solace — being close to nature — the trees and perhaps the silence.

The two youngsters hastened there hoping to find her. Judy ran to her and hugged her with tears in her eyes.

"Mom, please come back. We all love you ... We need you." It was an appeal that came from the heart. Alice was moved and so was Bernie, who hadn't suspected the depth of Judy's feelings.

When they got back to the house, Alice was hesitant, unsure of what kind of reception she would receive. But her husband got up and opened his arms. She said, "Please forgive me." Mark murmured something they couldn't hear. While the two hugged, Judy and Bernie decided to give them some privacy and went to Judy's bedroom. Judy was still moved, with tears in her eyes. The two of them hugged. Clearly there was still a strong link between them. Bernie had come to realize that for him their relationship had been more than a passing fancy. But they had been separated for too long. He had lost her as a lover, with Harold waiting for her in the wings.

******

Bernie hardly understood what had happened between himself and Judy during the years of their forced separation and when they interacted again. They had seen each other repeatedly but had held back and spoke to each other only in a formal way. It was an awkward situation for the both of them.

Eventually, a few years later, Judy had asked him to come to her college graduation. "It wouldn't be such a festive occasion without you," she had intoned on the telephone. He felt flattered and yet felt reluctant to go. Thinking about her still set his heart aflutter but also brought him regret and sadness. When he finally found her room in the dormitory, he had duly hugged and congratulated her. At the ceremony their proud parents were also there, sitting among the ebullient crowd with Bernie. After the usual boring speeches, a multitude of students stepped up to the podium one at a time when their name was called to receive their sheepskin. Judy was very dignified. He almost didn't recognize her until she regaled the college president with her brilliant smile. Defying tradition, it seemed to him that instead of the customary "thank you" or the such, she had said, "About time!" It certainly fit her personality. He couldn't be sure he had deciphered her words, his ability to read lips was very limited. Perhaps the words had formed in his own mind to match her perky personality.

At the celebration party, he found himself separated from her and in a jolly group, discussing silly things that hardly mattered. At one point he was asked point blank by a cute little brunette, "Do you agree with that?"

He realized that he hadn't been listening. It must have been reflected on his face because some kind soul repeated the question.

"Does one's first love fade right away?"

The answer came to him automatically as if it had been waiting poised on his lips. "You shouldn't ask me. I can't possibly be typical. I'm still in love with my first girlfriend."

Judy was not far away. When he realized that she might have heard him, he blushed. He wasn't even sure that what he had said was entirely true. Fortunately, his audience was likely to take it as a boast — the kind made at parties to attract interest. After a pause and some incredulous exclamations, the chatter turned to some other topic.

Judy had indeed heard him. The thought that he actually meant it was quickly dismissed, but after the party his words began to trouble her. What if it were true? They had been so young then! And later he hadn't seemed concerned about her life and dates. But what if it were true? What did she actually feel about him? She loved him, obviously, but was it the kind of love that binds a woman to a man? These thoughts came to torment her.

But it was not the end of the incident. Back in his room at the hotel a knock on the door summoned him. And there on the threshold was Judy. More attractive than ever.

"Did you mean what you said?"

There was no room for doubt about what she meant and something sang in his heart. "Of course."

"I love you too. That must be why I could never become interested in the boys I dated. I have been just too stupid to realize it."

And suddenly they were in each other's arms, kissing passionately as they had so many years before.

"Are you going to spend the night?" he asked.

"Why do you think I came? If you still find me acceptable, of course."

But she wasn't finished. "I think we should get married as soon as possible. That would do away with that brother-sister horseshit!"

He murmured something that sounded to her like, "One plus one is two." But it might have been her imagination, as she was overwhelmed by passion.

ANABELLE

Anabelle Elmay, who preferred to be called Anne, was confused. At sixteen, she was two years away from coming out so she was neither fish nor fowl — still a child and yet almost a woman. Not that coming out would make any difference. It seemed to Anne her elder sister, Jane, was just as bored after coming out as she had been before taking that step. Besides, the world was a puzzling place. The rules, the accepted facts, seemed to change, all driven by forces she couldn't even envision. She had been told that Saratoga in the year 1906 was no longer the place to go. Somehow, taking the waters, watching the races and gambling had lost its allure. This season they had favored the Grand Union Hotel, in Saratoga as in past years, but that was to change. Next summer they'd go to Newport.

Mother kept giving her silly instructions. Anne wasn't supposed to read newspapers which were simply too vulgar. Many topics of discussion were off limits as not being suitable for a young girl. Anne was lucky that Jane was the oldest of the two and the prettiest, because the admonitions directed to Anne were more casual. "Don't talk to this girl" (there was a rumor that Susan's mother had been divorced), favor this other girl (less competition, not as pretty as other girls). Of course half of the fun was to discreetly ignore those interdictions. "Dress is most important. Unfortunately, these days you can't tell a good woman of proper status from an actress." Anne supposed that the actress classification included women of ill repute. Anne wasn't sure what that meant but had derived a vague idea from casual eavesdropping on the chatter of matrons or talk between men of stature as they smoked their cigars discussing the races, horses or poker. God! She hated the cigar stink.

The veranda in the afternoon usually was awash with ladies and young women ready to play games or flirt gently with some beau, but it was entirely empty early in the morning. She had gone there before breakfast to enjoy the solitude and the Adirondacks's morning coolness. The daytime temperature had been in the nineties and during the night the heat had lingered in the rooms.

As she emerged onto the veranda, she suddenly realized that she wasn't alone. A young man was sitting in a rocking chair. He was dressed in a shirt and dark pants of questionable origin. No dress shirt, tie, vest or coat. Clean shaven, he wasn't bad looking and his brown hair was combed. He must have been close to thirty or thereabout — what she considered an old man. She was about to withdraw when his voice reached her.

"Good morning, young lady." The voice was refined with a trace of an accent she couldn't place.

She didn't know why she felt the need to answer. Perhaps she suspected a patronizing tone in his voice. "I'm not a lady, just as you are not a gentleman."

"Not a gentleman!"

"No gentleman dresses like a working man or speaks to a young woman without being properly introduced." She knew immediately that she must have sounded like a prig and couldn't mistake the amusement that showed mostly in his twinkling eyes.

"Ah! So after all, the clothes make the man!"

She recognized the sentiment as one of Mark Twain's drolleries that seemed to disguise deep philosophical quips. She could feel her lips trying to suppress a smile.

He continued, "Well, at least I can introduce myself. I'm Archibald Longbow, usually known as Archie. Horrible name isn't it? It wasn't for me to choose!" And then after a short pause, "You don't have to introduce yourself. You're Anabelle Elmay. Please sit down so that we can have a decent conversation."

Still standing, Anne had had no intention of introducing herself to a total stranger, but the surprise that he knew her name must have shown on her face.

"If you want to move about incognito, you must try to be less conspicuous!"

"Conspicuous?"

"You're rather pretty and besides I witnessed the episode with the maid, Mary. I was in the hallway at the time."

Anne felt herself blush. It had been drummed into her that she was rather plain and not at all in the same class as her sister. The incident Archie referred to was very embarrassing and her mother had berated her about it. Mary was one of the hotel's Irish maids who had been taking care of the rooms on their floor. Red-faced, sweating profusely and obviously forcing herself to proceed, she seemed overcome by the heat and shouldn't have been working. Anne had fussed about it. The manager made the mistake of underestimating her and had insisted that Mary should continue working.

"If she isn't immediately relieved, I will mention to everybody I see the possibility of typhoid." With those remarks Anne had succeeded in making her point, upsetting not only the manager, but her own mother and Mary herself. However, Mary was allowed to leave. Having tested Anne's mettle and getting no support from Anne's mother, who wouldn't involve herself in such a mundane matter, the manager didn't take any reprisals on Mary who returned cheerfully to work two days later.

"Young lady, you're quite a card ain't you," Mary had said with a roguish smile.

Anne had quickly recovered from Archie Longbow's impertinence and had a reply ready. "Don't try to flirt with me. I'm too young and besides I know I'm not pretty."

"You never looked in the mirror when your eyes are amused or ablaze with anger. Besides you look pretty to me. And beauty can be inside as well. You see, I know more about you than you realize. I'm Susan's brother. You're the only one who befriended her."

That she had done, but had been horrified by Susan's scurrilous gossip and cryptic references to mysterious goings on, supposedly between young women and some young men. What had the little wretch said about her? The thought troubled her yet she couldn't deny their friendship.

"She's my friend," she confirmed.

Anne decided it was time to withdraw. He interpreted her movements. "Maybe we can meet here tomorrow at the same time. You'll honor me by sitting down and talking to me some more."

"Not very likely."

He found her freshness and bluntness enticing. The young women he had known, including his own ex-girlfriend, had the dullness of dishwater. Her unawareness of her own attractiveness was also alluring. Too bad that Anne was too young for him — he felt he could grow to like her immensely.

During the whole day that followed, Anne gave some thought to that strange young man and each time she decided she certainly wouldn't show up again. Games such as checkers or card games didn't entertain her for long and she was deadly tired of the conversations with the other girls —how to sneak away to enjoy the illicit cigarette smokes that Anne despised — what young man had shown interest in them and which one was cutest — veiled references to flirting or even going beyond that. She wondered exactly what they meant. Her innocence which she would deny vehemently, made her navigation among the older girls rather difficult.

Luckily, she had her own room so that she didn't have to explain anything she did to anybody. Early the next morning, she washed and then dressed in a hurry and proceeded to the veranda, despite her firm decision, certain that she was making a fool of herself. First of all "he" certainly wouldn't be there. But if he were, how would she explain meeting him again despite her earlier declaration?

Indeed Archie was there. After greeting her warmly, he took her by the hand and led her to one of the chairs and sat next to her.

"I'm glad you could make it," he said.

First feeling vulnerable and slightly scared, she was soon at ease. Perhaps it was his friendliness and the way he talked to her as if he recognized her as an equal. Anne would have never imagined she could be so relaxed with a stranger and certainly not a young man. Some time before, she had come to the conclusion that men were unpredictable creatures who should best be avoided. But she found the two of them were soon chatting without any tension.

"I got tired of all the nonsense that comes out of girls my age. I needed a respite."

"Is their chatter any different than what you hear from grown ladies?"

"That's precisely the problem. They are mostly the same. They can only speak about inane matters."

"What should they talk about?"

"A slew of matters. I would be more interested in a discussion of the Seneca Falls Declaration. Surely that's a meatier matter that deserves deliberation."

"What do you know about it?"

"It contains resolutions arguing that women have a natural right to equality in all respects including the right to vote."

"How did you get to know about these things?"

"On the sly. I read newspapers very carefully. All the arguments against these ideas seemed to me to attack what was obviously right. And that's how I heard about them."

"You believe in the right of women to vote?"

"Of course! Most newspapers, men and even some women keep saying that women don't know enough to vote intelligently. Well, I don't see much intelligence in men's real interests but they certainly have the vote. What I hear from them is often very dumb, even when some of them are important! Anyway, women will get the right to vote soon. That's the way I see it."

"I have to agree with you."

The following morning they spoke about something entirely different.

"There are many topics respectable girls aren't supposed to talk about. When I mentioned "evolution" there was practically an explosion. 'That's not a proper topic for a young girl!' Well, that got me interested. I asked your sister who is on a looser leash to get me from the library a book written by Darwin

I'd heard criticized. I'm surprised that it wasn't banned from the library. She certainly got some raised eyebrows and I think she enjoyed that!"

"And you read it?"

"I most certainly did. It makes sense. Why wouldn't species evolve? Look what happened to dogs through the ages. They all descend from wolves and by selection, breeders created various breeds. Tiny dogs, huge dogs —breed of dogs of all colors. And in the same way, why can't nature do the selection the way Darwin says?"

"Why not, indeed. And you believe we are descended from apes?"

"I'm not sure Darwin said that, but why not? Some of the men and women I have observed behave as if they were apes."

Archie was laughing and she found herself laughing with him. Luckily there was nobody watching her. Her responses weren't very lady-like although she found them very satisfying. She hadn't been able to express her thoughts for too long. Until then, they had remained bottled up inside her. Her acquaintances and friends would have been shocked to hear them.

Anne wanted to draw out Archie's opinions. Many of the discussions she had heard involved disputations about President Roosevelt. "What do you think about Teddy Roosevelt?" she asked. Archie seemed ready to talk on that topic.

"A fine man. He was trying to make our economy work for everybody. And he showed that he's not a hypocrite like everybody else. I particularly admire his inviting Booker T. Washington, a Negro and a very distinguished scientist and educator, to the White House. But that must have been before you were able to read newspapers. There was quite a fuss about it."

Another morning Anne went on the offensive. She didn't quite know why but she felt at home with Archie and he could satisfy her curiosity about a number of worldly matters. "Now you know everything about me. The little there is to know. Tell me about yourself."

"Ah! I just listened to you telling me what you think and very interesting it was. But I didn't ask about you, although I'm the soul of discretion."

"Poppycock! Let me ask a few questions. Susan says you're not married. You play the role of a man of the world very well. But are you?"

"A man of the world? Obviously not. But I have been around some."

"Did you ever have a mistress?"

Archie almost choked with laughter. "Is that what a man of the world does?"

"That's what I have heard. Don' t avoid the question!"

"I guess then that I'm not a man of the world. Never, never had a mistress. Perhaps I should get started now. I don't want to be taken for a primitive. I had a girlfriend once, almost a fiancée, but that didn't pan out. Something to do with my scarcity of cash and her very disapproving parents!"

"So sad!"

"Not at all! It saved us both from making a terrible mistake!" And then he continued, "What are you planning to do with yourself?"

"That's a good question. My parents expect me to get married —after my sister of course. Then a husband supposedly will keep me busy, whatever that means."

"You're very bright and inquisitive. Have you ever thought of going to college? There are some excellent women's colleges."

"Mother and Father think it would be a waste of time. I certainly don't approve of their plans for me but I don't seem to be able to avoid them."

"Marry me and all your troubles will be over!"

"Sure, sure! Stop making fun of me. "

"I'm not making fun of you! Quite the contrary. What I said is part rhetoric and part sentiment."

"What does that mean?"

"It means that either you are too young for me or I'm too old for you!"

Anne couldn't stop her blushing. "You're funning again!"

"Why do you say that? I voiced the truth and nothing but the truth. But what I say is sometimes difficult to decipher — sometimes difficult for me too!"

Anne knew all along that their exchanges had to come to an end. Although they had met only for a few mornings, sooner or later Archie would get tired of her. All she had to offer was novelty and obviously that would wear out. Also, if somebody came to suspect she was meeting a young man secretly, her early morning jaunts would definitely come to an end. The end came one morning when Archie said, "I have to leave Saratoga now to stop being a freeloader. I'm very happy to have met you. I had come to see Susan. I'm very fond of my little sister. But you certainly enlightened my mornings!"

Actually, Susan was Archie's half-sister, born after their mother had remarried following a contentious divorce. She had been just a toddler when they first met. Archie had been taken by her smile and cuteness, picking her up and playing with her. She had been unable to hide her delight at meeting an attentive older brother. For the first time in his life he had encountered unlimited love and loyalty. It marked their relationship forever. His boarding-school environment and distracted parents had lacked warmth. Later, he had spent much of his time with his mother's older brother Herbert Massy and his wife Maryanne. A childless couple, they had reveled in his growing up. Still, Archie kept in touch with Susan through all her growing years, even while he attended Columbia College.

"What are you going to do now?"

"Supposedly I'll try to earn a living."

"How?"

"I have no idea. In the past I went West, ranching. I didn't make much money but I also learned a lot."

He remembered his cowboy days fondly. The Flying Ace was a ranch belonging to acquaintances of his Uncle Herbert, and Archie had been able to insert himself in the crew that worked there. It was a way of withdrawing from a burdensome world and a chance to enjoy a real adventure. He never would have suspected that being exhausted could be satisfying or that cattle drives, branding and other ranch tasks could be so demanding. In a way, it had made him grow up. Until then, his privileged and sheltered background had precluded interacting with the real world.

"You were a cowboy?" Anne thought that she was revealing too much naivete with her youthful enthusiasm.

"Very hard work. I acquired muscles and a suntan, but little money. And now I'll give gold mining a try. One of these days I'll give Wall Street a chance —hopefully making money by sitting on my behind."

She was amused — after all there is no other way of sitting, she couldn't resist teasing, "Gold mining! It seems a little boy's dream."

"I might not be a gentleman but I certainly can dream."

"And then you'll go from working man to parasite!"

He chuckled, "I hope so!"

They shook hands on parting. She must have noticed how rough his callused hands were, he thought. Yes, after all he wasn't a gentleman. Then they went their own ways and missed each other as soon as they realized they had really parted for good. Archie mused, "How could such a young girl have such an impact?"

******

After Archie's return from his mining adventure where he had spent the time in virtual isolation, New York City although familiar, also seemed very strange. At times he felt as if he were in a totally alien world — the chatter of crowds, the clanging of trolley-cars, the occasional roaring of the new automobiles or the raucous and rude sound of their horns.

Archie stayed with friends — young men as unattached as he was. Old habits and camaraderie can last a long time. His Mexican adventure where two friends from college had abandoned him should have argued against such a choice of companions. They were prone to frolicking and heavy drinking. Archie had other thoughts. At one time, he must have been as feckless as they were. His money wouldn't last forever, particularly after the dunking he had suffered in Mexico. He first examined what he considered the lay of the land. On Wall Street he visited his father's cousin Lawrence Coryell. A middle-aged man, well connected and experienced in financial matters. He might be able to direct him or even find him a job.

He had no trouble being admitted to his eminence. Lawrence Coryell was a dignified man. His gray hair and cheerless countenance conspired in making him appear important and older than he actually was. Lawrence didn't take his request kindly. His lips twisted to express his indignation. "After what happened with your gold mine venture, you expect me to help?"

At the time, Archie had been more intent on survival after his friends had abandoned him in the middle of the mountains without warning. Larry's share in the loss had been small. But men involved with money were never very forgiving.

Archie left without making a fuss or trying to explain what had happened. As he was walking along, he noticed four bootblacks setup under an awning in front of a tobacco shop — black men of various ages. He remembered as a child that with the exception of the older man, they'd behaved with customers as if they were part of a vaudeville act. Archie understood that their hard life had forced them into an undignified pretense. The older man was an unusually courtly gray-haired old Negro. Many a time, Archie had been with his uncle who had his shoes shined in a routine that had become almost a ceremony. Years before, his uncle had spent time and exchanged ideas, opinions and sometimes jokes with Mr. Fertel. Although many years had gone by, Archie was surprised to see how little the older bootblack had changed. Archie wondered whether the old man would recognize him.

"Good day Mr. Fertel."

The puzzled old man wrinkled his forehead and smiled. Obviously he didn't recognize him but something was stirring in his memory.

"I'm Herbert Massy's nephew. Remember?"

Archie was regaled by a big smile. "Archie. Now I guess, Mr. Archie!"

"No, it's Archie just bigger and dumber."

Mr. Fertel was laughing. "It's been a long time but I'm still here. It hasn't been the same since your uncle died!"

"You can say that again. I miss him too."

Archie had always been amazed by how promptly Fertel would switch from what white customers considered Negro talk to the words of a cultured man.

"Please stop any time to have a chat and a free shine."

"A chat sounds good. You always have something interesting to talk about!"

"Now I'd probably bore you."

Their next meeting happened sooner than either one of them would have thought and boring it was not.

******

After the financial disasters of his ranch and mining adventures, Archie was left with very little and also he didn't want to think about the debts incurred during his efforts. The money was owed to friends and relatives. Although none of them would ask for a prompt payment, he felt responsible for what had happened. A job had become essential and he'd started looking for one. But he felt he might be able to invest some money on Wall Street. After all, the stock market had been the source of his uncle's fortune and also the natural playground of the Longbows before their undoing by some incautious investments.

A visit to the brokers Brownell and Lacy assured him a way to trade in the stock market. His dealings were with a Mr. Belltone, a middle-aged well dressed man in a gray suit, the uniform of a banker. He was thin lipped with a gray tonsure surrounding a bald head. He showed little animation and handed Archie papers to be signed without a smile or a comment. Archie wasn't surprised that everything had gone so smoothly. The name Longbow still elicited respect in some financial circles. Nevertheless, the formalities were time consuming and Archie had stayed longer than expected.

The day had been dark even at its beginnings. With the progress of the afternoon the outside had turned even darker. As he left the building, his eyes strayed to the awning where the bootblacks were based. It was late, although the street bustle wasn't entirely gone; a drizzle must have discouraged them. Only Fertel was still there, picking up his box, ready to leave. A figure appeared wielding a cane and hitting the old man mercilessly. Without being conscious of what he was doing, in a cold anger, Archie found himself next to the attacker, grabbing and wresting the cane from him. He proceeded to hit him and the man quickly ran off yelling obscenities, including some words Archie hadn't heard before.

Archie was surprised at his own sudden anger and actions. In his previous encounter with violence, he had been choked with fear and nothing else. In the midst of the Mexican revolution he had been abandoned by his college friends, George and John, without any warning. At that time, Archie had yet to learn the difference between loyalty on the football field and loyalty in dangerous real-life situations. For some time, they had discussed leaving to avoid being trapped in the fighting. Even if distant, they could hear shots and occasional volleys from where they stood. However, leaving would mean abandoning the miners without the pay. Considering the miners' level of poverty, Archie had found such an alternative unacceptable. But he'd never expected to find himself alone, facing a silent, menacing group of men intent on violence. It had seemed most likely that his life was at stake. Swallowing hard he'd found the strength to yell, "El más macho solamente," "Only the most macho". It must have surprised and perhaps interested the angry men because they paused. A tall, brutish looking man had stepped forward. With no experience at knife fighting, Archie knife in hand had found himself facing the equally armed man. The dark face showed no expression. Archie guessed that his opponent had been involved in knife fights many times before and was anticipating an easy victory. Aside from school altercations when he was a boy, Archie's experience had been only in gentlemanly fencing with sword, saber or foil. Agility had been one of his talents.

Stifling his fear, he had gathered his wits. Assuming a defensive position, he stood with knife on the ready. His opponent suddenly struck. Estimating the man's speed and with his instincts taking over, Archie had dropped his knife and quickly swung his body to one side. As the attacking knife had grazed him, his right hand grabbed his opponent's arm and his raised knee delivered a lucky whack where it hurts most.

The "macho" man was left writhing in pain on the ground. Judging by the obvious amusement of the spectators, he must have been an unpopular bully. The unexpected laughter had given Archie time to explain in his clumsy Spanish that he'd do his best to meet the payroll. He wasn't sure whether he could keep his promise or why they had believed him. Much was disrupted in the closest town. Nevertheless, hurried telegraphic communications between the States and the local bank had allowed him to recover enough money to appease the miners.

But this time when an old man was being beaten everything was different, and he responded in a cold, primitive anger. The old man couldn't be abandoned. Fertel murmured that he wanted to be taken home. Waving money, Archie was able to stop a hansom cab and help Fertel into it. The hansom driver objected with his face gnarled in anger. Black men were not encouraged as fares. He first refused to go to the address the injured man had supplied. In anger, Archie practically lifted the man out of the cab.

"Okay! Okay!" the unfortunate man yelled.

Fertel lived in a part of town where tenements prevailed. Men and women of color were sitting on stoops and a few were braving the drizzle.

Archie helped the old man down and handed a generous tip to the driver, who nevertheless kept grumbling. He was surprised by the house, a neat single-family unit with a well-tended garden in front. In the house the furniture was functional and reflected a fairly significant investment. Fertel was obviously not poor and bootblack work couldn't possibly be his only source of funds.

"Surprised, ain't you? A black skin and poverty don't always go together."

The appearance of an attractive young black woman interrupted their exchange. "My God what happened?" She looked at the old man with concern, but then her eyes strayed to Archie intently and with suspicion. Well dressed, she was unusually pretty and well proportioned. Her dark skin seemed to enhance her beauty.

"What occasionally happens. Somebody decides to beat me up and take my money. My friend Archie showed him what for." Holding onto the back of a chair he stopped and then after a long moment. "This is Monica my daughter, or rather my niece who might as well be my daughter."

"Shouldn't you see a doctor?"

"What for? Haven't you ever been in a scrape yourself?"

"I wasn't in my seventies."

It was Monica's turn to speak. "He's as stubborn as a mule. We'll have to wait until he keels over. Then he may agree to see a doctor."

The old man was talking again. "That will eventually happen but not yet. Besides getting to a doctor is not simple for a colored man. What I need is a hot bath."

"May I help you? You shouldn't do it alone."

"I think I'd rather keep it in the family. Monica can help me. But look, there is no reason for you to wait. You'll have enough trouble getting a cab and might have to be content with a trolley. You'll have to walk several blocks. We have a lot to talk about. But not now. Come here tomorrow at about this time."

Their conversation on the next day was a revelation. Fertel himself opened the door. Although he moved hesitantly, he appeared to have largely recovered. Monica seemed to have disappeared. Archie was surprised by his disappointment.

"What happened to Monica?"

Fertel replied with a smile, "I miss her too. She's on her yearly trek to Negro colleges to distribute some of my money." Then he continued. "We have a lot to discuss. You might have wondered how a black man could live so comfortably, The answer is simple. My work, as menial as it is, puts me in contact with much important information. Your uncle showed me what to do with it. In fact, he's the one who set up an account for me and I have been playing the market ever since." Archie's amazement must have shown on his face. Fertel chuckled quietly in response before continuing. "Then when he got sick I acted for him. I'm well to do. And so are you."

Archie, not quite recovered by his surprise, laughed uncertain as to where the conversation was leading them, "How is that?"

"He set up a fund in your name and with his instructions and my efforts it accumulated 200 grand. After he died I couldn't find you."

"I was out of the city most of the time."

******

The next few days were very confusing for Archie. His sudden wealth made him feel that restitution was due to the friends and relatives who had funded the mining venture. With a good deal of trepidation he approached them. Since they might have expected a successful investment, he added five percent to the amount of their contribution.

After some polite chatter most of the people who had contributed in the gold mine were delighted to recover their investment. As he might have expected, Lawrence the cousin who had shown some resentment before, was an exception. He was incensed that it had taken Archie so long to come up with the money. If Archie had expected thanks or at least relief from the man's anger he would have been disappointed.

"Why didn't you tell me earlier that you'd recovered the funds?"

"As you must know, it takes time to complete an operation."

Aunt Maryanne, now in her seventies was a dream. She was a gray-haired woman with a severe expression who could stare down any imprudent soul when necessary. She could also break into a radiant smile when one least expected. That's what happened the instant she had seen him come into the room. She put down her book and they hugged. Archie kissed her on the cheek. Reading had been her major occupation since she had reached a ripe old age. His explanation of why he was there didn't satisfy her and she berated him for not visiting her as soon as he had come back.

"Aunt Maryanne, I was too ashamed not to have returned your money and I wasn't in a position to act until now."

"Nonsense! I always considered the money a contribution to your wild side! Gold mine! For goodness sake, I had never heard anything more absurd! You should have come to see me sooner. As if I expected money! Don't hide behind such a flimsy excuse."

"I apologize. I apologize. As you always say, youth is thoughtless!"

"That's not enough, you haven't even told me why you're not married yet!"

"Well, it's an enterprise that requires two people!"

"It's not too hard to find a charming young lady. And you're not that ugly." After a short pause and a mischievous smile, "Actually you're not ugly at all. Some misguided people might even consider you handsome."

She got up and fussed in a chest of drawers. She turned holding something in her hand. She insisted on giving him an extravagant diamond ring. "It's been in the family for three generations. Your Grandma had it and gave it to me when she was dying. As you know I was never blessed with children. You're my only hope that it will be used appropriately! Make good use of it. It would make a marvelous engagement ring."

Amused by her persistence, Archie thanked her profusely. He took the ring, knowing there was no way he could dissuade her.

******

After having discovered his small fortune, Archie figured that he could well afford staying at a hotel. The continual bacchanal of his friends was starting to disturb him. Perhaps he had outgrown them. At one time he must have been as feckless as they were. The hotel provided him with the privacy and all the amenities he needed, along with freedom of movement he desired.

One day returning from a walk, he was surprised to find his two erstwhile associates, George and John, with fatuous smiles waiting for him in the lobby of the hotel. Archie still felt betrayed by the two and didn't feel like exchanging niceties.

It was George who took the initiative, "We hear that we made a neat profit with the gold mine. You should have contacted us. You are a bastard for trying to cut us out of our share."

Archie had trouble containing his anger. "I thought you had dissolved the partnership. You're lucky that duels have gone out of fashion or I would have killed you both by now."

The phony smiles were gone. "You'll be sorry to have cheated us."

"I would be happy if you take it to court. You would be exposed for what you are: two cowards with no principles. It shouldn't be hard to establish when you came back to mama while I was left to face the music."

"You'll be sorry!"

"So be it! I'll be sorry. You're breaking my heart!"

Archie never expected to see them again. But it didn't happen that way. A few days later, returning to the hotel he found them waiting for him at the corner. He barely had the time to defend himself. With his hands up he hit one of them. The other man intervened with a cudgel. Archie was able to avoid being hit full in the face, however, the stick painfully grazed his face and he found himself on his knees and in pain. Two women on the opposite side of the street prevented further damage by loosening the most penetrating, shrill howls he had ever heard. The two startled men must have decided the occasion called for caution and they quickly disappeared.

Archie was much surprised by the course of events. He never expected to be attacked. Furthermore, ladies were not supposed to take notice of street scuffles and certainly not become directly involved in them. The two women were next to him in an instant as he slowly got up. They ignored the crowd that had been attracted by the noise. One of the two women handed him a handkerchief which quickly was tinged with blood as Archie held it to the side of his face.

"There is a pharmacy on the next block."

"Thank you very much!" Having been saved by the two gentle women left him more amused than embarrassed and most of all grateful, although he found it very difficult to express his feelings.

"Do you know those men?"

"There are no worse enemies than ex-friends."

The two solicitous women accompanied him to the pharmacy. He noticed that they were well dressed. As he expected the pharmacy was able to provide only some iodine and a small bandage. The spontaneity and audacity of the women triggered something in his mind and he looked them over carefully. One, the youngest he had never met. His memory stirred on the sight of the other and recollections flooded his mind.

"Anne ... isn't it? Have you forgotten me, the man you're affianced to?"

Surprisingly she remembered him as well as the incident that was amusing him.

"Archie Longbow. I remember you, but aren't you exaggerating?"

His impish side was aroused. "Not at all. I proposed and as I seem to remember you said ,'Sure, sure.'"

The other woman was disturbed, "You know each other?"

"Intimately," he said.

"He's a big joker. I was a young kid when I met him."

The woman he didn't know took the initiative. "A joker, that's what we need for our party. They are getting to be very boring. By the way I'm Laura Permuttit," and she shook hands with him.

******

The party was at Laura's house, a decorous brownstone where a whole floor seemed to have been set aside for frolics. The scene revealed mostly the presence of people younger than Archie. As many voices blended with the clinking of glasses, Laura took him aside flirting with him outrageously. In a way he was relieved that she had sequestered him. He thought he would have felt very strange addressing Anne. He didn't know what he felt about her. The intimacy he'd thought they had shared might have been in his imagination. Besides, many years had gone by and she might be an entirely different person. He searched with his eyes and looked at her surreptitiously. Well dressed, dark hair, glowing complexion without makeup and a shapely figure. She also seemed to be very sure of herself. With the passage of years, her attractiveness had grown and couldn't be denied even by herself.

After he had retreated from Laura's company, an eager young man quickly replaced Archie. Anne who also had seemed to have been avoiding him, suddenly appeared in front of him.

Surprisingly she hadn't forgotten their past exchanges and spoke as if she was continuing a recent conversation. "Did you really go to Mexico to mine gold?"

"Yes indeed." Archie was embarrassed by his past foolishness.

"Well? Is that all you can say about it?"

"It was a disaster and we didn't make any money. Remember what you said? It was like a little boy's dream. Do you remember? Nevertheless it was an adventure. I found myself in the middle of the Mexican revolution without any cash to meet our payroll."

"I'm sorry to hear that. But you weren't alone."

"No. For a while I was with two partners until they left me in the middle of the mess. You've had the privilege of meeting both already. Or rather you were so rude as to frighten them away."

"You are not very particular in choosing your friends."

"Sometimes you have illusions about comrades you meet in college."

"What do you do now?"

"Not much. For a change I seem to be lucky in my Wall Street investments." Uncle Herbert and Fertel didn't have to be mentioned at the moment.

The impact of her presence on him was surprising. The vivacious young girl with the large brown eyes was now a beautiful woman. Somehow he didn't want to lose her presence. As if he had any calls on her!

"I do other things as well. Not everything I do is making money. I would like to show you my secret life."

"Ooh! You're being so mysterious!"

"Well, I didn't want to introduce contentious subjects in this august gathering."

"The gathering may be august but you know me better than that. I haven't changed that much."

Archie thought, "You're just much more attractive." Then he continued, "I'm involved in a settlement house. You know a house in poor neighborhoods where poor people may find some solace — English language classes, schooling and food for immigrants' children, after school activities, health services, etcetera. I'd like to show you what I do."

"Why did you get involved?"

"I wish I could tell you that I'm a hero, but actually, I got involved because it makes me happy."

"A new Archie. I knew Archie the adventurer who had the patience to talk and listen to a lonesome young girl and then proceeded to dig for gold, but Archie the saint is entirely new to me."

Archie found himself blushing. Undoubtedly he had overdone it! Yet he was met by her brilliant smile.

"We've talked enough about me. I can show you around my haunts if you find it interesting, but what has happened to you since we last talked?"

"Nothing very exciting. My parents were strenuously opposed to my attending college. I was able to fake signatures and to attend Barnard secretly for two years. Eventually all my ploys were discovered. After all there was no reason for a girl of my social class to attend college and it might well interfere with my catching a husband. Then I was exposed to various desirable men. The latest, a British lord complete with lisp and fruity accent. My parents are threatening to send me abroad if I don't behave the way they want."

Poor Anne! She certainly was in a tough spot.

******

After that, Anne was frequently in his thoughts, he wasn't sure why. She was attractive in every way and he admired her vibrant personality. But he couldn't count on their previous encounter — people change. He wished he could see more of her but couldn't figure out how to do it discreetly. He couldn't think of any socially acceptable excuse to contact her and wasn't sure whether she regarded him only as an amusing recollection from her past. Obviously, he was inexperienced in matters relating to women.

Archie's sister Susan had asked him to have tea at her house. You shouldn't have to invite your brother to tea when you want to talk to him, he thought. And that is what he said as he entered her house. Susan, the existential non-conformist, had made a very conventional marriage to Tom Allbain, a wealthy and pleasant young man.

"You know, you shouldn't have to invite your brother to tea when you want to talk to him."

"I'm not sure what is the appropriate socially accepted procedure, after all you're only my half-brother!"

"Half is better than nothing. Besides, you have no other brothers!"

Impulsively, she hugged him. "You're my best brother regardless of technicalities. Come meet Tom and my little barracuda."

As they entered the room, Tom, bounced up to shake his hand. With him was a little boy of about three. Calling him a barracuda seemed a little far-fetched.

"Come and meet your Uncle Archie, Willie."

Willie gave him a smile and shaking Archie's hand solemnly said, "How do you do?"

Surprised by the greeting, Archie was strangely moved by holding the little hand in his.

"Willie loves relatives, particularly if they appreciate his precocious charm," Susan explained smiling.

It didn't take long before the little barracuda was on his lap with a book asking, "Will you read to me please." A request that could hardly be refused.

Then Susan intervened, "Stop reading when my other guests arrive."

"Other guests?"

"You didn't think you were the only person receiving my magnificence?" And then, "You might remember one of the guests, Anabelle Elmay. She was with us in Saratoga. The only decent person there. Be kind to her. At least then she had a crush on you or at least blushed whenever anybody talked about you."

He had to promise Willie to read to him later.

Guests came in, married couples and some unaccompanied single women, Anne with them. One of them, Agatha something or other, attached herself to him and he had trouble disengaging himself. Eventually he was able to approach Anne who smiled at him, pleased.

"Ah! My favorite buccaneer. The one with a heart! You'll have to show me more of your good side!"

Archie took it to mean that she wished to accompany him when he visited settlement houses. Somehow their conversation proceeded naturally from there and they arranged to see each other. One meeting led to another and pretty soon they were on more familiar terms. Visiting the settlement houses was one of their activities. Anne was amazed and shocked at seeing poverty first hand. Despite her success in avoiding the prejudices of her class, she had never been exposed to anything so raw. Archie had made himself responsible for providing good food to one of the settlements, knowing full well that he was avoiding the more demanding tasks. Good naturedly Anne quickly joined him in that enterprise and they saw each other frequently.

At some point or other Susan thought she'd better have a heart to heart talk with Archie. She warned him to clear his reputation. A rumor was circulating that he had a mistress. In their eyes, to make the matters worse, she was rumored to be a woman of color. Archie was amused. Gossip could be even more vicious than he had ever imagined. Nevertheless, he thought that Anne and Monica should meet. They were the most important women in his life apart from Aunt Maryanne.

The two of them visited Monica after one of their calls on a settlement house. Archie had simply said, "I would like you to meet a friend of mine."

Monica greeted them with a big smile. "Ah! Anne. I'm so glad to meet you at last. Archie talks about you all the time. I was dying to meet you."

Anne felt herself blush. The ice was broken in one scoop. Monica quickly explained that soon she would go South to attend Walden University College. It was her dream to continue in Meharry Medical College and eventually become a physician. She hoped that being a woman would not be an insurmountable obstacle.

"Isn't it amazing," she quipped, "the obstacles to common sense our world erects around us? Color, gender and other brands of intolerance!"

Since these had been Anne's feelings even when she was a little girl, it brought them together as if they had been lifelong friends. Archie was pleased at their chatter that followed. Monica was probably the first woman of color Anne had met socially. Their ease with each other marked the unusual character of each of his two friends. Their animation was contagious and he felt his spirits lift with theirs.

******

Anne and Archie went to the theater or attended a concert rarely, usually in the evening. Archie assumed that she didn't want to invite a clash with her parents, who probably would disapprove of their friendship. When they parted after one of their days in a settlement house, he usually would kiss Anne affectionately but in a reserved way. Then one day as their relationship seemed to become more intimate, Archie revealed with some trepidation what had been on his mind for some time. Her dynamic personality had become irresistible. "I love you. Will you marry me?" He had held himself back, afraid that she might say no. He didn't understand the passion that had taken him over and even less how to express himself.

"How do you know you love me?"

"Because I'm happy only when I'm with you."

A pensive Anne looked into his eyes. "You're certainly the only man I ever cared for. Please give me some time to think about it. You must understand that I have been avoiding getting married for quite a while. Besides, there would be much opposition from my family, and I have to figure out what that would mean."

"Why is that? The Longbows were always a respected family. I'm not exactly wild and I'm even somewhat wealthy."

"Your mother is a divorcée, God forbid! And they would consider you a Bolshevik. Imagine, interacting with the poor, intermixing with them and having friends of color. But believe me, I think you're well worth a fight. I just have to get adjusted to the idea." "Bolshevik" was a term that had been picked up with gusto by the press not long before.

The difficulties they were to face came to a head when he went to pick up Anne one morning. The elegant lines of the house always made he feel that they belonged to an earlier period, before the city had expanded northward. Anne was always ready and would meet him at the door. He had never been inside. This time Anne wasn't there. The maid explained at the door. Anne was not available but that her parents wanted to talk to him. He was surprised that the difficulties would surface so soon. Anne intercepted him before he had a chance to go upstairs.

"A family cabala is upstairs. It doesn't bode well."

He was amused by her choice of words. "I think I have the remedy. The decision is entirely yours." He pulled out of his pocket the ring that Aunt Maryanne had given him. "This will do as an engagement ring if it meets with your approval. If you don't want to get engaged just keep it in your pocket. There is nothing else we can do to block them. It's your decision."

"Oh! Archie." She smiled while taking the ring. Her mischievous look encouraged him, but at the moment he could only hope.

The maid didn't let them dawdle. "Please sir. I don't want to lose my job!" And so Archie followed her. The atmosphere in the parlor he had been led to was glacial. The expensive furniture called to mind cheerful occasions. The chairs were upholstered in bright colors — the walls of the room were apportioned with good paintings of Hudson sceneries. But Archie didn't really notice. A middle-aged man and a woman sitting in the room facing him looked stern and uncompromising. He had seen Anne's father and mother before but had never met them officially. They were dressed as if they were going to an important function, the man in a well-cut dark suit, the woman in a fancy but somber dress. Another man, less conspicuous was also present. Archie surmised he might be another relative or a lawyer. He felt like when still a young boy, he had faced the headmaster after a particularly nasty piece of work, either his or somebody else's. Archie did feel a slight twinge of intimidation but couldn't help being amused by his strange feeling. He was never surer of his love for Anne. It was for Anne to decide if she was ready to marry him as he hoped — she held all the cards.

Mr. Elmay immediately broke the judgmental silence. "Mr. Longbow, I'm afraid you'll have to stop seeing our daughter Anabelle. You are totally inappropriate as a suitor, even if we considered your intentions honorable."

"I'm sorry to hear you disapprove. My intentions are most honorable. I think I'm in love with her. May I ask you what brought you to such unlikely conclusions? "

"We don't have to explain ourselves. We have other plans."

"How are you going to enforce your edict? She's no longer a minor, having reached the age of twenty-one some time ago. Furthermore, we have recently become engaged. We were just holding back the official announcement until we had a chance to discuss it with you."

Red in the face, the two parents seemed close to exploding. "That's total nonsense. We can't permit it."

"Well, as I said there isn't much you can do."

Anne's father went to the door and called the maid. "Please ask Miss Anne to come here immediately!"

After a few tense minutes, Anne entered the room demurely, but with an impish smile. The large diamond ring on her left hand spoke for itself. Archie was delighted.

"We absolutely forbid you to go through with this."

"I'm sorry to have to go against your wishes, Father, but I don't need your approval. Besides Archie has much better prospects than the idiots you tried to foist on me."

It was the mother who continued the argument. "You can't disgrace us in this way. You just can't."

Then the father took over menacingly. "We can stop this. There are ways."

It was time for Archie to assert himself. In cold anger he said, "There are no legal ways. I'm afraid you're raising some very unpleasant possibilities. I can't trust you with Anne. And I'm taking her with me now. You could have avoided embarrassment had you taken a more reasonable stance."

"Edwin! Do something!" bellowed Mr. Elmay at the man sitting with them.

"I'm afraid they are right," the man muttered in reply.

By then Archie had taken Anne's hand and after a show of a dignified departure, they made a hasty exit.

"I'm afraid you'll have to get your stuff another time. As inconvenient as it might be, I'd rather if we didn't have another confrontation."

A cab brought them to the hotel where he was staying.

"I'm afraid this won't do Archie."

"Why not?"

"I want the works. After a dignified and expensive dinner, I want the bridal suite at the Waldorf-Astoria. And I understand there is an accomplished fashionable little store in the hotel which can provide me with new clothes tomorrow morning."

Archie laughed. "Are you saying what I think you're saying? You know we can't get married instantaneously."

"I don't want to bother with technicalities. I have been waiting for you for six years and I'm through waiting. I'm sure we'll have enough panache not to be challenged at the desk. Measured arrogance can get you whatever you want. I have seen it work. And then I will have turned my ring around first to appear as a very respectable wedding ring."

"Oh, God. You were in love with me that long?" The question didn't deserve an answer apart from an amused smile.

They followed her plan. In the hotel room, they quickly embraced. After that, she was absolutely not lady-like. They were both overwhelmed with a long felt passion.